EDO VAN BELKOM

MARTYRS

DESIGN IMAGE

THE DESIGNIMAGE GROUP, INC.

Inquiries may be directed to:
The Design Image Group, Inc.
P.O. Box 2325
Darien, Illinois 60561

ISBN: 1-891946-13-7

First Edition

THE DESIGNIMAGE GROUP, INC.

Visit us on the web at
www.designimagegroup.com

Printed in the U.S.A.

10 9 8 7 6 5 4 3 2 1

BOOKS by Edo van Belkom

NOVELS
Wyrm Wolf (1995)
Lord Soth (1997)
Mister Magick (1998)
Teeth (2001)
Martyrs (2001)

COLLECTIONS
Death Drives a Semi (1998)
Six-Inch Spikes (2001)

NON-FICTION
Northern Dreamers (1998)
Writing Horror (2000)
Writing Erotica (2001)

ANTHOLOGIES
Aurora Awards (1999)
Northern Horror (2000)
Be Afraid! (2000)
Be Very Afraid! (2002)

DEDICATION
For my uncle, Father Loek van Belkom.

ACKNOWLEDGEMENTS
I am indebted to several people whose help,
support and friendship made this book possible. Thanks to:
Thomas Strauch of the Design Image Group who
was interested in the novel before it was even written;
my agent Joshua Bilmes; and my beta testers,
Dr. Anthony Cagle of the Archeology Department of the
University of Washington, and fellow writers
Marcos Donnelly, David Nickle, Michael Rowe,
and Robert J. Sawyer, for their invaluable and
insightful feedback on the manuscript;
and finally my wife Roberta, without whose love
and support this novel and all my other books
could never have been written.

Wherever God erects a house of prayer,
the devil always builds a chapel there.
— Daniel Dafoe

PROLOGUE

1

The big grey bus came to a stop.

Its doors opened.

A small man dressed in dark clothes got off.

There was no one there to meet him.

The streets of Abbotville were empty, as darkness began to fall earlier and earlier now that the remnants of summer were dying and the cold chill of autumn was beginning to encroach upon the town. The sun had been shrouded by thick grey clouds for days and there seemed to be a constant threat of rain hanging in the air. People had already begun locking their doors and securing windows in anticipation of the storm they could all feel was coming.

The dark man stood on the sidewalk waiting for the bus to leave him. There was no real bus station in Abbotville, just a signpost and a park bench behind the Becker's convenience store where bus tickets were bought and sold.

It was all the town of five-thousand souls really needed. Sure, traffic got busy a couple of times a year, mostly in September and around the holidays when students came and went from Ste-Claire College, but the rest of the time the bus rarely even pulled off the highway.

Still, every once in a while, the bus stopped and a stranger would get off.

Like now.

"Take this road west," said the bus driver. "The college is just a few klicks out of town. Take you about half-an-hour to get there on foot. If you call the college, they'll probably send someone out to get you."

The dark man nodded his thanks. "I'll walk."

The bus doors hissed closed and a moment later the vehicle's diesel engine roared like some angry beast. The bus lurched forward – as if hesitant to leave the dark man alone on the sidewalk – then finally began to roll away.

Moments later, the sound of the bus faded, leaving the man by the side of the road.

Alone, and in the dark.

He turned his head once left and once right, as if to examine his surroundings, then began walking westward, his shoes clicking against the cement of the sidewalk like a pair of cloven hooves.

2

Abbotville was a small rural town situated between Haliburton and Bancroft in the heartland of Ontario. And, like most small towns in the province, Abbotville basically had one of everything.

One barber shop. One hairdresser. One beer store. One pizza parlor. One motel. One book store. One Chinese restaurant, one Mexican. One fire station. One cop shop. One hardware store. One software store. One library. One movie theater. One video rental place. One department store. One supermarket. One junkyard.

And one college.

There were a few things they had two of, but not many.

Two auto repair shops. Two banks. Two coffee shops. Two gas stations. Two bridges. Two churches. Two traffic lights.

People also said that Abbotville had too many town drunks, but since they all seemed to take turns at the job it was hard to tell how many were real pros and how many were simply part-timers. That's because like every college town, Abbotville had some things in threes. Three pubs. Three taverns. And three places to buy alcohol – a Liquor Control Board of Ontario store, a Beer Store, and an Andre's wine shop.

The dark man reached the edge of the town in a few minutes and took a moment to rest by the sign that read – *You Are Entering Abbotville*. There was a rotund, smiling abbot painted on the sign, dressed in a white blouse, black cassock and white cincture. At the bottom of the sign were the words, *All Are Welcome Here*.

The dark man read those words and a devilish smile appeared on his face.

Surely, not *all*.

Again he took a look around. Patches of farmland and forests stretched out before him, and a road – Highway 35 – cut through both in a slightly curved line thinned in the distance like the point of a knife.

To his right, just off the shoulder of the highway was a sign erected by the provincial government. It was a foot square, blue in color and made of metal. There was a big "U" on it, and a mortarboard cap, denoting that there was a post-secondary educational institution nearby.

Three kilometres further west, according to the smaller rectangular sign below it. Changing his shape might get him there quicker, but he had clothes with him so he was stuck with his present form.

And so the dark man started walking.

Toward the college.

3

By the time he reached the crossroads, the lights of the college had become visible against the backdrop of the now dark, dark night.

Ste-Claire College was a small Jesuit school with an enrollment of just over 1,000 souls. It was well-known for its undergraduate and post-graduate degree courses in theology and religious history, but it was also just as famous for its hockey team, the Ste-Claire Cardinals. While the school had helped train a half-dozen priests over the years – one of which had ended up working at the Vatican – they had also graduated two young men to the ranks of the National Hockey League, making the college as much a hockey shrine as a spiritual one.

The church steeple was clearly visible from the crossroads. It rose some twenty-five meters into the air, and its quarried white stone was clearly visible from a distance, even in the dark.

It was a beacon...for now.

To the left of the church were the white walls of Ste-Claire Arena. It was made of brick and corrugated steel, but it had been painted white to match the exterior of the church. There were some that said the arena attracted more faithful on Saturday night than the church did Sunday morning, and it was probably true. But whether someone entered the church or the arena, it was impossible to leave either without being touched by God in some small way.

That would change too, thought the dark man.

There were other buildings on the campus, some made of white stone, others of plain painted wood and brown bricks, but most of them were shrouded by trees and rolling hills.

He'd examine them later.

Right now he needed rest.

He made a left at the crossroads, turning onto a narrow dirt road that led over a rise in the landscape. At the top of the rise he could see the college better. It was nestled into the surrounding landscape as if it were a child in swaddling clothes and the forests and rolling hills around its edges were a blanket of security, protecting it from outside forces.

It looked cozy.

And easily torn apart.

He continued walking, now with more of a purpose to his stride, eager to reach his destination and get on with his task.

The trees on the left side of the road began to glow as lights appeared behind him. There was a car approaching, its motor making less noise than its tires as it rolled over the rocks and stones covering the dirt roadway. The movement of the car's lights against the trees began to slow. The dark man turned and watched the car pull up beside him, then the passenger side window roll down without a sound.

"Give you a ride?" asked the old man driving the car. He was hunched over the steering wheel as if it had something to do with holding him upright. His clothes were old but neat, as if he'd put on his good work clothes just for the ride into town. There was a rosary hanging from the rearview mirror, the cross on it still swinging back and forth in reaction to the car's sudden stop.

The dark man shook his head, declining the offer.

"Dark as hell on these roads at night," said the old man. "Plenty of animals out too. Won't hurt you, but some get spooked by noises and what not."

"I don't mind the dark," he said, nodding in thanks.

The old man looked past the steering wheel and out over the hood of his car, a six year-old Chevy. "Not much down this road but a few farms, and there a ways off."

"I'll walk, thanks."

The old man was obviously having trouble moving on, or else the dark man wasn't being as friendly as people around Abbotville were used to. "Wouldn't be neighborly of me to just leave you here when I'm going the same way and I got an empty seat in a warm car."

The dark man leaned inside the car and smiled. "Go," he said, his voice little more than a whisper. "Before it's too late."

The old man suddenly seemed to be short of breath, as if his chest were being squeezed by a pair of giant hands. "Yeah, okay," he wheezed. "I think I will."

The dark man nodded and moved away from the car.

The old man put the car into gear, then stomped on the gas pedal. The rear wheels spun for a moment – sending a stream of dirt and stones out behind the car like a fantail – before grabbing hold of the earth. The car shot forward and then glided into the darkness, its red taillights shrinking into a pair of tiny pin-prick eyes before vanishing in the darkness as the car drove over another rise in the road.

The dark man continued walking.

Alone.

And in peace.

4

There was nothing remarkable about the farm house. It was the same as any number of buildings he had passed along the way. It was made of wood, covered with wooden siding painted white and topped with asphalt shingles the color of a bullfrog's back. It had begun life as a two-story square, and then was added to generation after generation until it sprawled out on one side like a caterpillar's rear end, each addition slightly smaller than the one before, with the last add-on made of slapped-together bits of plywood and chipboard. There was a barn on the property complete with missing boards and rusting steel roof, a couple of old silos at one end that hadn't held grain for years, and a collection of old junkers that had been stripped, ravaged and forgotten like an old town whore.

And then there was the garage. There were cars parked in front of it and all manner of junk piled up by the doors as if it was all waiting to get inside. On top of the garage was a room, with a stairway and entrance hidden from the road, and only a single pair of windows to look out of…or to look in through.

That was why he was here.

There was a dull, dim light flickering inside of the farmhouse and the faint odor of greasy hamburgers was lingering thickly on the air like a fog.

He knocked on the door.

There was no sound or movement inside the house.

He knocked again, this time harder.

A curtain jerked aside at one of the windows, its space taken over by a pair of eyes. Then, just as quickly, the curtain fell back into place and there was movement inside the farm house.

Someone was coming.

The door opened slowly at first, but once the man inside saw the diminutive stature of the dark man and figured he'd probably be safe, the door burst wide open.

"What do you want?" he said. There was an angry scowl on his face, a dribble of hamburger grease on his chin and even more down the front of his dirty white t-shirt where the expanse of his considerable belly had acted like a trough catching everything that fell from above. In the background, a voice on the television reported that the Toronto Blue Jays were coming up to bat in the bottom of the sixth, down by a run.

"Good evening, Mr. Shepherd?"

Shepherd looked at the dark man strangely. "Do I know you?"

"I'm here about the room."

"What room?"

"The one you're renting over the garage."

"You sure I don't know you?"

The dark man shook his head. "No, I'm new in town."

"Then how do you know I'm renting out my room?" asked Shepherd, pushing the back of his hand across his chin, spreading the grease out into a shiny slick. "The ad doesn't come out in the paper until Wednesday."

The dark man ignored him. "The room *is* for rent, isn't it?"

"Maybe it is, maybe it isn't."

"I don't see anyone living in it at the moment."

Shepherd's eyes narrowed as he studied the features of the dark man. "You a student?" he asked.

"Not exactly."

"I wanted to rent the room out to a student, young girl, something like that...someone who had money for rent and wouldn't be no trouble."

"Well, I won't be any trouble," said the dark man. "Not to you."

"Is that right?" Shepherd looked unconvinced.

"Yes, you won't even know I'm here."

Shepherd was silent, scratching his chin. He noticed the grease on his hand and wiped it off on his t-shirt, putting a new stain on one of the few remaining patches of white.

"You got money? I like to have the first and last month's rent up front, if you don't mind."

The dark man reach inside his coat and pulled out a sheaf of red and brown fifty and one-hundred dollar bills. "I can pay you for the first and last month's rent, and three month's rent in advance...in cash."

A smile was beginning to form on Shepherd's face. "You need a receipt?" he asked.

"That won't be necessary."

Shepherd's smile got wider.

The dark man counted out several bills, and handed them to Shepherd. Shepherd took the money and shuffled the brown, red, green and purple slips of paper between his hands like some kid looking at hockey cards in a school yard.

The dark man remained standing on the stoop, unmoving. "The keys," he said.

"Oh, yeah." Shepherd's eyes finally came away from the money as he folded the bills over and dropped the wad into the right pocket of his pants. Then he reached into his left pocket and pulled out a steel ring bristling with keys. He singled out a small brass key from the jumble and began twisting it off the ring. "It's not much of a lock, but it'll keep people out. Not that anyone ever passes by or drops in to visit mother and me...'Course, I won't be poking around either, unless I have reason to, understand? You don't give me trouble, I won't cause you none neither, you get my meaning?"

The dark man didn't answer. He had his hand out waiting for the key.

"Here you go," Shepherd said, presenting the key as if it were for a brand new car, or some vault full of treasure.

The dark man reached out and grasped Shepherd's hand along with the key.

Shepherd's body went stiff as a cleric's collar.

The dark man pulled the key from his fingers, then backed off the stoop.

Shepherd remained standing in the open doorway, as if in a daze. His blinking eyelids were the only part of his body that was moving.

The dark man walked across the yard toward the garage, climbed the stairs to the upper floor, unlocked the door, and stepped inside the room.

5

When the light came on in the room over the garage, Pete Shepherd found himself standing in the doorway to the farmhouse looking out over an empty yard.

For a moment he wondered what he was doing there, but he fished inside his right pants pocket and pulled out the wad of money and it all came back to him pretty fast.

Some older guy dressed in black – a mature student, they called them – rented out the room, for cash. Not exactly the kind he liked living on the property but it sure beat what he usually rented the room out to – guys who'd been kicked off campus, or who couldn't afford school unless they lived four to a room, or rich kids who just wanted to party somewhere away from campus where the college priests couldn't see them.

Yeah, this would work out all right. Nice change of pace. And the cash, well that sure as hell wouldn't be showing up on any tax form. In fact, there was a woman in Abbotville he could get to know real well with the bulge that money had put into his pants.

He turned back around, closed the door behind him and headed into the living room. The baseball game wasn't on anymore. In its place was a repeat of *The Waltons*, a show mother couldn't get enough of.

"I was watchin' the game," said Shepherd.

"You was gone a long time, so I put something on that I wanted to watch."

Shepherd switched it back to the ball game, saw that the Jays were now down by five and flipped it back to *The Waltons* so he wouldn't have to listen to mother complain about watchin' losers, and not just on the television screen either.

"Who was at the door?" she asked.

"Rented out the room."

"To who?"

"Older guy," said Shepherd. "All dressed in black."

"He pay first and last?"

"And the first three months rent."

"You took a check?" mother said, her voice rising in volume and her stubby fingers digging into the armrests of her easy chair.

Shepherd hadn't wanted to tell her about the cash, but he didn't have a choice. "Paid in cash."

"Good," mother said. "Now you can have the roof fixed, and if there's anything left over, you can buy a television set for your room…used."

Shepherd slumped back in his chair and the semi-hard dick he'd been working on went soft as a jelly roll with the realization that there would be no woman from town. Still, a new television wasn't too bad. Maybe he could save on the roofing job and have enough to by a VCR too. Be able to watch pornos without mother knowing…

"You get that roof fixed properly," Mother said. "And not by any of your good-for-nothin' friends. You get a roofer from town that's got his own truck."

Shepherd was silent.

"You hear!"

"Yes mother."

6

It wasn't much of a room, but it would do.

There was a place for him to lie down when he was tired, a place to warm food when he was hungry and a place where he could wash-up and keep himself clean. The room felt cold, but that was only because it hadn't been lived in for a while. There was a pot-bellied stove set against one wall and some firewood piled up on the floor beside it. Although it would be a few more weeks before he'd need a fire to keep the place warm, it was good to know he could light one any time he needed.

He walked over to one of the windows, pulled aside its heavy curtain and looked out. It was a western facing window and would let in plenty of light in the late afternoon. It also overlooked the driveway, and had a view all the way down to the road which would be handy if things got tight, but he didn't think they would.

He checked the other window on the southern wall. He could see the yard and the farmhouse across it. He would be able to know when Shepherd and his mother were up and about, and he'd have a bit of warning if anyone, namely Shepherd, decided to saunter over for a chat.

With only two windows, and both of them on the second floor, there wasn't much chance anyone would be looking in on him. And the curtains were heavy and opaque, which would prevent Shepherd from spending much time wondering if he was in, or awake, or asleep. He was happy to think there was some older student renting out the room, but that would eventually wear thin. Sooner or later he'd get curious, but by that time it would all be over.

The dark man continued to walk about the room, inspecting the items and articles that the previous tenants had left behind over the years. There were a few Ste-Claire Cardinal banners pinned to the walls and a set of cross-country skies by the door. A bookshelf near the kitchen had plenty of textbooks on its shelves, but none of them seemed very current. There was a writing desk pushed up against the wall near the door and a single lamp on one of its corners. The framed pictures and prints pinned to the walls seemed out of joint. There were shots of high-flying skiers, one bathing beauty, a calendar's worth of old warbirds and a carnival poster from somewhere in east Texas.

He left them where they hung, not caring about them one way or another.

The slight chill in the room continued to bother him, though. The room seemed unnaturally cold, colder inside than outside, and that just wasn't right.

He began searching the room.

Starting from the windows, he worked his way around the room, searching the walls for the source of his discomfort.

He found it hanging above the door.

And to think, he'd walked right under it.

It was a small crucifix. The cross was made of wood and

the bastard nailed to it, plastic. And it had been blessed, he could feel that like ice-water in his veins.

He reached into his coat pocket for a pair of leather gloves. He pulled them on carefully, checking for any holes or tears in the seams. There were none.

He approached the doorframe slowly, as if there were danger all around him. Seconds passed as he steadied himself with his left hand and reached up over the frame with his right.

And then he grabbed it.

The thing felt cold in his hand, as if it were going to freeze his fingers solid if he held onto it for too long.

With a hard jerk of his hand, he ripped it from the wall, the nail that had held it in place coming out of the stud with a squeak before tinkling loosely on the floor like a shard of glass.

He rushed over to the pot-bellied stove, holding the crucifix as far away from his body as possible, like a dead animal. His left hand fumbled with the latch on the front of the stove, but after a few clumsy attempts it finally gave way. And then in one swift motion, he drew his arm across his body and threw the crucifix into the stove with all the strength he could muster.

The crucifix thudded against the firebricks inside, splintering and coming to a rest amid the ashes of long-dead fires at the bottom of the stove's big steel belly.

And then the broken pieces of the crucifix suddenly burst into flames.

The dark man took off his gloves and warmed his cold, cold hand on the flames.

There was a hellish fire aglow in his eyes.

And for the first time since stepping off the bus, he was beginning to feel at home.

PART ONE: MISSION

These poor, distressed people forsook their lands, houses, and villages, in order to escape the cruelty of an enemy whom they feared more than a thousand deaths. Many, no longer expecting humanity from man, flung themselves into the deepest recesses of the forest, where, though it were with wild beasts, they might find some peace.

– The Jesuit Relations and Allied Documents

CHAPTER ONE

1

Karl Desbiens glanced at the clock on the wall of his tiny dorm room and felt his stomach tighten. It was ten minutes to ten and Father Dionne was surely on his way, walking slowly across the campus with his familiar gnarled rosewood walking stick in hand. The stick was a yard long, deep reddish brown and was said to have belonged to one of the Jesuit martyrs who founded the college back in 1750. Karl doubted that, and had often thought about scraping a bit of the wood from the bottom of the stick and have the sample radiocarbon dated.

That would put an end to the mystery once and for all.

It would also help him make up his mind.

Father Dionne was on his way over to ask Karl if he had decided on his future, if he knew what he wanted to do with his life. He'd enrolled at the college in his mid-twenties after working a variety of jobs that weren't for him. Now, after studying at the at the college for six years and receiving his Master's Degree in Theology, he found himself at a crossroads. He had completed the requirements of philosophate, and was now embarking on three years as a regent where he would either work in a foreign mission or teach at a Jesuit school.

It was a tough decision to make, especially when he wasn't sure if becoming a Jesuit priest was even for him. He enjoyed some aspects of the order like meditation and the pursuit of knowledge and academic achievement. He also had a fascination with the Spiritual Exercises of St. Ignatius. It was all so mysterious that it sometimes seemed that it had all come right out of *The Twilight Zone*, rather than the writings of a holy man.

But was it for him?

As a Jesuit priest Karl would have to take a vow of celibacy and that had been easier to accept than he'd thought since he'd never been much of a ladies man. And coming from a family of modest means, a vow of poverty wouldn't change his life all that much. But there was also a vow of obedience and that was the one Karl thought he might have trouble with. Would he be able to accept and follow orders from his superiors absolutely and without question? Karl had always been the type who wanted to know the reasons behind things, who needed to understand before he could act. It was an obstacle to be sure, but perhaps it was something that further study would help him to understand.

If he decided to become a priest, his life would always be a simple one and he would have to follow orders and like it, because he had *chosen* to live his life in that way.

Chosen to serve God.

That was the thing, wasn't it? It was a poor and humble life, but there was no more noble a calling on Earth than to serve God, and do His work.

It was almost enough to tip the scales in favor of the priesthood.

Almost.

But Karl needed to be sure.

He'd been told by other priests that when the time came he would know what the right choice would be, without a doubt and without hesitation. That moment hadn't come yet, and he wondered if it ever would.

And if it didn't, there were other options.

He could continue his studies and work toward ordination, but remain a lay person living his life as a Jesuit, but not as a member of the order. That was an alternative, but it seemed a pretty poor one since the main reason he'd studied and already put up with so much hardship was to eventually become a priest.

There was also the possibility of becoming a priest *and* something else, sort of like the bestselling novelist, Father Andrew Greeley. Greeley was both a fiction writer *and* a priest. From what Karl had read about the man, his superiors didn't like it all that much, but Father Greeley seemed to enjoy doing both jobs, and there was no law, either inside or out of the Church, that said he couldn't.

It wasn't all that new an idea.

Church scholars and philosophers had long ago figured out that in order to matter in today's society priests needed to have a second profession. Hyphenated priests, they were called, and they could be everything and anything they wanted to be, from Jesuit-lawyers to Jesuit-engineers, Jesuit-psychiatrists to Jesuit-journalists, Jesuit-poets and Jesuit-musicians, even Jesuit-construction workers. There were no limits, and in fact, because of his training and discipline, it was quite likely that if he were to become a Jesuit-lawyer, he might be a better lawyer than the non-Jesuit variety. He'd certainly be a more honest one. The idea appealed to Karl, but even if he picked the hyphenated priest route, he still wasn't sure what should come after the hyphen.

It might as well be Jesuit-skeptic, because the more he considered and wrestled with his future, the less he believed in Ste-Claire College's place in the whole Jesuit order.

For example, just a few years ago the college celebrated its two-hundred and fiftieth anniversary, but they had no artifacts from the original settlement, which had supposedly been located some seventy-five kilometers north of the college. While an earlier nearby Jesuit settlement, Ste-Marie among the Hurons, was more than a hundred years older than Ste-Claire, that site had been a treasure trove of stone structures, iron tools, artifacts and old bones. So celebrated were the martyrs of Ste-Marie that a Shrine was erected to them in 1926 complete with the reliquary of the martyrs. The martyrs themselves had been canonized in 1930 and made secondary patrons of Canada ten years later. In 1950 the site of the mission was excavated and archeologists found the hard-packed floor of the Church of St. Joseph. By 1964 the entire site had been uncovered and reconstruction of the original settlement had begun. It was finished by 1967, Canada's centennial year, and now the shrine and the settlement attracted tens of thousands of tourists and pilgrims from around the world each year. Pope John Paul II even visited the shrine in 1990. But even though Ste-Claire was less than three hours away by car, it hadn't even merited a drive-by in the Popemobile.

And there was more.

The names of the Ste-Marie martyrs were part of Canadian history – Jean de Brébeuf, Gabriel Lalement, Anthony Daniel, Noël Chabanel – and countless schools across the country had been named in their honor. Even two Jesuit martyrs who had been killed in what later would become New York State – Isaac Jogues and René Goupil – were considered to be martyrs of Ste-Marie. With the reconstruction of the mission and the shrine built to honor their memory, the Ste-Marie martyrs were very much alive in people's hearts and minds. In fact, it appeared as if they were going to live forever.

But what of the Martyrs of Ste-Claire: Daniel Sernine, Joël Champetier, and Jean-Louis Trudel?

No shrine. No ruins. No canonization. No schools. No rusted tools. No old bones. No artifacts.

Nothing.

Nothing, except for a few books detailing the Ste-Claire martyrs' struggles in the forbidding Canadian wilderness, a couple of graphic accounts of their torture and deaths at the hands of savage Iroquois raiders, and a college named after the martyrs' patron saint.

And even that didn't make any sense. Ste-Claire wasn't a Jesuit saint. She was an Italian saint, and had been a follower of St. Francis of Assisi. Other than establishing the Order of Poor Clares, Ste-Claire's only accomplishment of note was being proclaimed the patron saint of television in 1958 by Pope Pius XII, because in 1252 she had apparently been able to see the Christmas services held in the Basilica of St. Francis while lying in her sickbed inside the convent.

Just another mystery to be solved.

Which, combined with the rest of the facts, or lack thereof, made it seem as if the martyrs had never existed.

Or no one wanted anyone to know of their existence.

So what difference would one more Jesuit priest make at a college that already had enough of them to field a hockey team called "The Flying Fathers" that played in charity events all over Southern Ontario? Why should he stay at the college and become a priest when all he'd be doing is teaching other similarly directionless youths about a "house" in the Order of Jesus about which few people knew and even fewer cared?

Just then there was sound on the other side of the door. The squeak of door hinges swinging open, and then the sharp tapping of a rosewood walking stick approaching. The sound of the stick against the hallway floor grew louder with each tap.

Tap.

Tap.

Tap.

And then silence.

It was Father Dionne.

He wanted to know what Karl was going to do with the rest of his young life.

Karl didn't know, and that wasn't going to be good enough for Father Dionne.

There was a firm knock at the door.

Karl didn't want to answer it, but he had no choice.

2

Karl cleared his study chair of books and papers so that Father Dionne could sit down. When the priest was seated, Karl took his walking stick and set it gently by the door.

"Thank you," said Father Dionne.

"My pleasure," answered Karl. "Can I get you something? Juice? Coffee? Tea?" Karl would have to go down to the cafeteria or one of the pubs on campus to get something to drink, but it was right to make the offer to the priest.

"No thank you, Karl." The tone of Father Dionne's voice was firm, letting Karl know that he hadn't come to socialize.

"Did you have a pleasant walk? It looks like a nice day out."

Father Dionne said nothing for a few moments, staring at Karl with a hint of disappointment on his face. "Still haven't made up your mind yet, eh?"

Karl sat heavily on his bed, his shoulders and head drooping down like a man who was utterly defeated. "No," he said weakly.

"Do you know what the problem is? Perhaps I can help you in some way. I have been known on occasion to provide guidance to wandering souls..."

Karl lifted his head and looked at Father Dionne. He was an old man, in his late sixties or early seventies. Already a short man in his youth, he had withered with time rather than grown stout. There was a band of white hair that ringed the back of his head, but he kept it cut short so that it was hard to tell where his bald pate ended and his white hair began. His eyes were a light shade of blue, which gave him a bit of a mysterious air and made it difficult for anyone to look him directly in the eye for more than a few seconds. Father Dionne had been a priest at Ste-Claire for almost half a century, teaching the same classes year after year with hardly ever a change to the curriculum. After all, the Bible and the letters and communiques of Order of Jesus founder Ignatius Loyola had never changed during that time, why should the instruction about them? The yearly routine and repetition seemed to suit the priest, giving him the chance to keep in touch with his students while leaving him time to oversee the more mundane aspects of running the college, such as operating budgets, tuition fees, building maintenance and the like. In addition, Father Dionne was also the college's spiritual leader, but that was a task he seemed to perform with great stealth. Karl often wondered if Father Dionne ever had any doubts about the role of the college within the Jesuit Order, because if he did he had never let them show.

"Come on, Karl," said Father Dionne when the silence in the room had gone on too long. "What's bothering you? If you can't tell me, I don't know who else you'll be able to turn to."

That was true, thought Karl. He couldn't see himself talking to his parents about this. His father was a sheet metal worker, and his mother a banquet waitress. Together, they had made all sorts of sacrifices to send him to Ste-Claire and the intention had always been that he would be a priest at the end of it all. Karl *wanted* to be a priest, but he wanted to be a priest that really mattered, not the kind that only came into people's lives at weddings and funerals, Christmas and Easter.

"I don't know, I just can't make up my mind...or maybe I don't want to," he said, still stalling. "It's such a big step."

"You don't want to become a priest anymore?" There was real surprise in Father Dionne's voice.

Karl shook his head. "It's not that, I still want to be a priest, but...no offense father, I want to do more than spend my life trying to convince young people that God matters, or that he even exists." Karl glanced over at Father Dionne and was relieved to see he didn't look upset by the comment.

"Is that all you think we do here?"

"No, of course not..." Karl said, under his breath. He felt embarrassed and a little ashamed. What he was basically telling Father Dionne was that he didn't want to end up being a priest *like him*, doing the same thing day after day, year after year, to the point where the fire in his heart that had first made him want to serve God had been snuffed out by bureaucracy and routine. Being a priest wasn't supposed to be something you could do simply by going through the motions.

Father Dionne's face remained impassive. "If you want to become a priest, I mean really want it, then you'd become one and let God decide how you would best serve Him."

Karl knew in his heart that Father Dionne was right.

"Sounds to me like you're having a crisis of faith, not just trouble making up your mind about the priesthood."

"You think so?" Karl asked.

Father Dionne smiled. "Mine was named Sophia."

"A childhood sweetheart?"

"Hardly." Father Dionne shook his head. "I never met Sophia Loren, but when I saw her up on the screen I was in love...or as in love as a teenager can be. I thought, if I lust after a woman – because, let's face it, that was what I was experiencing, lust rather than love – how could I possibly be worthy of becoming a priest."

"How did you resolve it?"

"I visited my parish priest to talk about my 'problem', which wasn't an easy thing to do for a fourteen year-old, especially when the priest was older than my grandfather. Anyway, I went to see him and he told me that he thought Sophia Loren was gorgeous too. He even had a picture of her up on his office wall. He pointed to that picture and said, 'I may be a priest, but I'm still a man, eh.'"

Karl joined Father Dionne in a laugh.

"Well, that settled it for me. Since there wasn't any reason I couldn't be a priest and still appreciate feminine beauty, I decided to serve God...and admire his handiwork whenever he'd produced beautiful things...like Sophia Loren."

Karl breathed easier. This was a side to Father Dionne he'd never been aware of and it came as a bit of a revelation.

"Now, if you still want to become a Jesuit, but not serve the college, I can arrange for you to be sent anywhere you like. We still have missions in Africa, South America, and plenty of inner cities across the United States. Just tell me where you want to go..."

"No, that's not it, I like this college. I love it, the grounds, the campus, the atmosphere, the people..."

Father Dionne nodded in acknowledgement.

"I'd just like to do something important *here*, maybe something to make people take notice of this school and what it's accomplished outside of the hockey arena."

"That's a tall order, you know. Coach Chambers has a good team this year. He's talking about a run at the national championship."

"A tall order," said Karl, feeling the fire warming up in his heart, "but not impossible."

Father Dionne shifted in his chair, making himself more comfortable. "No, not impossible, but I am curious about how you would propose to do it?"

Karl was silent for a long time, thinking the question over. Here was his chance to make his pitch and he had to make sure he was as convincing as possible. He took a deep breath, let out a sigh, and said, "Why is Ste-Claire College here?"

Father Dionne's response was immediate. "We instruct young people in matters of history, philosophy, and theology with an emphasis on the Catholic faith."

"That's from the school brochure, isn't it?" Karl asked. "That comes just a few lines above the part that says Ste-Claire College has a champion hockey team."

"The Cardinals do play an important part in the way the school is perceived by the rest of the world."

"Yes, Ste-Claire College, the school that takes young people in at one end and pumps out priests and hockey players at the other."

"They say that about the school?"

"No, they say that the only two things that come out of Ste-Claire College are hockey players and perverts."

"Oh," said Father Dionne. Obviously he hadn't been aware of the college's reputation outside Abbotville's borders.

Karl tried to keep things moving. "I mean, why was the mission located here in the first place, especially after Ste-Marie among the Hurons failed so miserably more than a hundred years before?"

Father Dionne looked at Karl curiously. "To establish the Catholic faith in lands distant, barbarous and strange, where the name of God is not invoked—"

Karl shook his head and waved his hands like a referee calling back a goal. "I know the royal patent as well as you do Father."

Father Dionne gave a slight shrug. "Well, that is why the mission was founded."

"Was it even founded in 1750?"

"That's when all our documents say it was."

"So where's the proof? I mean the real proof? Do we have an axehead? A sawblade? Door hinges? I don't even know of a single Indian artifact that's been found in the area."

"No one has looked for any of those things."

"Why not?"

Father Dionne hesitated, then shrugged. "I don't know."

"Well I'd like to."

"Like to what?"

"Look for those things."

"You're not an archeologist."

"No, but I know how to shovel dirt."

Father Dionne said nothing for a long time, as if considering what Karl was suggesting. "All right, what do you have in mind?"

"We already know the general area of the mission," said Karl, feeling a tingle of real excitement beginning to build inside him. "I could take some students up there and start digging and sifting through the earth. If we find something–"

"If you find something you might very well ruin the site."

"Is that supposed to be a pun?" asked Karl.

"What?" Father Dionne looked at Karl curiously, as if thinking.

"*Ruin* the *site*."

"No it's not a pun. The Ste-Claire Mission is a sacred site, recognized by the Vatican and three levels of government in this country. If you and a bunch of undergraduate students go poking around up there, you might destroy something of great value."

"I don't want to excavate the site, Father. I just want to find something, *anything*, that I can use to convince the government, or maybe private sponsors, that there had in fact been a mission on the site two-hundred and fifty years ago, and that there are a great number of historical, cultural, and spiritual reasons to undertake a proper archeological dig."

Father Dionne was smiling now. "Does this mean you want to be ordained and remain here at the college?"

Karl thought about it. "Yes, I guess it does."

"Excellent," Father Dionne said. Then, after a pause, "You know as well as I do that the college doesn't have the money for things like archeological digs."

"Of course not, father. I'll raise the money for the preliminary dig myself."

"How?"

"I don't know. I'll think of something."

"All right. If you can raise the money to fund say...a two-week exploratory dig on the site, I'll give you my blessing and whatever help I can."

"Like use of the Cardinals' team bus?"

Father Dionne shifted uncomfortably in his chair, then said, "Yes."

"And letting the students I take with me out of class for two weeks, with school credit for their work on the site?"

Father Dionne hesitated, his lips pressed tightly together in a thin white line. "All right."

"Great! Excellent! Thank you!"

"Don't thank me yet. This could all turn out to be a big mistake."

"No, this is going to be wonderful."

"I hope you're right," Father Dionne said, clasping his hands together, as if in prayer. "Now, how do you plan on getting things started?"

Karl looked about the room and saw Father Dionne's walking stick by the door. "With this," he said, picking it up. "I'd like to take a small piece off the bottom and have it dated. If it's really two-hundred and fifty years old, it would give the mission study a terrific start."

"All right."

Karl watched the priest struggle to get up from his chair. "Let me help you," he said, walking Father Dionne to the door.

"My walking stick," said Father Dionne, a hand against the wall.

"I'll bring it back to you as soon as I'm done with it," answered Karl.

"And how am I supposed to get across campus without my walking stick? It's not just for show, you know."

It was a good question, especially since Karl didn't want to give it up until he had a proper sample, and he wouldn't know how much of a sample he'd need until he'd made a few calls.

"Why...I'm going to escort you all the way back to your office. That's how."

Karl held his arm out.

Father Dionne grabbed hold.

Together they headed out of the dorm and across campus.

3

In the darkened doorway of a lecture hall, a dark figure leaned against a brick wall, shrouded in shadow. He watched the two men walk by, the younger one guiding the older one along the path, as if hurrying him toward his grave.

Thinking of how close it was to the truth brought a smile to the dark man's face. If he had known it would be this easy, he wouldn't have waited so long to return.

CHAPTER TWO

1

It was almost a three-hour drive into Toronto, and then another half-hour to find a parking spot, but Karl knew it would all be time well spent.

When he'd first called the Royal Ontario Museum, he'd expected to get the run-around and a lot of uninterested administrators acting as if he were bothering them. But once he told the woman who first answered the phone who he was and explained what he wanted, he was transferred directly to the office of Doctor Cornelius Bos, who headed up the Ontario branch of the museum's Archeological Department.

It turned out that Dr. Bos wasn't in, but Karl left a message for him on his machine and the good doctor returned his call less than an hour later. Then, after a bit of small talk, the doctor listened patiently while Karl explained what the walking stick looked like and related a few of the stories surrounding it. He asked questions only when Karl was done.

"If you bring it down," said Dr. Bos, "I'd love to take a look at it."

"Will you be able to determine its age?"

"If you can leave it with us for a week, and don't mind us taking a small material sample from an inconspicuous spot..."

"No problem."

"All right then," said the doctor. "When can you come down?"

"How about today?"

And so Karl had rolled up the walking stick in bubble wrap and took Father Dionne's Ford Tempo down into the city. By the time he'd arrived at the museum the doctor had already gone for the day, but Karl left the walking stick with someone else in the department, filled out and signed some paperwork, and made an appointment to return in a week's time.

That was seven days ago.

He'd had no contact with the doctor in the interim so he had no idea if the walking stick was the genuine article or a seventy year-old item out of the Eaton's catalogue. Not knowing made it all so exciting, like opening up Pandora's Box.

He climbed the wide stone steps, entered the museum through one of the six main glass doors, and found himself in the museum's large octagonal lobby, which the museum called the Rotunda. He scanned the Rotunda quickly finding the Garfield Weston Exhibition Hall on the left and a gift shop and Druxy's deli on the right, then moved to the far side of the Rotunda, between the admissions desk and the membership-services counter, and spoke to the security officer standing at the entrance to the main galleries.

"My name is Karl Desbiens," he said, nodding politely. "I'm here to see Doctor Cornelius Bos."

"One moment please," said the security guard, an elderly East-Indian man wearing a blue-blazer and dark blue turban.

The guard went to the membership-services counter and picked up the phone. Then he punched in a few numbers, and after a short wait, said a few words into the phone. He laughed then, as he and Doctor Bos shared a joke. A few more words and the guard hung up.

"He'll be right down to meet you."

Karl nodded and waited.

Several minutes passed before a tall, middle-aged man in tan slacks and long-sleeved denim shirt appeared in the foyer and began walking toward Karl. He looked strong and powerful, and judging by the dark tan on his weather-beaten skin, he liked to get out of the museum and into the field as often as he could.

Karl took a few steps and the two men met in the middle of the Rotunda.

"Karl Desbiens, I presume?"

"Yes."

"I'm Doctor Bos...and please remember, that's just my name, I don't run the place."

Karl just looked at the man for a moment wondering what he was talking about. Then all at once he understood, and laughed.

"Good to see you have a sense of humor. That's a help if you're going to be digging up the Earth and working with ancient artifacts. Dead people tend to have pretty grim expressions on their faces, so it's usually up to us to provide the smiles."

Karl nodded politely. "About the walking stick, is it old?"

Doctor Bos inhaled a breath, held it, then said, "Let's get back to my office so I can explain things properly."

"It's not old, is it?"

"This way," said the doctor.

2

"So why is it again that you brought the walking stick here to be dated?" the doctor asked.

"Well, I'm thinking of doing a survey of the site of the Ste-Claire mission and I thought that if I could prove the walking stick once belonged to one of the Jesuit martyrs who were killed on the site, I might be able to raise the funds to get started."

The doctor nodded. "Well, I think the ROM would be very interested in such a survey, perhaps even a proper archeological project. If you need any advice or help, I'd be glad to assist you in any way I can. It's what we're here for, after all."

"I'll keep that in mind, uh…Doctor Bos." Karl stumbled on the name. Somehow it didn't sound right to him.

"You can call me Cornelius if you like, but some people find that just as awkward. My friends call me Cor."

"I'll keep it in mind, Cor." That didn't sound right to Karl either.

"Ah, here we are." The doctor took a key from his pocket and opened the door.

Karl followed the doctor inside.

For Karl, the doctor's office was a bit of a disappointment. He had hoped to be led back into the laboratory where the actual testing on the walking stick might have been done, and where all of the museum pieces were cleaned, restored or just plain dusted off. Doctor Bos' office was like any one of a hundred offices he'd seen before – a room with four walls painted white, a couple of filing cabinets and a desk that seemed too cluttered to be any help getting any work done.

"Please, take a seat." The doctor pointed to a small chair in the middle of the room, then stepped around the desk and sat down in the large office chair behind it. "I would have taken you to the lab and given you the grand tour, but we're in the process of rotating a few major collections right now and it's a bit tight back there. The curators don't want anyone around that doesn't have to be..."

"I understand."

"Anyway, I can tell you about this walking stick of yours just as well in here." Doctor Bos reached down and took a long, slim cardboard box off a shelf behind him. It had the look of a flower box, but the cardboard was plain brown, and corrugated. He placed the box on top of his desk and carefully opened it up.

The walking stick was nestled inside the box wrapped in a thin, textured sort of tissue paper. The doctor reached in and gently lifted the stick out of the box by the thick, elaborately decorated end. That end featured a crudely carved face that was believed to be a likeness of Father Jean-Louis Trudel, the first of the Ste-Claire martyrs to be tortured and killed by the Iroquois. Above the head were a set of curved lines that depicted Father Trudel's thick shock of flowing black hair, while below the head the figure's arms were crossed over its chest in a sort of burial position, suggesting it was carved by one of the other Jesuits in honor of Father Trudel following his death.

But all of that was purely speculation.

Doctor Bos was a man of science.

"I first thought I'd be able to take a sample from the bottom," the doctor began, "but there was too much contamination there from grass clippings, dirt and who knows what else."

"Father Dionne uses it every day."

"Really." Something like a shudder seemed to course through Doctor Bos' body. "Well, having few options, we scraped away enough material from the back of the figure's head, here where it meets the collar–" He pointed to a spot that was slightly lighter in color than the wood around it, then held the stick out to Karl so he could get a better look at it.

There was a faint mark on the wood, but if the doctor hadn't pointed it out, Karl might never have noticed it. "You can hardly tell."

"I'm glad to hear you say that," the doctor said with a smile as he carefully laid the walking stick back in the box. "Some people are furious when we do such things, but even bits of the shroud of Turin had to be cut off in the name of science, eh?"

Karl nodded, wondering if the doctor's reference to the shroud was meant to be a hint to the veracity of the walking stick's age. When the shroud had been tested in Switzerland in 1988 it was revealed that the linen dated back to between 1260 and 1390 – old, but certainly not the burial shroud of Jesus Christ some had believed it to be. "I hope the results are better in this case," Karl said.

The doctor looked thoughtful. "That all depends on what you're looking for. The test doesn't pinpoint exact years, but instead gives us an indication of a time span. You see, living plants take up carbon dioxide gas from the atmosphere and incorporate it into their tissue, and some of that carbon dioxide contains the radioactive isotope of carbon, which is Carbon-14..."

Karl wanted to cut the doctor off and make him get to the point, but there was a chance that doing so might make him start all over again.

"...When the plant dies, it stops taking up Carbon-14, and the Carbon-14 that it took up during its lifetime begins to decay at a known rate so that the elapsed time from the plant's death to the present can be measured by the amount of Carbon-14 that's left in the plant's tissues. It's good up to 120,000 years, but your little walking stick isn't quite that old."

Karl had had enough of the doctor's beating around the bush. He had to know, and he had to know now. "Doctor..." he began to say, then corrected himself. "Cor, is it two-hundred and fifty years old?"

The doctor looked at him strangely. "A bit more than that."

"How much more?"

"This piece of wood is over one-thousand years old."

CHAPTER THREE

1

Karl made one stop on his way back to the college, and when he arrived at Ste-Claire, he went straight to the rectory to return Father Dionne's keys and thank him for the use of the car.

"Well, someone looks very happy," said Martine Ayres, an elderly woman who had been Father Dionne's secretary and assistant for as long as anyone could remember.

Karl had been trying to keep his exuberance hidden, but the closer he got to actually telling someone the good news, the less he was able to contain himself.

"Is Father Dionne in?"

"Yes," she smiled, as if Karl's happiness was contagious. "He's in his office. You can go right in."

Karl rapped on the heavy wooden door to Father Dionne's office and turned the knob even before the priest gave him permission to enter.

"Come in," said Father Dionne when Karl was already three steps into the room. The white-haired man was sitting behind his desk, looking over the summer issue of the *Ste-Claire Sentinel*, the school's student newspaper that was monthly during the summer, and weekly during the school year.

"I'm back from the ROM," Karl said, stopping in front of the priest's desk.

"It says here that even the coach of the Varsity Blues at the University of Toronto is picking the Cardinals as one of the favorites for the national title," said Father Dionne, not looking up from the newspaper. "Seems we've got a new defenseman from Timmins, six-four, two-forty...That should keep the front of the net clear, eh?" He looked around the side of the paper at Karl.

Karl was still standing there. Still smiling.

"The news must be good," said Father Dionne.

"It is," Karl nodded. "But first, I have a little gift for you."

"For me?" Father Dionne neatly folded up the newspaper and laid it on the top-right corner of his desk. "You shouldn't have."

"Well, I didn't really have a choice."

"What do you mean?"

Karl placed a long rectangular box on Father Dionne's desk. "I *had* to get you this."

"Why, what is it?"

Karl said nothing, watching Father Dionne open the box.

"A cane?" the priest said with a mix of surprise and confusion. "I don't need a cane."

"You do now," Karl said, sitting down to explain.

2

Karl had done well in the little time he'd had.

After he'd made the decision to stay on at the school, he enrolled in a few post-graduate classes, and was quickly assigned to teach several undergraduate theology tutorials. He'd done a small amount of academic preparation during the last two weeks of August, but most of his time had been spent organizing a used book and bake sale that was to run all of Orientation Week – the first week of school where students become familiar with the campus and comfortable with their surroundings by drinking large amounts of alcohol on each of the week's seven days.

He had scoured the entire campus for old books – most of them on the college's course lists – and he had begged and badgered all sorts of people to make baked goods and donate them to the cause.

The cause was, of course, the preliminary survey of the mission site, or *The Mission Study* as he had come to call it. The three words were simple to say and easy to understand, and most important of all the fifteen letters fit perfectly on the dormitory bed sheet he'd used to make a sign urging people to give.

The makeshift banner was strung between a pair of pressure-treated four-by-four posts Karl had found lying around the campus's small maintenance yard. He'd made a pair of heavy wooden bases for the posts and so far the banner hadn't wavered, even though the wind had been getting stronger over the course of the week. A couple of workers from maintenance had eyed the wooden posts suspiciously on Monday, but didn't press the point after he offered them free coffee and a few butter tarts.

While there were activities going on all week across campus, Karl had managed to secure a central location for his little booth. He was set up in the courtyard between the church and the arena and there was no one on campus who didn't have to pass his table full of cakes and confections at least twice a day.

But despite his efforts, no one seemed to care much about the mission. The baked goods had sold well enough, and most of the books on the course lists had gone, but no one felt inclined to donate any loose change or even stop by to ask questions about the study.

No one, except for one strange man that stopped by on Tuesday afternoon.

Karl had been on a lunch break when the man came by, but Mary Jane Mendes, one of the few students who seemed to share Karl's interest in the study, told him all about the man when Karl returned to the booth to relieve her.

"He asked a lot of questions," she said. "And I mean, *a lot* of questions."

"Really?" After a day of apathy, Karl was happy to hear someone, anyone, cared. "About what?"

"Oh, all kinds of things…like, if we were sure we knew where the mission site was, when we were planning on going, how long were we going to be up there, did we know what we're looking for..." Her voice trailed off and she shrugged. "That sort of thing."

"Anything else?"

Mary Jane shrugged again. "Not really." She paused as if to think. "Well, he was curious about the walking stick."

"What about it?"

"He wanted to know where it was."

That was curious.

Karl had been tempted to put the walking stick on display in the booth along with the documents from the ROM verifying its age, but he'd decided against it. The artifact was just too valuable now to leave out in the open where it could fall victim to the elements, or to some freshman running down an errant football from one of the nearby tracts of grass. Hell, it could even wind up stolen by someone looking to make their entire undergraduate tuition in the few seconds it took to run from the courtyard to a waiting car. Instead of presenting the actual walking stick, he'd opted instead to photograph it from all angles and create a science-fair sort of display for it, complete with plenty of text about the walking stick and its relationship to the mission site. He'd thought the whole thing looked pretty good, but no one had seemed to care...until now.

"So what did you tell him?" asked Karl.

"Since I don't know where it is, I told him I don't know where it is."

"Did he give you a donation?"

"As a matter of fact, he did." She picked up the jar on the table and shook it. There were a few paper bills inside it now to go with the coins Karl had dropped in there Monday morning.

"What'd he look like?" Karl asked, scanning the crowd in the courtyard.

"I don't know, he was dressed in black, but I don't think he was a Goth or anything like that."

"And?"

"And what? Some of his clothes were black, some were dark black." She looked at him with an irritated expression on her face. "He was all in black."

"What about his face?"

She thought for a moment. "You know, I must have talked to him for fifteen minutes, but I can't remember anything about his face."

"Well if you see him, let me know," said Karl. "I'd love to meet him."

"Sure, I'll let you know," said Mary Jane. "But you'll spot him just as easily as me. He really didn't look like a student, if you know what I mean."

Karl watched the crowd intently for the rest of the day...and the rest of the week, but the dark man never returned.

3

The wind that had been blowing through the campus all

week long finally began gusting on Friday afternoon, scouring
the courtyard clean of students and forcing everyone manning
the booths and displays into a mad scramble to keep things from
blowing away. Karl remained at the Mission Study booth alone
since everyone else, including Mary Jane, had given up on the
basically apathetic student body, deciding instead to spend her
last afternoon of Orientation Week in the warmth and comfort
of one of the campus pubs.

Karl hated to admit it, but he'd lost some of his own
enthusiasm for the study over the course of the week too. He'd
thought that once informed of his plan, everyone would be as
gung-ho as he was about the project, but that hadn't been the
case. Far from it, in fact. Comments from students during
the week had ranged from "That's old stuff" to "Is there any
money in it?"

For days Karl wondered if he'd gone about it all wrong. In
hindsight, *The Mission Study* banner looked like just what it
was...cheap and homemade. Used books and baked goods were
fine for raising money for scout troops and minor hockey teams,
but this was a serious archeological dig and it would require
similarly serious money to do it right.

He needed equipment and supplies.

He needed manpower.

He needed sponsors.

He needed to get people excited about a dig.

He needed to create a buzz, make it interesting, and maybe
just a little bit sexy.

And to accomplish all that, he needed...the media.

If he made the public aware of what he wanted to do, surely
some corporation would back the project, maybe provide a little
seed money so they could connect their company name and logo
to something that would unearth the heroic story of courageous
young Jesuits who unselfishly paid the ultimate price to bring the
word of God to a brave New World.

And that was just how he would phrase it in the release, too.
Yes, that was it...

On Monday he would send out a press release announcing
the discovery of the one-thousand year-old walking stick. Then
he would take the artifact out of the vault in the rectory
and make it available to news photographers and cameramen

who would be driving to the college from Toronto, Ottawa and Montreal to cover the story. Once he had their attention, he'd make mention of *The Mission Study* and by the end of the week he'd be in contact with a dozen or more philanthropists and major corporations.

By the end of the month, they'd be breaking ground on the site and getting ready to do some real digging.

The wind picked up again, and this time it was joined by a bit of drizzle. Karl scrambled to pack everything up, especially the photographs of the walking stick that he'd need to include with his release.

He had most of it in bags and boxes and was just about to take down the banner when Father Dionne stopped in front of the booth and rapped on the table top with his new and rather plain-looking hardwood cane.

"Hi Father," said Karl.

"I'm just on my way to give my last 'Welcome to Ste-Claire' speech of the week and thought I'd drop by to see how well you did with your sale."

"Not so good," said Karl, picking up the donation jar and giving it a shake. "A couple of hundred dollars. Enough for gas money and donuts for the crew, that's about it."

"It was a good idea, though. Showed some real initiative."

"But it didn't produce any results."

"You're sure of that, are you?"

Karl just shook the donation jar again and shrugged his shoulders. "I've got a great idea for next week...The media." He raised his eyebrows as if he'd just suggested something sneaky and a little bit dangerous.

Father Dionne looked unconvinced.

"I'll show them the artifact, tell them about the study and–"

Father Dionne shook his head. "I wish you wouldn't do that."

"Why not?"

"You'd only be wasting your time."

Karl didn't know what to say. Father Dionne had been so supportive until now, and here he was shooting down Karl's new idea before he'd even heard it out, or had a chance to talk it over. "Why?" he said at last.

"Because about a half-hour ago, I received a rather large

envelope from an anonymous patron. It was stuffed with more than enough cash to fund a two-week survey of the site, *and* begin plans for a full-scale archeological dig."

Karl was once again speechless. After a long silence, he said, "Who would do something like that?"

"If I knew that, then the patron wouldn't be anonymous."

Karl sat back on one of the hard plastic folding chairs he'd been sitting on all week. "No, I suppose not."

The rain began to fall.

CHAPTER FOUR

1

On Monday morning, after morning prayers, breakfast, and celebration of the Eucharist, Karl decided to forego the press release and prepared a sign-up sheet for the school's main bulletin board instead. With bold type announcing *The Mission Study* would begin in earnest in two weeks, he posted a brief explanation about what they would be doing and for how long, and scheduled a meeting for that Friday afternoon in one of the school's common rooms. He held back on divulging that the study would be worth academic credit because he'd hoped that everyone that signed up would want to be part of the study because they believed it was important work. Afterward, when he was sure they were seriously interested in uncovering the college's history and not just looking to get out of classes, he'd inform them the trip would be worth college credits. That way it would be a reward, not a come on. But by Wednesday afternoon there were just two signatures on the sheet and there was no way he'd be able to begin planning the trip without having at least a rough idea about how many would be coming along.

So on Thursday morning he put the words "Accredited Field Study" in a callout on the sign-up sheet. It looked like the kind of thing the makers of creams and lotions put on their bottles that say, "1/3 More Free," but it did the trick. By lunch-time there were twelve names on the sheet, more than what he'd need to start making plans.

At the meeting on Friday afternoon, only eight people showed up to actually find out more. Karl would have liked a few more students to choose from, but at least he had a good sampling from the student body…a bit of brawn, a bit of brain, and a rather neat four/four split of gender. Karl introduced the students to Doctor Bos from the Royal Ontario Museum – who Karl decided would be an invaluable person to take along on the trip – and after explaining to the group what he hoped to accomplish, he let Doctor Bos explain how they would be achieving their goals, mostly with shovels and trowels. The doctor made sure everyone was aware of the sort of conditions they'd be living under for two weeks and the hard work that would be required of them. Karl fully expected two or three students to back out upon hearing this, but thankfully none of them did.

That weekend Karl did the paperwork to pull all eight students out of their regularly scheduled classes for the week prior to the trip, freeing them up to help him fill the wish list Doctor Bos had given him. They'd be on the site for the third and fourth weeks of September, which would be comfortable weather for digging, and just about the right temperature to make evening campfires a pleasure. A few of the students' professors complained about the lost time from their classes, but most were supportive and encouraging, especially the Jesuit priests who would be taking on Karl's class load during his absence.

Coach Chambers stressed that safety be a top priority, and that Karl return the team bus to him in one piece. Karl asked him if he wanted Father Dionne to bless the mission, to which Coach Chambers answered, "It wouldn't hurt."

2

Karl decided the study team should leave early on Monday morning to give them enough daylight to get to the mission site, unpack, set up camp and store their provisions. Karl had celebrated the Eucharist at midnight on Sunday to allow him to forego the Monday morning mass with the other Jesuits and get an early start to the day. But when Karl pulled the Ste-Claire Cardinals team bus into the arena parking lot at six-thirty a.m. Doctor Bos was the only one waiting for him. He was sitting in his van sipping a medium-sized Tim Hortons coffee, and looked as if he'd been waiting there for hours.

Karl joined the doctor in his van, and was delighted to learn that the doctor had picked up a coffee for Karl on his way in to the college. The coffee was still hot, which was a good thing since Karl had plenty of time to let it cool as the first of his eight-member student crew didn't show up for another thirty minutes.

"Here comes one now," said Doctor Bos.

Ronald Henschel was a fine arts student who had earned the highest grade-point average at Ste-Claire College in each of the past three years. He was a tall, thin young man with mid-length blond hair who wore a pair of thin wire-rimmed glasses. Ronald was a visual artist – or more appropriately, a conceptual artist – who created bizarre objects and images and insisted they were pieces of art. One of his most famous pieces was an antique tea kettle that had been filled with a pound-and-a-half of tiny letter Ts cut out of bits of colorful paper and foil. He photographed the kettle pouring out the Ts in front of a huge clock and called it "T-time." Everyone on campus thought it was merely clever but Lowden Bros., one of the largest tea packagers in Canada thought it was brilliant and bought the rights to the photograph for six figures and put it on all of their boxes of "No-name" teas.

Ronald was dressed in a pair of rather new-looking beige denim pants, matching Tilley hat and jacket, and a new pair of Wolverine hiking boots.

"You look all ready to go," said Karl, guessing the outfit had set Ronald back a few hundred dollars.

Ronald pointed skyward. "I think there's a chance that conditions might be less than ideal, so I want to be prepared for the worst."

Karl glanced up for another look at the thick grey clouds hanging over the campus. "Don't worry, I spoke to God this morning and he's assured me that as soon as we get there the clouds are going to open right up for us. The sun's just waiting til we get there, Ronald. That's all." Karl had tried calling Ronald, 'Ron' in the past, but it had never sounded right. He'd tried 'Ronnie' as well, but while Karl liked it better, Ronald hated it with a passion. Apparently his mother had called him 'Ronnie' throughout his childhood.

"You keep a good thought," Ronald said wrinkling his nose at the sky. "And if God doesn't make good on his promise, I've got a pair of heavy hip-waders in my bag, just in case."

Karl watched Ronald get on the bus and heard him say hello to Doctor Bos who had finished his coffee and was doing a final check on the equipment already loaded onto the bus.

Karl looked around the lot for any of the other seven students. None were in sight, but he did catch a flash of light coming off the front door of one of the nearby school dormitories and minutes later he recognized Mary Jane Mendes making her way across campus. Since there was no one else around, Karl started walking toward Mary Jane so he could meet her halfway and carry her bags back to the bus for her.

They met at the edge of the parking lot.

"Good morning," she said.

"Here, let me take those." Karl reached out for her bags.

"It's okay, I can manage."

"Nonsense, it would be my pleasure."

"All right, then," said Mary Jane, flashing Karl an odd smile. "If you insist."

He hefted the bags easily. "You're traveling light."

"I tried not to bring too many clothes…only what I needed." She paused a moment, then said, "And of course, I sleep in the nude, so I didn't need any clothes for at night."

Mary Jane's odd smile had grown wider and Karl couldn't help but think she was flirting with him – coming on to him, actually. Why else would she tell him such a thing? "I don't know, you might get cold during the night," said Karl, not sure if what he'd said could be considered a *double entendre* or not.

"Then I'll just have to figure out some other way of keeping warm, won't I?"

Karl was at a loss for something to say, but judging by Mary Jane's response to what he'd said just a few moments before, perhaps it was for the best. Mary Jane was an A student with a major in English literature and a minor – like most other students at the college – in theology. She wasn't exactly a beauty, but she wasn't overweight either and she had a face that could probably be made quite attractive with the right hairstyle and some make-up if she ever decided to go that route. Karl wondered what she might look like in a dress, or in a pair of heels, or even asleep without any clothes on…

Mary Jane was looking at him rather coyly, as if she were waiting for a response.

"Well…we can always build a bigger campfire," Karl said rather abruptly. It wasn't like he wasn't interested, far from it. He was *too* interested, and that wasn't a good sign since he was already having enough trouble making up his mind about becoming a priest without this added bit of temptation to complicate matters.

"Oh, that's so cute," Mary Jane said, climbing onto the bus.

Karl tossed her bag into the baggage compartment underneath the bus where the hockey team usually stowed their equipment. There was plenty of room in there, especially since their supplies had only taken up the back ten rows of seats inside the bus.

Karl turned to see if any more of his crew were straggling in, and found Lucy Bartolo and Diane Darby climbing out of a late model Ford driven by a third similarly attractive young woman Karl didn't recognize. "See you in two weeks," Lucy said.

"And remember, not a scratch on my car," said Diane, pointing an admonishing finger at the driver.

The woman inside the car nodded rather tiredly, then drove away. Lucy waved, then started over toward the bus, but Diane stood there watching her car exit the lot.

"All ready to go?" asked Diane.

"No," said Karl. "I was ready twenty minutes ago, now I'm just waiting for the rest of my crew to arrive."

"We're not late, are we?" Diane asked as she came up behind Lucy. "You weren't going to leave without us, were you?"

Karl watched Diane bat her eyelids at him, as if that was going to change everything. Lucy and Diane were a pair of knockout blondes who knew they were pretty and used it to their advantage at every turn. They were average students at best, but always seemed able to earn top marks, especially in classes taught by men. Even Karl had fallen victim to their charms in a communications lab he'd taught last year. Karl knew they were no better than C students, but when he'd checked his final marks, they had both somehow managed to come away with a B.

Lucy and Diane lived in a private residence off campus in Abbotville with two other girls. Lucy was a communications major while Diane was studying journalism. Diane had arranged to do a feature article on the mission study for *The Ste-Claire Sentinel*, but that was just the start of it. With Lucy's help, Diane had already interested *Canadian Geographic* in an article, and they would be videotaping throughout the weeks with the hopes of selling a piece to either TVOntario or the Outdoor Life Network. Karl wondered how they could manage such a coup, but knew that if they wanted something, nothing would stand in their way. Karl often thought that the rest of the world didn't stand a chance against them.

"No, I wasn't going to leave without you," he said, trying not to lose his angry edge, but knowing he was failing miserably. "There are four more still to come after you."

"I can't understand why people can't be on time," said Lucy, dropping her bags at Karl's feet and climbing into the bus.

"Yeah," said Diane. "It's not like they didn't know we had to be here at seven this morning."

"Six-thirty," Karl muttered under his breath.

He reached down to pick up the women's bags and load them onto the bus when they were suddenly lifted off the pavement and out of his reach by a pair of strong, beefy hands.

"Let me get that for you, Father."

Karl looked up and saw it was Chris Wahl, a star defenseman on the Cardinals hockey team. Somehow he'd been able to sneak up on him without making a sound.

"I'm not a priest," said Karl.

"Not yet, right."

"No, not yet, and maybe not at all...who knows." Karl felt uncomfortable talking about it with a hockey player. "Technically, you can call me Regent Desbiens if you like, or just plain Karl would be fine too."

"No problem...Karl," he said, tossing the rest of the bags into the baggage compartment, including his own, which was a large red equipment bag with the Cardinals name and team logo embroidered on the side.

"I'm glad you could join us," said Karl.

"What? You thought I was going to back out?"

"It did cross my mind."

Chris Wahl was a big blueliner whose nickname was "Brick" and whose rights were owned by the National Hockey League's Detroit Red Wings. The Wings had sent him back to Ste-Claire so he could play another year without the Wings having to put him on their payroll. A little rough around the edges, he probably wouldn't make the big team next year either, but they wouldn't be giving up on him. The word around the arena was that the Wings planned to send him to their American Hockey League farm club after he finished at Ste-Claire. But even though it wasn't the NHL, he had already received a large signing bonus and had a low six-figure salary to look forward to. As a result, he wasn't all that worried about his academic standing and would probably be showing up for more hockey games than classes this winter.

"I wouldn't miss this for anything," he said. "Two weeks of camping, *with* chicks and *without* textbooks…and course credits on top of it all. If more courses were like this one I'd be a straight A student."

Karl smiled, unable to resist the chance to give the big man a playful jab. "It's good to have dreams, Chris."

"Call me Brick. Everyone else does."

"All right, Brick."

"Besides," he shrugged, "Coach Chambers asked me to keep an eye on the team bus for him."

Karl's smile faded at the thought of Coach Chambers not trusting him with the bus.

"You sure you know how to drive it?" Brick asked.

Karl had earned his "B" license while working as a counselor at Kilcoo Camp two summers ago. He hadn't made much use of the it while at the camp, but he was glad he'd upgraded the license since it was something that could always come in handy.

Like now.

"Yeah, I know how to drive it. Do you know how to work a shovel?"

"Well, Coach Chambers says I'm always digging myself a new hole."

"Yeah, I've heard that said about you."

"Gentlemen."

Both Karl and Brick turned to see Alexandre Sauve standing behind them with a dirty black duffel bag slung over his shoulder.

Karl let out a slight sigh.

Brick said, "Glad to see you're dressed for the occasion, freak."

"Get on the bus…Brick."

"We're going to dig up some ruins, not commune with the

dead."

"I said, get on the bus!"

Brick shook his head, then turned to get on the bus.

Alexandre Sauve was one of Ste-Claire College's few true Goths. His hair was dyed black, far too long, and often spiked. His body had more piercings than a dart board and his black clothes were studded with all sorts of steel clips, pins, and chains. His black pants had holes in them and his boots looked as if they'd actually seen combat. Karl had hoped Alex would have dressed down for the trip, but that hadn't been the case.

"How do you expect to roll around in the dirt dressed like that?"

"This is the way I dress every day."

"Yes, but you don't spend every day looking for the ruins of a Jesuit mission."

"Relax," said Alexandre. "This is my travel outfit, you know, to tell everyone who I am." He gestured toward the bus, and smiled as if he were rather pleased with himself. "The hockey dude sure freaked out, didn't he?"

"Yes, he did," Karl said, conceding that Brick's buttons had definitely been pushed. "But you can't work dressed like that."

"Of course not. I've got sweats and workboots to change into after we get there."

"Okay, good," Karl said, breathing easier.

Alexandre tossed his bag into the baggage compartment and turned to get on the bus.

"Just stay away from Brick til we get there, all right."

"Sure thing, but at least let me show him my tongue?" Alexandre stuck out his tongue to show Karl the two studs that were lined up down the center of it.

"I don't think so—"

Alexandre was smiling gleefully...

"—it might entice him to grab hold of your tongue and rip it out of your throat."

...then suddenly shut his mouth and got onto the bus with tightly pursed lips.

Karl looked at his watch. Ten after seven.

Where were they?

The answer was in their car.

It was parked at one end of the lot and there were two people inside of it. They were obviously having a rather heated discussion, but about what, Karl couldn't say. He watched the two argue inside the car for several minutes before one of the doors opened and a man got out of the driver's side. He went around to the back of the car, popped open the trunk and took out two travel bags. Then he headed for the bus, with a woman – his girlfriend – bringing up the rear.

"Morning, Karl," Geoff Willett said as he neared. He was a grad student like Karl had been, but some ten years younger. He was in good shape and would be a handy guy to have around.

Unfortunately, he came with a bit of baggage.

Karl didn't know all that much about Charlotte Harriotte-Reid other than she was Geoff's girlfriend, studied drama and theater arts, and had been in every play that had been performed at the school in the last three years. Karl's guess was that after graduation they'd both move to Toronto or Los Angeles and spend the next few years pitching ideas up against the network walls until one of them stuck and they'd be overnight celebrities with their own television show. Knowing them, they'd be millionaires by the time they turned thirty, if – and it was a big if – they didn't kill each other first. The couple hadn't even left the college parking lot and she was on him like red on roadkill. Worst of all, she didn't seem to be letting up even though Karl could clearly hear everything she was saying, and the right-side windows of the bus had filled up with a gallery of faces eager to find out what all the commotion was about.

"Sorry we're late," said Geoff, looking rather tired.

"We would have been here on time but he had to call some girl this morning," Charlotte said, scolding Geoff as if he'd slipped in the playground and torn his brand new pair of pants.

"She's my lab partner," Geoff explained to Karl. "I forgot to let her know I'd be gone for two weeks so I had to get in touch with her this morning, which took a little more time than I thought it would."

Charlotte stood behind Geoff with her arms crossed and an expression on her face that said she didn't believe a word of it.

Karl could feel his skin starting to get itchy under his clothes. "The main thing is that you're here now and we can get this show on the road."

"You had a whole week to tell her before this morning,"

Charlotte continued on like some pit bull that has its teeth firmly sunk in the postman's ass.

"Forgot," said Geoff with a shrug.

Charlotte was about to say something more, but Karl cut her off. "There's plenty of empty seats on the bus, Charlotte...why don't you find one before we loose any more time."

She let out a sigh that said this wasn't over, and reluctantly got onto the bus.

"Help me with the doors, will ya?" said Karl, keeping Geoff behind.

Geoff helped Karl get the baggage compartment doors closed and locked. "Sorry about that," he said. "Diane's a bit of the jealous type, and we've been having a few arguments lately."

Karl nodded as if he understood, but he really didn't. "You know what they call women like that in Las Vegas?"

Geoff shrugged. "What?"

"Two-legged cats."

Geoff smiled broadly at that, as if a lot of his built-up tension had suddenly been drained away.

It was a good sign.

"Okay," Karl said, clasping his hands together. "We're losing daylight, so let's get moving."

Doctor Bos stepped off the bus. "You got everything I asked for," he said with a bit of an incredulous tone to his voice.

"We got lucky with a patron."

"Who?"

"I don't know."

Doctor Bos had a confused look on his face. Then after a moment he shrugged and said, "As long as whoever it is, they're on our side."

Karl nodded. "Meet you up there?"

"No, I think I'll just follow you, so if we get lost, we'll both get lost together."

"Okay, then. I'll try not to lose you."

"Thanks."

Karl climbed onto the bus, closed the door, turned the key and waited for the engine's glow plugs to warm up and the Wait to Start light to go out. When the indicator light faded, he started up the engine and threw the bus into gear.

A moment later they were moving.

3

As Karl drove the bus out of the arena parking lot, he eyed a dark figure heading toward the rectory. It was a bit early for Father Dionne to be up and about, but perhaps he'd gotten up with the sun so he could see them off.

Karl waved at the figure.

The figure did not wave back.

CHAPTER FIVE

1

The first day proved difficult.

They had to carry most of their supplies a half-mile into the woods to the mission site and that took up most of the morning and early afternoon. The guys all carried their share of the load back and forth from the bus to the site, but getting the women to carry supplies – Lucy, Diane and Charlotte, especially – turned out to be an ordeal. Lucy broke a nail, Diane twisted her ankle and Charlotte, well, she just didn't want to work very hard. In the end, Karl put the women in charge of preparing the camp site, and had the guys bring in what they'd need for the first few days, leaving the rest of their supplies on the bus where they would stay dry, and away from bugs and animals.

While Karl spent the rest of the day setting up the three rented tents that would be their home for the next two weeks, Doctor Bos trekked out to the mission site to do a preliminary survey that might shed some light on which locations would be most likely to yield evidence of the mission's existence. Karl had offered to send a student along with Doctor Bos, but the doctor preferred to work alone. That suited Karl, since he'd need all the help he could get pitching tents. The men and women would each have a tent of their own, while the third and largest of the three tents would serve as a mess hall and meeting room where they could eat, discuss their progress, or just keep out of the rain.

It was during the pitching of this last tent that the first injury occurred.

The first thing Karl heard was the heavy *thud* of a mallet hitting something that wasn't a tent spike.

The second thing he heard was a scream.

Karl ran around to the other side of the tent and saw Alexandre Sauve standing there with a shocked look on his face. There was a mallet in his hand and streak of blood splattered across his sweatshirt.

"I thought he was ready," was all he said.

Ronald Henschel was rolling around on the ground at Alexandre's feet. He was crying out in pain and covering his face with a pair of bloody hands.

Ronald had been holding the spikes for Alexandre to pound into the ground with the mallet. They'd done a great job on the first two tents, but had obviously gotten careless with the third.

Karl moved in and knelt by Ronald's side as the rest of the crew gathered around.

"Way to go, freak," said Brick.

"I don't know what happened," Alexandre said. "He must have looked away for a second...I caught him on the upswing."

Karl put a hand on Ronald's shoulder to stop him from moving, and then gently pulled his right hand away from his face to assess the damage. Alexandre had hit him square in the nose with the heavy end of the mallet. The skin had been split open, and everything was swollen and bloody, but at least nothing looked broken or bent out of shape.

"It's your lucky day," said Karl. "Your nose doesn't look broken."

"It hurts like hell!" Ronald said with a bit of a twang to his voice. There were tears leaking from his eyes and flecks of blood covering the lenses of his glasses.

"Maybe," answered Karl, "but look at it this way...Now you won't have to do any digging for a couple of days if you don't want to."

"Hey, that's not fair," said a female voice, probably Charlotte's.

Karl ignored the comment. He looked around for Brick and Geoff. "Help me get him into one of the tents."

The two men lifted Ronald off the grass and held onto him while he tried to steady himself on his decidedly wobbly legs. When it was obvious he was unable to stand on his own, the two men lifted him and carried him away.

Karl followed them, just a couple of steps behind. "And, I

thought this trip was going to be fun," he muttered under his breath.

2

Father Dionne returned to the office in the rectory just before ten in the morning. After morning prayers, breakfast, and celebration of the Eucharist, he'd done his usual walk around the campus and was finally beginning to get used to the cane Karl had bought for him. He didn't mind giving his walking stick to the young man, especially if it was over one-thousand years old. If it kept Karl in the Order of Jesus and at Ste-Claire College, then using a cheap drugstore cane as a substitute was a small price to pay.

Karl was an energetic and imaginative young man, just the sort of new blood both the Jesuit Order and the college needed to be relevant in this new, fast-paced and ever-changing world. Even though Karl had yet to be ordained, and he would have to be appointed Rector of Ste-Claire College by the General of the Jesuits, Father Dionne couldn't help thinking of Karl as his replacement. Having Karl piece together the college's history would make him an obvious choice for the position, and would make the transition that much easier and acceptable to the other priests at the school.

"Good Morning, Martine," said Father Dionne as he entered the rectory's reception area.

"Did you enjoy your walk, father?"

"Yes, the new cane is working out nicely," he said, hanging the cane on the coat rack near the door to his office, then covering it with his jacket. "You know, even if I'd kept the walking stick, I'd never be able to put any weight on it again knowing how old it is."

Martine nodded. "Would you like a cup of tea?"

"Only if you'll be making one for yourself."

"Of course."

"Then, yes."

Father Dionne opened the door to his office and immediately knew someone had been in there. One of the drawers to his desk was half open and several papers on the desktop were askew. In fact, there were countless items around the office that had been moved. It was as if someone had gone through the office lifting things up to either check them out or look underneath them. The effect was that the entire office looked as if it had been shaken by a mild tremor.

And then there was the vault. It was really more of a safe, but a very large and strong one, dating back almost to the founding of the college. It was made of heavy gauge steel and the key that opened it was enormous. Out of habit, Father Dionne kept that key on his person at all times even though there was rarely anything of value inside the vault.

But now there was something valuable inside the vault – a one-thousand year-old walking stick.

Obviously, somebody had been looking for the key that opened the vault.

Father Dionne wondered who it could have been.

3

That night it rained, dousing their campfire and sending everyone into their sleeping bags early. So far, the radio's forecast of scattered showers throughout the week was turning out to be bang on. Of all the times for the weatherman to be right, Karl thought, shutting off the radio before it had the chance to give him any more bad news.

Karl stayed up late that night talking to Doctor Bos – he'd given up on calling the man Cor, something about the name just didn't feel right – about where they might start digging in the morning.

"It's rather odd," said the doctor after spending most of the day on the site. "Although there is definitely a clearing there large enough to have housed a Jesuit mission, there's absolutely no clue as to where the buildings might have been. I mean, usually I wouldn't have agreed to come unless there were already indications that there was something here…like surface artifacts, artificial landforms, that sort of thing."

"But two-hundred and fifty years have passed."

"Yes, of course, but even over such a long time a stone wall or fireplace might still be left standing, or if they fell over there might be a pile of similarly shaped rocks on the ground."

"And there's none of that on this site?"

"None that I've seen."

"Is that unusual?"

"It doesn't happen all that often, but it's not impossible. To give you an example, for years archeologists had been looking for an ancient city called Ubar. It was mentioned in all sorts of texts as being a major trade center but no one had ever found it."

"Did they ever find it?"

"Yes…Someone took a look at satellite images of the Arabian peninsula and saw a bunch of caravan tracks converging on a spot called Ash Shisr. They dug a few holes on the spot, and…there was the city."

Karl sighed. "I don't know if there are satellite images of our site."

The doctor seemed to find Karl's comment amusing.

"Relax," he said, putting a hand on Karl's shoulder. "It's quite possible we have the wrong site, or that the entire place was destroyed by the raiding Iroquois so that not even a trace of the Jesuits remained. Or, the Jesuits themselves might have burned the whole thing to the ground so as to not leave any spoils for the raiders."

"Except for the walking stick," Karl reminded the doctor.

"Look, you don't have to convince me that there's something here. If you did, I wouldn't be helping you. But you do have to prepare yourself for the possibility that we won't find anything, and that some hunter might stumble upon a headstone lying in the grass a kilometer to the south of us twenty years from now…"

The doctor seemed to think that was funny too, but Karl didn't appreciate the irony.

"All I'm saying is that a lot of times, major discoveries happen by chance or simple dumb luck."

"No!" Karl said, surprised by his own conviction. "This isn't all happening simply by chance. There's a reason we're here, I can feel it. There's something in the ground, and we're going to find it, whatever it is."

The doctor looked at him curiously. "Let's just hope the thing we find is the thing we're looking for."

CHAPTER SIX

1

By next morning the rain had stopped and the sun was peeking through the clouds, only to shed light on a new problem. Most of their food had been picked over by raccoons during the night, forcing Karl to send Brick and Alexandre back to the bus for some breakfast food. The crew eventually ate well, but they'd lost a couple of hours and a bit of enthusiasm for the task ahead of them.

After the crew had eaten their breakfast – and Karl spent some time in prayer – he led them down the path that had been created over the years by a handful of hikers, a few tourists and sightseers, and the odd pilgrim like Karl himself. The path wended leisurely through the woods before opening up onto a roughly trapezoid-shaped clearing that had been partially overgrown with trees. The north end of the clearing was narrowest and was bordered by a stand of birch and long-needle pine trees. The eastern edge was lined with boulders and a jagged rock face that seemed to have erupted from the ground like extrusive igneous rock as opposed to the eroded Precambrian formations that were usually found at the southern rim of the Canadian Shield. At the southern end of the clearing, the land dropped off and there was a steeply pitched slope covered with small trees and jutting rocks that led down into a narrow ravine. On the western side, the clearing was walled in by a forest of incredibly tall pines that seemed to be in competition with each other for the affections of the sun.

Since there were no stone ruins on the site, and all of the wooden structures had likely been hauled away by scavengers or burned to the ground by the Jesuits or their Iroquois raiders, the crew would be forced to look below ground for clues that would tell them about the shape and locations of the buildings and structures that had once stood on the site.

"Post moulds," Doctor Bos told the crew gathered around him, "or stains of rotted wood in the soil should be the easiest things to find."

"We're looking for stains in the ground?" one of the girls asked incredulously.

"That's our best chance," said the doctor. "If we get lucky and stumble upon a building, like say a blacksmith's shop, you'll come across metal scraps, axe heads, nails and spikes...things like that."

"Nails and spikes," said Alexandre. "All right."

Brick gave him a gentle push from behind to shut him up.

"If it's a carpenter's shop, you might find a broadaxe or scratch awl, even charred bits of wood. And the cookhouse will be sure to have plenty of animal bones, forks, fish-hooks, even carbonized kernels of corn."

Charlotte Harriotte-Reid put up her hand.

"Yes?"

"What if we find, like...human remains?"

Karl had been expecting everyone to make a joke at Charlotte's expense, but they were all silent, as if eager to hear the answer themselves.

"Then call the Discovery Channel and tell them to send a crew right away, because we'll have hit the jackpot."

Everyone laughed, including Karl.

"You're likely to find the animal bones because they would have been left lying around. Human remains would have been buried pretty deep to begin with so they'll be that much further down in the ground after two and a half centuries. If we find the other stuff, a proper archeological project would likely turn up the bodies of the martyrs themselves later on."

Everyone seemed relieved.

"All right," the doctor said when there were no more questions. "We're not digging ditches here, so pay attention."

He then proceeded to explain how best to dig so as to not damage the things they were looking for. Shovels would be fine early for the top layers, but they would likely have to do most of their fieldwork with trowels.

"This is a Marshalltown trowel," he said, handing a seven-inch long pointed trowel to each of them. "Troweling is slower than using a shovel, but much more detailed." He held up his hand. "Most archeologists in North America have a permanent callus on their right hand from wielding this type of trowel. Luckily for you, you'll only be here long enough to get a decent set of blisters."

A laugh trickled through the group.

Doctor Bos showed them the basics of using a trowel and explained a little bit about how to define sediment. "But if you think you've found anything significant, let me know as soon as you do. Any questions?"

When there were none, he gave everyone a shovel to get them started, then said, "Let's get busy!"

2

By the end of the second day they had nothing to show for their efforts except sore backs, aching muscles, and hands that were rubbed raw. Doctor Bos had mapped out the site with a grid that would ensure that, as long as they dug in each square of the grid, they would eventually find *something* – a post hole, a doorway, a stone step – in the ground...if there was actually anything there to find. There were four pits in the ground now, the deepest being two feet deep and the others ranging in depth between a foot and a foot and a half.

After dinner Karl started a campfire. When it was burning brightly and giving off warmth, he made himself comfortable on a nearby log and watched the flames dance against the backdrop of night. In the corner of his eye he could see Geoff Willett and Charlotte Harriotte-Reid sneaking off somewhere alone. He knew he probably should have stopped them, but he also knew that there was nothing they could do out here that they couldn't do just as easily back on campus. As long as they came back from their *liaison* in the woods at a decent hour and were ready to dig in the morning, he'd be happy.

"Hi Karl..."

Karl turned to his left and saw Mary Jane Mendes approaching. She had an odd sort of smile on her face, one that Karl knew could only mean trouble. He should have gotten up, moved away, or busied himself with some task, but he was too sore to do anything but sit. "Hi M.J."

"Coffee?"

Coffee, even though it was the instant variety, sounded good. "Yes, please."

She handed him a steaming aluminum cup, then sat down next to him on the log. She must have noticed Geoff and Charlotte wandering off because she nudged him in the elbow and said, "Want to see where they're going?"

There was a playfulness in her voice that Karl wasn't used to. Because of it, Karl couldn't tell if she were suggesting they wander off into the woods together as well, or just spy on Geoff and Charlotte while the couple did their thing. "No thanks," Karl said politely. "My legs aren't up to a walk in the woods."

"I'm pretty tired too," said Mary Jane. "Besides, it's nice just to sit here together."

As long as sitting is all you have in mind, thought Karl. "Yeah, sitting's nice."

Mary Jane gave a little laugh, and slid closer to him.

Karl was about to move over and restore the distance between them when he heard it.

A woman's scream, ripping through the fabric of the night, accompanied by the rustle of leaves and the snapping and knocking of twigs and branches.

Then, a jumble of voices.

Karl jumped to his feet, and ran away from the light and into the darkness.

CHAPTER SEVEN

1

"It's Charlotte," Geoff said.

"What happened?" asked Karl.

"She fell down the slope, there!" He pointed down into the shadows below.

"I can't see her," Karl said, trying to catch some movement in the darkness. "Somebody bring a–"

A flashlight suddenly beamed down into the ravine, guided by Doctor Bos. In the dim light, Karl could just make out Charlotte's tan jacket at the bottom of the slope, some fifty feet away. She was sitting upright, and moving.

Thank God, she was moving.

Still, her movements were slow and hesitant and she seemed disoriented from bouncing from tree to tree on her way down. Worst of all was that she'd landed in the ravine and was sitting in a couple of inches of water. If they didn't get her out of there soon she could suffer hypothermia.

Karl turned to face the members of the crew who were just arriving. "More lights," he told them. "And a rope. No, two ropes."

He turned back around and shouted down into the ravine. "Charlotte, are you all right? Can you hear me?"

No answer.

"If you can hear me, wave a hand."

Charlotte's left hand came up off the ground and moved awkwardly from side to side.

"Okay, just sit tight, we're going to get you out of there."

At Karl's left, Geoff looked ready to head down the slope after his girlfriend.

Karl grabbed him by the arm. "Wait!"

"But I've got to help her."

"Fine, but the last thing we need is to have two of you down there needing help. Just wait until we have some more light and a couple of ropes."

Geoff's body hesitated, then lost a lot of its tension as he realized that Karl was right and things had to be done cautiously.

"Now, tell me what happened," Karl said.

Brick arrived with another flashlight and a coil of rope. The others were behind him with Coleman lanterns, flashlights and a second length of rope. And then Lucy and Diane arrived with a powerful video light and their palmcorder, recording the rescue for posterity.

"We were just walking along and she slipped. Fell right down the slope. I didn't think we were that close to the edge, but...God, I hope she's okay."

Karl wound one of the ropes under Geoff's arms and around his chest and tied it off. Then he slung the coil of the second rope over his shoulder, keeping one end of it at the top of the slope with the rope that was tied to Geoff. "When you get down there, tie the end of this rope around Charlotte and we'll help pull both of you back up here."

Geoff nodded and tested the knot on the rope around his chest. It was secure. "I'll be right back," he said.

They watched Geoff head down the slope, feeding him line as he went from tree to tree. It was a controlled sort of fall, since the slope was still wet and slick from the rain the night before. There was plenty of light shining down the ravine now and Charlotte looked to be moving easier, even standing up and leaning against a tree.

When Geoff reached the bottom, he ran to Charlotte's side.

And then as everyone watched, she slapped him hard across the face.

"Looks like she's fine," announced Karl.

Everyone at the top of the slope laughed nervously, then breathed a deep sigh of relief.

2

"It was so dark," Charlotte said, an hour later as she sat in front of the campfire wrapped in a blanket and sipping a hot cup of tea. "I thought I could see where I was stepping, but there was just nothing there. It was like someone had pulled the ground right out from under me, or maybe even given me a push."

"So why did you slap *me*?" Geoff asked.

The rest of the crew that had gathered round all leaned in, as if they were intent on hearing Charlotte's answer too.

"I don't know...I was frustrated and angry and sore and I was mad that I was the one who'd fallen down there instead of you...and, oh...I don't know."

"Well, the main thing is that you're all right. Tomorrow we can all get back at it."

Charlotte winced slightly. "I don't know if I'll be well enough to dig, Karl."

There were groans of disbelief from the rest of the crew, but Karl wasn't about to confront her on the matter. There were other things Charlotte could do to help, and it wasn't as if one less shovel was going to make all that much difference to the dig.

"Then you can help with the meals," Karl said at last.

Charlotte seemed pleased by this, but there were rumblings among the rest of the crew and Karl didn't blame them. Digging was hard work, and after just one day of it they had lost ten percent of their work force. At this rate, they'd be lucky to last out the week.

"Chin up, Karl," said Doctor Bos. "And look on the bright side."

"There's a bright side?"

"No one's gotten killed."

Karl laughed under his breath. Even the bright side seemed pretty dark and forbidding. "Yeah, not *yet* anyway," he said.

It had been meant as a joke, but no one was laughing.

3

"Did you hear that?"

Brick opened his eyes, but it was so dark inside the tent that there was little difference between having them open and having them closed. "Hear what?"

"That," said Ronald, his voice still suffering from a bit of a nasal twang.

Brick held his breath a moment...and heard it. The snap of a twig. And the faint squish of something against the damp ground. "Yeah, I heard it."

"Think it's a bear?"

"Maybe. Maybe it's raccoons again."

"Or a skunk."

"Yeah, a skunk."

"Wanna check it out?"

Brick was so warm and comfortable inside his sleeping bag that the thought of stepping out into the cold, cold night and chasing away wild animals was definitely not on his "wanna-do" list. "You go ahead if you want."

"Me?" asked Ronald.

"No, the other asshole I'm talking to at three in the fucking morning."

Ronald said nothing, but his breath was coming in quick little bursts, like he was about to shit his pants with fright.

Just then, whatever it was outside snapped a tree branch. A thick one by the sounds of it. And it snorted, low and throaty, like a bobcat, or mountain lion, maybe even a bear.

Brick suddenly felt more awake. "C'mon," he said, pulling Ronald's sleeping bag open. "Let's check it out."

He grabbed a flashlight and stepped over the rest of the occupants of the tent. Before he headed out, Brick pushed a toe gently into Karl's back to wake him.

"What? What is it?"

"Something outside."

"What?"

"Don't know," Brick said, sticking his head out the tent.

He switched on his flashlight and swept it across the campsite, but could see nothing out of place, nothing out of the ordinary. Then he shone the flashlight onto the muddy ground around the fire pit. There were tracks in the mud, the water within them shining like glass as it caught the light.

Brick slipped on his boots and stepped out of the tent dressed in an undershirt and pair of boxers. He checked out the mud around the fire pit and saw that the tracks had been made by some sort of hoof.

"Are you all right in there?" That was Karl checking on the women.

"Is it gone?" Mary Jane asked, sticking her head out of their tent.

"I think so," answered Brick.

"I saw it," said Mary Jane, climbing out of the tent. "It was snooping around the camp site. I think it was a deer."

"Gave you a scare, eh?"

At that moment Brick heard something rustling through the trees to his left. He swung the flashlight around to bring the beam onto the spot, but only caught a branch swishing back and forth in the light.

He continued to search the woods with his flashlight, then saw it…something black moving through the trees, hopping like a deer, but smaller. Much smaller.

He set off after it.

"Do you see it?" he heard someone say.

He ran toward the trees, following the sound of movement as best he could.

And then all went silent.

Nothing moved.

Brick was sure he'd lost the thing's trail.

But then it snorted again. He panned the flashlight left to right, and saw it clearly. It was black, hoofed and had a pair of fair-sized horns on its head.

And it was looking right at him.

He took a step closer for a better look, but by then the thing was gone, darting through the trees for a moment before being swallowed up by the blackness of the forest's shadows.

Brick turned and headed back to camp.

"Did you see it?" Mary Jane asked, when he returned.

Karl put a hand on his shoulder. "Was it a deer?"

"Yeah," said Brick. "A deer."

It had to have been a deer, because what he thought it was didn't make any sense at all.

Not here.

In the woods.

And so far north.

What it really looked like was…

A big black goat.

But that was impossible.

"A deer," he said again. "Must've been a deer."

CHAPTER EIGHT

1

Karl had hoped that things would improve as the days passed, but that wasn't the case.

If anything, they were getting worse.

On Wednesday, Lucy Bartolo was stung by a bee on her left arm. It swelled up at the elbow and she wasn't able to work a trowel, taking another member of the crew out of action. The next day, Diane Darby's right eyelid was bitten by a black fly, causing it to balloon up like she'd gone three rounds with Lennox Lewis. Diane proved to be a trooper though, and kept working, but on the whole Karl's crew was beginning to look as if they'd been on a trip through hell.

With sixteen pits in the ground, they still hadn't found any evidence that a mission had ever stood on the site. When the crew talked this over amongst themselves around the campfire Thursday night, Doctor Bos told them the story of archeologist Howard Carter who had spent thirty years of his life searching Egypt's Valley of the Kings for the tomb of the then little-known boy Pharaoh Tutankhamen.

"Yes," said Ronald, whose nose now sported just a single bandage, "and once he found the tomb, twelve of the fifteen people who'd been present at the uncovering of Pharaoh's chamber died under mysterious circumstances over the next ten years."

"What?"

"Really?"

Ronald nodded. "The most famous was Lord Carnarvan, the man who'd bankrolled Carter for six years. After they found

King Tut's tomb, the guy was bitten by a mosquito. Then he nicks the bite while he's shaving and the cut gets infected. He dies six weeks later of what they said was pneumonia."

"Cool!" That from Alexandre.

Doctor Bos put up his hands, as if he were reassuring an angry mob. "Newspapers, books and motion pictures of the day got a lot of mileage out of the curse of the pharaoh, but all of those deaths – including Lord Carnarvan's – were purely coincidental. And even if there was a curse of the Pharaoh's tomb – which there was definitely not – I'm not aware of any similar curses that have been placed on the ruins of Jesuit missions. If anything, these places were cursed before they were built."

No one said anything in response to the doctor's little joke. The only sound was the scratch of crickets in the surrounding grass and the snap of pine resin crackling in the fire.

Karl stared into the fire, his face and chest warmed by its flames, but his back – especially the back of his neck – was left cold and dimpled with goosebumps.

2

By the weekend, they had made two discoveries.

One was a disappointment, the other simply curious.

Mary Jane had been digging near the center of the grid and struck something hard with her shovel. She used a hand tool to dig further, and when she was sure she'd found something other than a rock, she spread the word.

"I think I've found something here!" she shouted.

The rest of the crew dropped their tools and came running. Doctor Bos was the first into the area and looked at the smooth side of whatever was embedded in the ground with great interest. He carefully scratched at the earth around it with smaller and smaller trowels until a substantial portion of the object was free. And then, after a smile broke over his face, he put his hands on the thing and gave it a good hard yank.

The object came out of the damp earth with a bit of a sucking sound, and after he'd cleared away most of the dirt from it with his hands, he held it up for the rest of them to see.

It was a short, fat bottle made of brown glass.

"A beer bottle," the doctor said. "Molson Export, I believe."

"Hey, Molson's has been around since 1786," Brick offered

hopefully.

"Yes, but if I remember correctly stubby bottles like this were used between the 1960s and 1980s. So this is only somewhere between fourteen and forty years old."

"Well that's encouraging," said Geoff Willett. "Isn't it?"

"Oh yeah," said his girlfriend, Charlotte. "At that rate of settlement, we've only got another hundred or so feet to dig before we reach the ruins of the mission."

Karl looked at Doctor Bos so the doctor could shake his head and discount what Wendy had said.

But he didn't.

All he said was, "It's possible."

†

The second discovery was made off site.

Geoff had been digging through a bit of sandy soil on the eastern perimeter of the site when he decided to stop for a pee break. For most of the week they'd been trekking out into the forest to answer nature's call, but Geoff and the other guys had gotten tired of the long walk when it was so much easier for them to take a few steps off the site, find a spot that was out of sight of the others, and let go.

He stepped over the jumble of igneous rocks, heading toward an overhang about fifteen yards away. He liked the rock formation here, because it reminded him of the rocks he'd seen in Hawaii. Those rocks were supposed to have been put there by the volcanoes under the islands, but while these rocks were similar to those in Hawaii, as far as he knew there wasn't a single volcano in Canada, and the nearest one had to be thousands of kilometres away.

So how'd these rocks get here?

Geoff thought about it while he unzipped his fly and drained the snake.

And that's when he noticed something strange.

There was an indentation in one of the rocks, almost like a cross, but more of a diamond or star shape. Geoff finished his business, zipped up and examined the rock more closely.

The indentation was deep, like a hole, but its sides were straight and smooth, as if someone or something had cut the slot into the rock with a modern cutting tool.

He hurried back to the site and called Karl Desbiens and Doctor Bos.

"There's something I think you should see," he said.

"What is it?"

Geoff shook his head. "I don't know. You better come and take a look."

The two men climbed up out of the pit they were working on. "How far down is it?" asked the doctor.

"It's not in the ground." Geoff pointed eastward. "It's in the rocks over there."

Geoff led them to the spot.

"What is it?" Karl asked the doctor.

The doctor stuck his finger into the slotted rock, gauging its depth and feeling the smoothness of the inner walls. He looked up at Karl and shrugged. "I don't know."

"Do you think it has anything to do with the mission?"

"It might have been something like a church pulpit, I mean, it's vaguely the shape of a cross..."

"If it's a cross, it looks upside down to me," said Geoff.

"Then again it could just be a very curious natural formation. Maybe some crystal-shaped minerals were stuck inside the rock, then eroded away over time, leaving this hole. Or, maybe years of rain pounded out the softer material in the center of the rock..." The doctor shrugged. "Who knows?"

"So what should we do about it?" Karl asked.

"Right now, not much other than make note of it in the journal, and take some pictures in case it turns out to be important later on."

"Okay, we'll give Lucy that job," said Karl.

Over the course of the week, Diane Darby and Lucy Bartolo had been taking pictures, and Lucy in particular had proven quite meticulous in her effort to document the dig on video tape.

"What about the rest of us?" asked Geoff.

The doctor smiled. "Keep digging."

3

Sunday morning, the rain came in earnest.

They'd been lucky with the weather for most of the week. The downpours that had been forecast had always held off long enough for them to get the day's digging done before drizzling through the night, keeping them inside their tents and in each other's faces. In the morning the ground was that much muddier than it had been the day before, and a lot of the pits were filled with a foot or more of water. Every day walking around the site was getting more and more difficult. Some places weren't just slippery, they were downright dangerous.

So when it began to rain on Sunday after Karl performed a Eucharistic service in the big tent complete with pre-consecrated hosts that Father Dionne had given him, morale among the crew was as low as it had been since the day they'd arrived.

"And I thought it couldn't get any worse," said Lucy Bartolo, slumping over one of the tables in the main tent.

"At least you have a pair of rubber boots," moaned Diane. "My feet have been wet all week, and now I'm going to be picking mud out from between my toes."

"If you need a hand doing that, I'm available," offered Brick.

"Me too," said Ronald.

"Me three," said Alexandre.

"In your dreams, schoolboys."

"All's not lost," suggested Doctor Bos. "We've got plenty of tarps that we can set up over the active pits to keep them dry."

No one seemed to be keen on the idea of going out into the rain to set up tarpaulins, because even if they could set up something to keep the pits dry, the rain that had already fallen would ensure they wouldn't be getting much work done today.

Karl could feel the entire dig falling apart around him. Although he was almost twice as old as most of the students, he understood exactly how they were feeling. They were all young adults who'd grown up in the era of sound bites and music videos. They'd come on the dig expecting quick results and something to show for their labors at the end of each day. They wanted to sprint when this type of work was more like a marathon. And as much as he hated to admit it, Karl was guilty of having that feeling too. He'd thought they'd dig a few pits in the ground and find a doorway or wall or building foundation. He'd been looking forward to returning to the college with a few artifacts, a map of the ruins, and a plan for the wholesale excavation of the site which would be undertaken within the year...under the direct supervision of Karl Desbiens.

But none of that was happening.

Not even close.

Instead, his crew was growing miserable and the dig seemed doomed to failure. He needed to lift their spirits, somehow. And that's when the thought occurred to him.

"Why don't we just take the day off?" he said. "You've all been working hard and have earned the right to take a break. Why don't we set up the tarps so the site will be dry for us tomorrow, and I'll take the doctor's van into Chalk River and see if I can bring us back some hot pizza and cold beer."

Karl looked over at Doctor Bos and was relieved to see the man nodding in agreement. The group needed to unwind a bit, and the rain was providing them with the perfect opportunity to have some fun without losing much time on the dig.

"Now you're talking," said Brick.

Mary Jane smiled at Karl. "That would be nice."

"Can we spend the day in bed if we want?" asked Diane.

"Sure, anything you like," Karl answered. "But let's get the tarps up first so we'll be ready bright and early tomorrow morning…rain or shine."

There were smiles around the tent for the first time in days.

Karl hoped it was a good sign.

CHAPTER NINE

1

The day off was good for the crew.

Even though by the time Karl returned to the site, the four party-sized pizzas he'd picked up at a mom and pop place in Chalk River called *Gusto's* were cold, no one seemed to care. After eating their meals out of cellophane bags and aluminum foil all week, they were happy to have something that had been freshly made.

The beer went down well too. The Beer Store in town was located right next to the pizza place and that seemed like too much of a coincidence to be ignored. He bought a two-four of Molson Export – of course – and a six-pack of President's Choice Honey Brown Lager. With ten people in total that gave three beers to each person. Not enough to get anyone drunk, but just enough to get everyone feeling good. Even when Mary Jane, Lucy and Diane opted for just a single beer each, their beers were divided evenly amongst the rest of the group without any trouble or fuss.

After everyone ate, Doctor Bos told them a few stories about archeological projects that had gone wrong, most of them in Egypt, but a few that went on in Europe undertaken by the Nazis who'd been looking for something that would help them win the war and take over the world.

Lucy and Diane were persuaded to do a few Cardinal cheers, with Brick doing most of the encouraging. They did the first couple of cheers reluctantly, but when they saw that no one was laughing at them, they did ten minutes worth of their basketball halftime routine, replete with choreography.

Getting into the spirit of things, Ronald recited a few poems
by Edgar Allan Poe, including as much of "The Raven" as he
could remember. Some in the group had heard the poem before,
most likely in the Roger Corman film of the same name staring
Boris Karloff, Peter Lorre, Vincent Price and a young Jack
Nicholson, but none of them were aware of the author's name.

When the topic of Poe came up, Alexandre mentioned that
he'd written a few scary stories of his own, but had never had any
published in *Relations*, the college literary magazine.

"Why not?" asked Mary Jane.

"Not good enough," quipped Brick.

Everyone looked at Brick disapprovingly. They were
becoming friends and cheap shots like that were quickly
becoming out of place.

"I don't know," said Alexandre, his black hair hanging
loosely about his head after a long day of work. "My stuff isn't
about navel-gazing feminists struggling with their inner selves, or
about middle-aged English professors trying to figure out the
meaning of life."

"I've read stories like that in there," Lucy said. "Lots of them."

Alexandre shrugged. "Not by me you haven't."

"His stuff's weird," Ronald offered. "But it's good."

"You've read some?" Mary Jane asked.

"When he lets me."

"Then you have to share one with us, Alex." Mary Jane
seemed to be telling Alexandre, rather than asking him.

The rest of the crew joined in, urging Alexandre on.

"I don't have anything with me, so it's going to have to be
from memory."

No one seemed to mind.

"All right then, this one doesn't really have a title yet, so I'm
just calling it 'The Gunslinger' for now."

Everyone got comfortable.

The campsite grew silent, except for the tapping of the rain
against the tent canvas.

"The story opens with a gunslinger in a bordello in some
desert town in Nevada right after a gunfight. He's in a room with
a woman who works there and she's busy telling the gunslinger
how great he is…especially since it had looked as if the other guy,
the dead guy, had caught the gunslinger square in the chest with

his first shot.

"The gunslinger doesn't say anything to this, he just slowly gets undressed, taking off his vest and then his shirt. With his shirt off the woman can see there are wounds and holes in his chest, all over his body, in fact. He's been shot plenty of times over the years, but no one's ever killed him. She looks at him strangely and is a bit repulsed by what she sees. 'What are you?' she says.

"But before the gunslinger can answer, someone knocks on the door. The gunslinger tries to send whoever it is away, but the guy on the other side of the door is persistent. 'There's an ornery fella down here looking for you, and he looks like he won't be told no to.'"

Alexandre tried to do the voices as best he could, but it was clear that he was a much better writer than he was an actor.

"The gunslinger is tired of being a target for every young gun who's looking to make a name for himself, but it's the price he knows he has to pay for the life he's chosen to live. 'Tell him I'll be down in an hour.'"

There were some knowing laughs among the crew.

"But the guy outside the door, he doesn't go away. 'He's not going to wait that long. If you don't come down, I think he's gonna be coming up a'gunnin' for you.'

"So the gunslinger gets dressed, tells the woman he'll be back and heads down to the bar to meet the young gun.

"'You killed my brother,' the young gun says, only he's not really so young. In fact he's sort of old, and his hands are shaky and he needs a cane to help himself get around.

"When the man gives the gunslinger a name, the gunslinger shakes his head saying he can't remember killing anybody by that name, but that doesn't mean he never did, just that he can't remember. The man doesn't let up, he says the gunslinger killed his brother and now he wants the chance to make things even.

"The gunslinger says, 'I ain't got no brother, so how you gonna even the score,' but the man doesn't think the gunslinger's joke is so funny. Eventually, the gunslinger agrees to a gunfight out on the street. He's even feeling sorry for the man and tells him he'll let him take the first shot. A free one.

"And so they go out in the street and the man hangs his cane on his left elbow and takes aim at the gunslinger with his right hand. He shoots...and the gunslinger falls down in the street."

There was an audible gasp from a few people in the tent, making Alexandre smile.

"While the gunslinger is rolling around on the ground, the man holsters his six-shooter and walks over to the downed man.

"'What did you shoot me with?' the gunslinger gasps.

"'Hollow point bullets,' the man says, 'filled with garlic paste.'

"The gunslinger laughs, exposing his two long fangs. 'It'll take more than a little trick like that to kill me...' But the gunslinger hesitates, because from his new perspective on the ground he can see that the man is wearing a cleric's collar. 'Preacher?' he gasps. Then his voice gets angry. 'You ain't even close to killing me. All you're doing is pissing me off...preacher.' He sort of spits out the last word like it tastes bad in his mouth.

"'I know,' says the preacher. 'But I'm not finished yet.' So he breaks his cane over his knee and thrusts the jagged end of one of the wood pieces through the gunslinger's heart.

"The gunslinger wails in agony, but he doesn't die. In fact, he's still smiling up at the preacher, showing him his fangs. But then the preacher, unbuttons his fly, whips out his pecker and starts peeing on the downed gunslinger. 'It's not exactly holy water,' the preacher says, 'but it'll do.'"

The crew laughed out loud, some of it coming from deep down in the belly.

Alexandre beamed with pride as he finished off the story.

"The gunslinger's body sizzles as the holy water rains down on him. He gives one last baleful cry and then his body becomes still. In a few hours, the body will be gone, scattered across the desert like dust in the wind.

"The man, or 'The Preacher,' as he comes to be known, stands on the edge of town and looks down the main street with narrowed eyes and says, 'All the young men you killed, they were *all* my brothers,' and then walks off into the sunset."

Everyone clapped in appreciation.

"That was good," said Mary Jane.

"Yes, very good," Karl said, patting Alexandre on the back. "I especially like how good triumphed over evil...well, sort of."

"The gunslinger, he was a vampire, right?" asked Brick.

Alexandre nodded.

"Excellent."

The mood in the tent was suddenly light, and Karl thought that maybe their luck was about to change.

He couldn't be more wrong.

CHAPTER TEN

1

Karl awoke Monday to find that the rain was continuing without abatement. And as he said his morning prayers, it seemed to come down even harder.

And the wind was starting to pick up.

As the crew huddled inside the large tent eating a breakfast of fruit, toast, instant oatmeal and coffee, the wind and rain seemed to find every hole and opening in the tent's canvas. Water dripped in on them from above and the wind seemed to pass through the sides of the tent as if it were made of mesh. And then, every once in a while the wind would pick up and the tent would shake as if the whole thing might fall down on top of them.

Digging would be difficult today to say the least, but Karl wasn't about to give the crew another day off. They had to come away from this dig with some evidence, *something* that would convince people like the Royal Ontario Museum, or the Catholic Church, or the provincial government, that there was real history buried on this site and a full-scale archeological project needed to be funded. Another day without digging while the rain continued to fall would be like conceding defeat.

They simply had to resume digging, even if it was on a limited basis. They had tried to keep the active sites dry with the use of tarps, but all of them had become soaked overnight. Maybe they could double up the tarps and concentrate them on just a couple of pits, keeping those going at the expense of the others.

Karl talked the idea over with Doctor Bos. "If you really want to keep working, I suppose we could do it that way," said the doctor. "Just remember that when this soil gets wet, it's as slippery as oil and as heavy as cement. And..."

The doctor hesitated.

"What is it?"

"Well, these students aren't the most experienced crew I've ever worked with. They've already had plenty of accidents in the dry, asking them to work in the rain, well..."

"What about just one location, then?"

"Then we'd all be getting in each other's way."

"Two then. We'll dig in two places, rotating crew so that everyone can dry off and rest when they need to."

"That might work," said the doctor.

"All right." Karl got up to tell the rest of them the plan.

But when he told them they'd be digging, no one was very eager to head out into the rain. Karl really didn't blame them. After all, it was already cold enough inside the tent. Add some rain to the cold and the crew members would be thinking about hot showers, warm dormitories and cold drinks in the pub. That is, if they weren't thinking about those things already.

Karl needed to set them straight, bully them if he had to, make them feel guilty if he had to...whatever it took to get them outside and digging on the site.

"We could take another day off, sure...but tomorrow's forecast doesn't look much better than today's. So, if we don't dig today, we won't dig tomorrow. That will bring us to Wednesday, and who wants to start digging on Wednesday when we'll be packing up on Friday."

No one said a word. Many of them were looking at their boots, or to the ground, anywhere but at Karl's face, or in his eyes. Karl wasn't going to let them off so easily.

"We have the chance to do something important here..." he began. "Really important. Men gave their lives on this spot because of what they believed in. Martyrs, dying because of their devotion to God, because of their dream of spreading God's word to the rest of the world. They traveled thousands of miles, overcame all kinds of hardships, only to be brutally murdered by the very people they were trying to embrace...And here we are two-hundred and fifty years later, not wanting to honor their heroic legacy because it's raining outside."

Karl shook his head, and said nothing more.

The tent was silent.

Even the rain seemed to have eased up while the crew thought about what he'd said.

"Karl's right," said a voice.

Karl looked up and saw it was Mary Jane.

"So it's raining. So what. We've come all this way, and we're doing something we all know is important, are we going to stop it because we're going to get a little wet? Well, I'm not."

Mary Jane zipped up her raincoat, tossed her hood over her head, and stepped outside.

Karl watched her leave, wondering if she'd supported him because she believed in what they were doing, or because she was just trying to get closer to him. But then he realized that it didn't matter. She thought enough of him *and* the dig to support him and that's all that mattered.

"Shit!" said Brick, pulling the hood of his raincoat over his head. "She's going to need some help."

He left the tent.

The others, including Doctor Bos, followed Brick outside.

Karl made a mental note to remember to thank Mary Jane for what she'd done. Even if that meant sitting close to her around that night's campfire and being tempted by her charms.

The more he thought about it, the more he felt it wouldn't be so bad. In fact, maybe he was even looking forward to it.

2

Father Dionne thanked Martine for the tea she'd brought him. It would go down well after his morning walk had been cut short by heavy rains and high winds.

"Here's your mail," she said a moment later. "I've also forwarded you your morning emails. There's one from the General in the queue."

Father Dionne thanked her again, sipped at his tea and then unwound the elastic band from the thick jumble of envelopes. He began flipping through the white and beige pieces of mail to see if there was anything that needed his immediate attention. There were the usual things like invitations requesting the college send students to the annual Jesuit conferences in Pennsylvania, information about opportunities at Jesuit missions in East Africa, and a letter from a college in New York state wanting to start an exchange program with Ste-Claire with the aim of strengthening their school's hockey program.

All of those paper letters could be handled later, or by someone else. Father Dionne was curious to read his emails, especially if one of the letters was from the Vatican and the General of the Society of Jesus himself.

Two weeks ago, he had written to the General feeling him out about Karl's plan to survey the Ste-Claire Mission site, and inquiring about the possibility of financial help from the Society for the site's future full-scale excavation.

The email had to be the General's answer.

Father Dionne turned on his PC and waited impatiently for it to boot up. Once the screen was blue and all the program icons were in place, he logged onto the College's server and accessed his mail. The letter from the General was third in the queue.

#: 14262 S0/ClaireServe Mail
    14-Sept-01 08:13:04
Sb: Ste-Claire Mission Site
Fm: INTERNET:GeneralSJ@vatican.it
To: Gilbert Dionne, S.J. [gdionne@Ste Claire.on.ca]

Dear Gilbert,
As always, I was happy to receive your letter, although I found the news it contained rather troubling.

In regards to your question, the Society of Jesus has neither the funds nor the will to help finance, or otherwise aid the study or excavation of the site of the former Ste-Claire Mission.

Furthermore, we strongly urge you not to proceed with any other plans you may have for the site. As you know, the Order of Jesus considers the land to be Holy Ground, and we do not wish for the site to become another Martyrs Shrine, like the one down the road from you built to honor the martyrs at Ste-Marie Among the Hurons. Having one gleaming monument to one of the Order's more spectacular failures is more than enough in your part of the world.

Yours sincerely,

General Barthelme Rousseve, S.J.
Society of Jesus Headquarters
Vatican City, ROME

P.S. What are the Cardinals chances like this season?

Father Dionne had trouble believing what he'd read to be true, so he went over the letter again, this time reading it more carefully.

It still said the same thing.

The Society of Jesus wasn't willing to help them. More than that, they were basically ordering them not to do anything to the ground at the site. While it was true that the Jesuits' attempt to convert the natives in the New World proved to be a disaster, it was still part of the history of the Order, the Catholic Church, even of Canada. It didn't make sense to simply ignore the fact that something important happened at the Ste-Claire Mission.

But while it didn't matter to Father Dionne if they couldn't excavate the mission site, he knew that Karl would be devastated by the news. Over the last few weeks, uncovering the mission site had become something more to him than simply a reason to stay on at Ste-Claire College. It had become a kind of obsession and in time it would surely become his life's work. He would remain at the school, teaching his classes and spending weekends and summer breaks working at the site, uncovering the secrets that had been interred with the martyrs, and sharing them with the rest of the world.

Karl was going to put Ste-Claire College on maps other than the ones used by NHL hockey scouts and player agents. He was going to make the school mean something to the rest of the world, and people would came from all over to visit its museum, to study, and to learn about the long-forgotten heroes of the Jesuit Order.

But none of that was going to happen now.

Karl would be heartbroken. The study would be called off and Karl would transfer to some inner-city church, or South American mission where – and Father Dionne didn't blame him for wanting it – he would make a real difference in somebody's life.

And, Father Dionne feared, if someone as bright and resourceful as Karl Desbiens didn't take over Ste-Claire College, it would surely be doomed to a slow, agonizing death as enrollment continued to drop, the school's funding kept evaporating away in a neverending series of budget cuts and downsizing, and the number of new Jesuits joining the order trickled down to nothing. Eventually the college would be sold to developers and made into the Ste-Claire Golf and Country

Club, putting millions into the Orders' coffers back in Rome while leaving this part of the world spiritually and historically bankrupt.

Without Karl's energy driving the school, it would only be a matter of time.

Father Dionne looked at the papers scattered across his desk for the slip that he'd written Doctor Bos's cell phone number on. Both Karl and the doctor had encouraged him to call them regularly to keep in touch and to monitor how things were going with the dig. Father Dionne had been reluctant to call them, first of all because he couldn't be sure when would be the right time to call – envisioning himself bothering the men during a moment of terrible stress or physical exertion – and secondly he didn't want them to think he was checking up on them. He trusted Karl without reservation and Doctor Bos worked for the Royal Ontario Museum so surely he knew what he was doing. And so he'd left it to them to call him, but they never had.

Perhaps, Father Dionne thought, things were going too well for them to bother calling an old priest.

But as much as he hated the idea of telling them to stop digging and return to the college, he couldn't go against the will of the General.

And so, reluctantly, he picked up his phone and started dialing...

There was a strange noise coming from the ear piece, like information being sent over a phone line, but mixed in with a faint scream of someone in terrific pain. Father Dionne listened to the sound for several seconds, then hung up and tried again. The sound was there again, only this time the scream sounded louder and clearer, and more agonized.

Finally the line went dead and an emotionless female voice informed him that the service was unable to connect him to the number he'd dialed.

The voice encouraged him to try again later.

Father Dionne smiled as he hung up the phone. The General had told him not to proceed with plans to excavate the mission site, but an even higher authority would not allow him to get in touch with Karl and Doctor Bos.

Of course he would try again later as the woman's voice had suggested.

Maybe tomorrow.

Maybe in a couple of days.

In the meantime, he'd write a letter to General Barthelme asking him to reconsider.

3

Karl could feel the rain dripping under the neck of his raincoat and chilling its way down the length of his spine.

They shouldn't be out on a day like this, he thought, but after the speech he'd given and the effort the crew was putting out, he wasn't about to call them back inside.

Maybe he'd end work early today.

That seemed like a decent enough compromise. They could work for a few hours, and then he'd keep them in the tent after lunch to dry off.

But for now they'd work.

The rain was coming down harder now, the individual drops hitting the plastic of his raincoat and the vinyl tarps overhead like tiny bullets from a scattergun.

And the ground was getting slippery.

The path leading to the site had gotten slick with mud and Lucy and Ronald had both fell on their asses on their way to the site. The rest had managed to stay on their feet, but the level of mud had been rising steadily and was now up to their ankles and the quagmires beneath the surface of the water were getting deeper and deeper.

"I hate this!" shouted Diane, grabbing onto a nearby tree to keep herself upright.

No one paid any attention to her. They all probably felt the same way, but were thankfully keeping it to themselves, soldiering on.

Karl and Doctor Bos decided to concentrate on the two pits at the north end of the site. They were at the highest points in elevation and therefore the driest. The two pits were also closest to the camp, so if things got worse, they wouldn't have far to run to reach shelter.

Doctor Bos supervised the pit at the foot of the trail, while Karl oversaw the work on the pit nearer to the center of the site. They had tried to double up the tarps covering each pit, but the wind wasn't co-operating with their wishes. Every time they stretched out a tarp, the wind would pick up and blow it out of their hands. And if they hung onto it when the wind got strong, those on the corners would be dragged across the site, while desperately trying to get a foothold on the impossibly slippery ground.

Karl decided to lead by example, doing most of the dirty work on his site himself, but his digging just seemed to make things worse. While it was fairly easy to cart away dry earth in wheelbarrows or throw shovelfuls of it up and into screens for sifting, trying to do the same thing with wet, muddy ground was an arduous and messy task. Brick had proven to be the best – or at least the strongest – at transporting the earth, but even he had to struggle under the extra weight of all that water. He'd already slipped and fallen several times that morning, pulling and stretching his legs in ways they were never meant to go. Karl was worried that the hockey player might end up twisting a knee, or breaking an ankle, putting his career in jeopardy and Karl on Coach Chambers' most wanted list...but they had to keep working. They just had to.

Karl dug another chunk of earth out of the wall of the pit he was working. At one point he'd thought he'd come across some sort of pottery, but nearly an hour's worth of delicate digging had revealed it to be just an oddly shaped stone. Karl lifted the tarp in front of him and flung the stone across the wet earth and got back to work. He was sure there was something here in the ground, something that wanted to be found as much as Karl wanted to find it. They just had to look in the right place, was all.

"Hey," cried a voice. "There are people out here."

It was doctor Bos. He had the oddly-shaped stone in his hand.

Karl stood up in the pit and waited for the man to join him.

"How are you doing here?"

"I just spent close to an hour digging out that rock."

"And a beautiful rock it is."

Karl nodded. "What's up?"

"I need to talk to you." The doctor's expression was grave. "I think you should consider cutting short the project."

"What?"

"I think you should end the mission study early..."

"How early?

"Like today."

"Why?"

"Take a look around you, Karl. The ground is too wet, the conditions aren't safe anymore, and the forecast is calling for more rain, and wind. Lots of both."

Karl didn't want to give up, not yet. If he stopped now, the study would be a failure, but if they kept working, there was always a chance they'd find something.

"Look Karl, I went along with you because you seemed intent on continuing the project, and I was impressed by the focus and dedication to duty the Jesuit Order has instilled in you, but let's face it, three more days here isn't going to make any difference to this project. Not in the rain."

Karl looked at the doctor, studying him. "You think we're wasting our time, don't you?"

Doctor Bos shook his head, but Karl wasn't convinced.

"I'm not saying that at all," the doctor said. "There very well may be something here, and if you continue looking you might find it, or you might not. The one thing I can guarantee you is that if you keep going in this rain, somebody's going to get hurt...seriously hurt. These kids have had enough, and quite frankly, so have I."

"But there *is* something here, I know it. If we leave now, we've failed. I've failed."

"You haven't failed." A pause. "Try looking at it this way, at least now we know where the mission was *not*. When you come back next time, like in the spring, you'll know where not to look, and you can try someplace new."

In his heart, Karl knew the doctor was right, but he still couldn't let go of his dream. "What if we keep digging just for today, then pack up first thing tomorrow morning?"

"I really don't think–"

Just then a frantic voice called out to them.

"Karl, Doctor Bos, come here!"

The two men looked into each other's eyes for a moment. Karl wondered if maybe this was it, the breakthrough they'd been waiting for. It was certainly the way things like this often went, just when they were about to give up, they discovered the very thing they were looking for.

Doctor Bos helped Karl out of the pit and the two men ran to the other site.

"What is it?" Karl asked.

"It's M.J.," said Alexandre. "She's been hurt, real bad."

Karl hurried over to where Mary Jane had been digging with the others, almost wiping out on the slippery ground when he tried to stop. Judging by the looks on the faces of the people surrounding the pit, Karl figured it was serious.

But it was even worse than he'd feared.

The mud at the bottom of the pit was a sickening shade of reddish brown. Brick and Geoff had managed to pull Mary Jane up onto her feet, but they were having trouble getting her out of the pit.

One of Mary Jane's hands was covering the left side of her face. Blood dribbled through the spaces in her fingers, staining the back of her hand before it flowed down into the sleeve of her raincoat. Mary Jane looked to be in a lot of pain, but she wasn't letting anyone know it. She let out a moan every once in a while, but anyone else in her condition would have probably been screaming in agony. Karl was sure of it.

"Get her out of there!" he shouted.

Geoff held onto Mary Jane while Brick jumped out of the pit. Then Karl, Brick and Doctor Bos, helped Mary Jane up onto the grass.

"How are you?" Karl asked, knowing it was a stupid question, but not knowing what else to say.

"I think I slipped, and I hit my head..." she began. "My face..."

"Yeah, her feet just went out from under her," Diane offered. "And her head hit the spade, the part at the back of the blade that's pointy. It was hidden in the mud and water...I think it caught her in the eye."

"I'm sorry, Karl," said Mary Jane.

"Sorry? For what?"

"Ruining your trip."

Karl felt his heart break for the woman. She'd supported him unselfishly when he'd wanted the crew to dig in the rain. And now because of that, because of her support for *him*, she might be seriously injured. And yet, here she was apologizing to him for ruining the study. For an instant Karl thought about how wonderful a wife Mary Jane would make for some lucky man. Maybe even him. But the thought was gone just as quickly as it had come as Mary Jane moved the hand covering her face and a spurt of muddy blood squished through her fingers, spattering Karl in the face.

"Let me see it."

She nodded and allowed Karl to slowly pull her hand away from her eye.

Karl nearly fainted.

The sharp part of the shovel had caught her in the corner of the eye socket. The skin had been torn open, but worse than that, the bone at that end of the eye had been smashed, leaving a huge open rent in the left side of her head. And the eye...the eye was floating around in a deep pool of blood, as if it suddenly didn't know where it belonged anymore.

Karl put Mary Jane's hand back over her face.

"Someone get some clean towels!" he barked. "Let's get her up to the camp. Doctor Bos, can you take her to the hospital in Mattawa, maybe even North Bay?"

"Yes, of course."

"And I want someone to ride with M.J. and the doctor to show him how to get to the hospital."

"I can do that." It was Charlotte of all people. "My parents had a summer home on Lake Nosbonsing. I spent a lot of time in North Bay when I was a kid and know my way around, at least well enough to find the hospital."

"Fine."

"Aren't you coming with us?" the doctor asked Karl.

"No. I'm staying here...to pack up the bus."

"You mean we're going back to the college?" Ronald asked.

"That's exactly where we're going."

It should have been a happy time, but no one seemed very cheerful.

CHAPTER ELEVEN

1

It took four of them to carry Mary Jane up the path to the campsite. Through it all she showed impressive grit, but toward the end of the trek she was crying out in pain each time someone slipped or had to make a sudden movement to stay on their feet.

The short trip from the camp to Doctor Bos's van was easier, only because the ground was more level. Doctor Bos ran ahead of the group carrying Mary Jane and started up his van to let it warm up before she got there. Karl, Brick, Geoff and Alexandre carried Mary Jane while Charlotte brought up the rear carrying her bag and belongings.

"I'll see you tonight," Karl said, as they eased her into the passenger's seat.

"I won't be seeing anybody tonight," Mary Jane said. "Not with this eye anyway."

"You know what I mean," said Karl.

"I'm looking forward to it...no pun intended."

Karl did up her seat belt and nodded to the doctor. "Drive carefully."

"Of course."

Karl backed out of the van, and pressed the door closed.

Doctor Bos stepped on the gas, but the front wheels of the van just spun on the grass.

He tried it again, this time more slowly, and the van began to move.

"All right," said Karl. "Let's get out of here."

2

The rain didn't let up.

And the wind kept getting stronger.

Karl put Brick and Geoff in charge of pulling down the smaller tents, while he would work on the larger one with the others, but before they could start pulling pegs, they had to empty out the tents and carry all of their unused supplies back to the bus.

This simple task seemed to take forever, especially when everyone's clothes had become fully soaked and they were carrying around an extra fifteen pounds of water in addition to everything else they had to move.

But no one was complaining.

They were, after all, getting out and going home. That made the work at least bearable.

By the time they had the big tent empty, the wind was already helping them take it down. The whole thing was leaning westward as if it were about to pull up its stakes by itself and leave the earth behind.

Karl considered leaving the tents where they stood, hopping on the bus and coming back for them in a couple of days when the storm had blown over, but the wind was beginning to tear at the tents' canvas and having to replace or repair one of these rented tents would use up all, or perhaps even more, of the money he had left in the Mission Study fund.

"Just pull out the stakes and wrap it up," he said over the driving wind and pounding rain. "We can dry it and fold it right when we get back to the college."

Karl took down the center spar of the large tent and the whole thing suddenly billowed to the right, covering Geoff and Lucy who had been working on the leeward side of it.

Karl ran around to where the two students had been and began lifting up the canvas. "Are you all right? Are you okay?"

"Fine," said Geoff.

Lucy didn't answer, but he found her lying on the ground next to Geoff, a miserable look on her face.

"Okay, let's just get this thing on the bus any way we can," Karl cried. He lifted the edge and began rolling it with his hands like a carpet. The others joined in and the tent canvas began getting smaller and easier to manage. Water gushed out from each end of the roll and eventually, they had the tent rolled into a ten-foot length that they could just get their arms around. Then the seven of them all picked up the roll, hefted it onto their shoulders and began the trek up toward the bus.

When they reached the bus, Alexandre ran ahead, opened up the rear emergency exit door and helped guide the tent into the aisle between the seats.

"There, that wasn't so hard," Karl said. "Just two more to go."

They headed back down to camp to retrieve the other tents.

Being smaller, the two other tents were easier to manage, but they still had to wrestle with the wind-blown canvases to get them down to the ground, especially the women's tent which at one point filled up like a balloon by a gust of wind and dragged Ronald a half-dozen feet across the campsite.

When they finally pinned the third tent to the ground and had it rolled up like some giant's cigar, Karl sent it up to the bus with Geoff, Alexandre, Lucy, Diane and Ronald.

"I'm going to take one last look around the campsite," he said. "Brick, I want you to head down to the site and check if we've left anything behind. I don't want to lose any tools, especially those that belong to the doctor."

"No problem."

"All right, go!"

Five students headed up to the bus with the third tent resting on their shoulder.

Brick headed down to the mission site for a last look around.

And Karl stayed where he was to check out the campsite, wondering if this was how his dream was going to end.

3

Brick slid most of the way down the path, just like he used to do on patches of ice in the schoolyard as a kid. It was easier than trying to walk the route now that it was covered over with mud, and it sure was faster.

And he was all for anything that would get him back onto campus sooner. He'd gone ten days without a hot shower, without a quarter-pounder, and he hadn't had his dick sucked since four days before this little field trip began.

That was two whole weeks ago!

Christ, no wonder he was feeling so lousy.

The first thing he'd do when he got back was take a long hot shower. Then he'd go down to the cafeteria for a couple of burgers and big order of fries smothered in gravy. And then he'd head over to Miriam Brown's dorm room and wait for her to get back from class. Oh, wouldn't she be pleased to see him. The last time he paid her a visit, they hadn't left her room for two days for anything other than hot showers and warm food. The way Brick was feeling, maybe this time he'd stay a week.

The mission site looked like it had been picked clean.

The first thing they'd done was take down all the tarps and fold them up so they could carry them back to the bus. That little job had been almost as hard as rolling up the tents, but they'd managed it. All that was left now was a dozen or more pits in the ground, a few other taped off areas that they hadn't gotten to, and plenty of mud.

After the ground had absorbed as much water as it could handle, each of the pits began filling up like muddy brown swimming pools. If there was a digging tool submerged under any of that water, there was no way Brick would be able to see it unless part of it – a handle maybe – was sticking up out of the water. Had to be that way, since there was no way he was going to go slopping around in the mud looking for trowels.

He made a quick circuit of the site, looking down into each pit, but not spending more than a few seconds on any one of them. But as he neared the southern edge of the site, he heard a sound that was different and distinct from the falling rain and blowing wind.

It sounded like...a river.

There was a ravine at the bottom of the slope at that end of the site and with all the rain the area had received in the past few days that tiny creek had probably swollen into a churning, roiling river. But as he reached the edge of the site and looked down the slope, he could see that while the creek had definitely gotten bigger, it was flowing easily, and in almost complete silence.

So, where was the sound coming from?

Brick checked the rest of the pits, especially the ones at the southern edge of the clearing.

"Holy shit!"

The southern most pit had been completely washed out and the side of it that had been part of the slope was gone. Water sluiced down the walls of the pit, out the hole in the side and then down the slope of the ravine to the ever-expanding creek below.

The pit was huge now, as water from all over the clearing was making its way to this one spot where it could escape the higher ground. Water was flowing through the pit like a torrent, carrying away gallons and gallons of water, and dozens of cubic feet of earth with each passing second.

If this went on for any length of time the flowing water would cut a swath down the middle of the site, dividing it neatly in two.

Brick thought about the way the rain was reacting with the earth and figured it was probably one of the reasons they hadn't found anything. If there had been anything left behind by the Jesuits it probably would have been washed away over the years, not only by rain like this, but by heavy spring thaws as well.

He was about to head back to the bus satisfied that there was nothing left on the site when he saw it...

The skull appeared first, moving slowly out of the earth as if someone, or something, was pushing it out of the ground from the other end, from below. Water sluiced around the skull, as well as through it, sending dirty brown jets spurting up through the eye sockets, nose and mouth.

"What the fuck–" Brick mumbled, leaning in closer before a slip with his right foot caused him to take a few steps back.

The water kept flowing around the skull, washing away the earth from the neck and collar bone, leaving the bones a shiny yellowish-white.

It was obviously a skeleton.

The right arm had come free now, the water pushing it roughly up and away from the trunk as if the skeleton were saying hello. The arm waved in the water as the current moved it back and forth in a motion that was almost regal.

"I gotta tell Karl," said Brick out loud, knowing what this discovery would mean to the older man. He'd be...in heaven.

Brick turned with the intention of running back to the bus and calling everyone down here to see this, but something stopped him.

No!

It was a voice.

But it made no sound.

It was a voice inside his head, and more than just talking to him, it was telling him something.

Take it! the voice said.

"What?" Brick wondered. "Take what?"

More and more of the skeleton was appearing out of the muddy ground, almost as if the earth was taking a crap, getting rid of its refuse.

The ribs began to appear, one after the other.

Take it! the voice said again. *It is yours.*

There was something stuck between the skeleton's fourth and fifth ribs on the left side of its ribcage. It was long, dirty and rusted and was stuck right through the ribs piercing them both at the front and back of the ribcage.

Hurry now! the voice was almost screaming.

Brick stepped into the pit. Water was flowing all around his foot. Every once in a while the current would surge and water would flow down into the top of his boot. The footing was treacherous and if he wasn't careful he'd slip and be carried away by the draining water, bouncing off trees all the way down the slope, unable to stop himself.

But the mud beneath his boot held.

He put more weight on the foot in the pit and reached down for the skeleton. He grabbed at the eye sockets and pulled, and the skull broke free from the rest of the bones and sent him reeling backward. He tried to hang onto the skull but it slipped from his fingers and tumbled down the slope where it slammed into the trunk of a birch tree and shattered into dozens of tiny shards.

Brick knew he should go find Karl before he destroyed whatever else remained of the martyrs…but the voice inside his head wouldn't let him.

Now, more than just telling him, it was commanding him, compelling him to do its bidding and not allowing him a single thought of his own.

Take it! the voice instructed. *It is yours.*

Brick set his foot again and reached down into the pit.

In the time that had passed, the pit had opened up even wider and now the remains of the skeleton had moved even further away. Brick reset his left foot closer to the churning water and dug the fingertips of his right hand into the soft grass and sodden earth above him.

And he reached down.

But not for a bone, or any part of the skeleton.

This time he reached for the dark object wedged into the skeleton's ribs, right where the heart must have been so many years ago.

He closed the fingers of his left hand around the object, and was surprised by how warm the thing felt, like the outside of a coffee mug. It was also comfortable in his hand, as if it were meant to rest in his palm, clenched by his fingers…his fingers alone.

Yes hissed the voice. *Take it! Take it now!*

Brick pulled with as much force as his tentative foothold allowed him, and the object slowly came away from the bones surrounding it.

Amid all the noise of falling rain, sluicing water and wind racing through the trees, there was a sound of great wrenching, as if lengths of heavy gauge steel was being twisted and broken. There was a scraping sound too, like metal against rock.

He kept pulling, harder and harder.

He could feel his hands and feet beginning to give way. In another few seconds he'd be without a thing to hold onto and tumbling headlong down the slope.

He gave the thing one last hard jerk…

And it came away.

Brick landed heavily against the mud at the side of the pit.

The headless skeleton came out of the earth more quickly now as if there was no longer anything holding it back. The bones seemed to be vomited out of the earth, and were sent hurtling down the slope, smashing and crashing against trees all the way down to the creek below.

By the time they reached the bottom, the bones were ground into fragments and carried away by the creek – grown into a raging river now – for who knew how many miles.

Brick looked at the thing in his hand.

The part in his hand was about five inches long and as thick around as a hockey stick. It was also bumpy, malformed, and dark as night. The surface of it was pitted as if it were made of some low-grade iron and had gotten rusty over the years. Funny thing was that it wasn't heavy enough to be iron. It felt more like the weight and density of a thin gauged steel, or maybe even aluminum. The other end was about six inches long and tapered away from Brick's hand to a blunt point.

Brick turned the thing over in his hand, noticing how the raindrops burst into droplets as they struck it.

What the hell is it? he wondered.

It had the right size and shape to be a dagger, or some sort of large knife. It could also be a sword, the blade broken off in defense of the mission. Then again it could be a kitchen tool, used to cut bread, or stir soup.

One thing was for sure, it had once been a murder weapon, used to stab someone straight through the heart.

Brick knew he should show the thing to Karl, or better yet, Doctor Bos, but something inside him told him not to.

It was the voice.

It is yours the voice said.

Brick just stared at it.

You will use it!

"For what?" he said under his breath.

You will know when the time comes.

"I will."

Give it what it needs and it will serve you well.

Brick looked at the object one last time, then lifted his raincoat and slid it into a pocket.

The thing was warm against his chest.

It was a good feeling.

4

Karl waited by the side of the road with the bus's diesel engine running. He kept the engine revving since it took forever to warm up and the crew in back were all wet and shivering against the cold.

He'd almost decided to send a couple of people out looking for Brick when the young man appeared between the trees and came running toward the bus.

It was about time.

Karl didn't think it was possible, but the rain was coming down even harder now. Looking out the front windshield, it seemed as if someone were standing on top of the bus with a garden hose, pouring water directly onto the glass. Water was leaking inside too, dripping constantly through the bus's body seams and pouring freely in through a few small holes. The wind had also gotten stronger too, gently rocking the bus as if there were a band of drunken homecoming revelers outside intent on pushing the behemoth onto its side.

Brick was splashing his way through the mud, his vinyl poncho being blown away from his body and offering him little protection against the rain.

As he neared, Karl opened the bus's doors, allowing Brick to run directly up the steps into the bus without stopping. The moment he was inside, Karl shut the doors.

"Well?" Karl said.

"Well, what?" Brick answered, a little out of breath, but not as much as Karl thought he'd be after such a long run over treacherous ground.

"Did you find anything left on the site?"

"Like what?"

Karl looked at Brick strangely. It was as if he were having trouble remembering what he'd been sent down to the site to find.

"Anything...like tools and supplies, I don't know, maybe somebody's hat."

Brick shook his head. "No, nothing like that down there."

Karl nodded. "All right, then." He put the bus into gear and lifted the clutch. "Let's get out of here."

The bus lurched forward, then hesitated, as if one or all of its wheels were stuck in the mud.

Karl pressed more firmly on the accelerator and released the clutch slowly.

Reluctantly, the bus began to move.

CHAPTER TWELVE

1

Just as Karl pulled onto the highway, a gust of wind rocked the bus, making it feel as if the right rear tires had momentarily lifted off the pavement.

Karl slowed his speed and brought the bus under control, but the steering wheel seemed loose, as if the front wheels were slipping and sliding over a sheet of ice rather than a watery windswept roadway.

There were leaves blowing everywhere too, landing on the windshield and sticking to it as if they were pasted on with glue and a brush. The bus's windshield wipers were slow at the best of times and now they were practically useless. The blades slid over the leaves as if their job was to press them more securely to the glass. Leaves were also falling onto the highway, shaken loose from the trees and sprinkled over the asphalt by a wind that seemed to be coming at them from all directions at once.

It was also getting dark. The clouds had turned from grey to black and with all the rain it looked as if it were early evening instead of the middle of the day.

Karl switched on his headlights, and headed into the darkness.

Karl could feel the bus slipping out from behind as he negotiated the first few turns, but he was doing a decent job of keeping it on the road and between the lines dividing the lanes. If he could keep it going at this speed for a while, they might just get through the worst of the storm without a scratch.

If they'd been farther from Ste-Claire, Karl might have looked for somewhere to spend the night, but they were just over seventy-five kilometres from the college and even driving at a crawl he could be there in a few hours. Besides, four hotel rooms for the eight students would put a serious dent in what little was left in the budget and he was already thinking about what he was going to do differently when he returned to the site in the spring.

The chatter that had droned on in the background during the ride up to the site was gone. The inside of the bus was silent except for the patter of the rain on the rooftop, the whistling of the wind through cracks in the body and windows, and the dull, but reassuring thrum coming from the diesel engine up front. They've probably figured out that getting back to the college wasn't going to be that easy, thought Karl, or maybe they were all thinking about Mary Jane and saying a prayer so she might not lose her eye.

Or maybe they were just scared.

Like him.

Whatever the reason for the silence, Karl appreciated it since driving the bus was getting more difficult by the minute, and it was requiring more and more concentration to keep the vehicle on the road.

Perhaps he should pull over and wait out the storm.

But even if he did, he first needed to find a safe place to stop.

Up ahead, there was a car approaching in the northbound lane. Although Karl's vision wasn't affected by the oncoming car's lights, the driver courteously flicked off his highbeams as he passed. Then a second set of lights appeared in the distance. They were larger, set higher up off the road. Obviously a transport, thought Karl.

He automatically eased off the accelerator.

The bus slowed.

From somewhere behind him came the faint sound of a horn, a car's horn. Karl looked in his outside rear-view mirror through the rain-streaked window and saw a big black sedan approaching quickly from behind. The sedan's lights were low to the ground, weaving back and forth across the two-lane highway as if the driver was impatiently searching for a way to pass.

Up ahead, the truck was nearing, its highbeams flickering down as the approaching driver prepared to pass the bus.

At the same time, the car's horn grew louder in Karl's ears. He glanced into his mirror and saw the two balls of light growing larger behind him, pulling out into the other lane.

The guy behind him was going to pass...

"No!" Karl cried out. "There's not enough time."

...and would surely be killed making the attempt.

Karl lifted his right foot completely off the accelerator and put both his feet down onto the other two pedals. He needed to slow the bus down to give the car more time and room to pass. He shifted into a lower gear and disengaged the clutch while his right foot remained firmly on the brake pedal. He was desperately trying not to lock up the rear wheels but with so much rain and leaves on the highway, he doubted he'd have much traction for long.

Behind him, the students cried out and shrieked as they slid off their seats, or were tossed into the aisle by the force of his sudden braking.

The black car was almost past now, Karl couldn't find it in his mirror anymore, but he saw it as he glanced down through his side window.

The oncoming truck was less than fifty metres away. Its lights had been flickering ever since the car had pulled out to pass, but now the truck driver was blowing long hard blasts on his air horn. The truck was on a slight downgrade and was obviously going too fast to even attempt stopping in time.

Carl pushed harder on the brake pedal.

The back wheels of the bus locked up and the rear of the bus started to slide ever-so-slightly to the left...into the oncoming lane.

Through the rain-soaked windshield of the bus, the huge chrome grill and long shiny bumper of the truck looked like a monstrously unforgiving wall of steel as it approached. The high-set lights seemed to grow brighter with each second until they looked as if they would bore into the tiny car and smash it into a gnarled and tangled mess of rubber, steel, and gore.

Karl anticipated the moment of impact between the truck and car and braced himself for it.

But the moment never came.

Instead the car darted right at the last possible moment and continued on its way as if nothing had happened.

But as the car continued down the highway Karl realized that he was looking across his left shoulder at it. With his foot still firmly on the brake pedal the rear wheels of the bus had skidded left on the rain-slicked highway.

Now the vehicle was sliding down the highway sideways, its full length stretched across both lanes.

"Hang on!" Karl shouted.

It was all he could do to warn the students at the back of the bus.

Karl braced himself for the impact.

And this time it came.

2

Brick opened his eyes but saw nothing.

Everything was dark and black.

People were screaming and moaning.

He had trouble moving his arms and legs, but at least he could feel them. Each of them hurt like hell and, like it or not, that was a good sign. Hopefully he was just banged, bruised and sore, and nothing important was broken.

With some effort Brick managed to get his arms free, then by pulling on the seats on the other side of the aisle, he was able to get his legs loose of the seat he'd been sitting on.

He looked around. The bus was on its side and most of their supplies had been thrown all over the place. Some of the other students had been thrown around too. A group of them were climbing out through the emergency exit windows on the upturned side of the bus. Karl was there, helping the others get out of the bus.

Brick sniffed at the air and for the first time he could smell it.

Diesel fuel.

It was almost a sweet smell. And strong. Too strong to have come from the bus alone. The truck had probably been carrying plenty of fuel and now it was leaking all over the crash site.

Brick realized that the bus could be engulfed by flames at any second...

But he wasn't worried.

A little fire wasn't going to hurt him.

Not now.

He crawled over the seats toward the back of the bus. In the midst of the panic and screams he saw that the bus's body had been twisted and bent by the collision with the truck. At the midway point, the thing had been pinched, squeezing the middle of the bus like a tube of toothpaste.

Through the front and rear windows he could see people outside, passing motorists probably, all of them eager to help the others climb out of the wreck.

Brick took another quick look around.

"Help me!" the voice cried softly. "I'm stuck."

Brick turned, his eyes scanning the darkness for the source of the voice.

"Help me."

He crawled toward the back of the bus and behind the last empty seat he saw Ronald Henschel pinned under a twisted piece of metal.

"Brick, thank God," Ronald said weakly. "My jacket. It's caught on something and I can't tear it free. I can't even move my legs and arms. Maybe you could cut me loose."

Ronald looked to be in good shape, just a few scrapes on his arms and a small gash across his face. His legs were pinned down by a seat that had been wrenched back when the bus went over. The seat could be forced loose, but he'd need two or three more guys to do that. Maybe Ronald would be able to get free if he cut him out of his jacket.

He will be the first.

The voice was firm, yet comforting. It would guide him through this, all the way to the end.

"Get something to cut me out of here?" Ronald cried, a little more frantic this time.

Brick reached under his raincoat and padded at his jacket pockets until he felt the object he'd found in the pit. One end of it was long and thin and had a flat edge to it.

Maybe it would be enough to cut Ronald free.

Maybe it wouldn't.

Sacrifice him.

Brick took the object out from inside his jacket and clenched it firmly within his fingers. He was amazed at how much it felt like a knife in his hands.

Like a dagger.

"I'm caught under my arm," Ronald said. "Start there."

Kill him.

Brick held the dagger before him like a sword, the tip pointing away from his body, knuckles pointing down. Holding it that way, he felt like he was about to join in on some knife fight on a street corner.

And then without another moment's hesitation, he slashed the dagger from right to left across the young man's throat.

The sound of the blood flowing out of the gash in his throat was lost amid the pounding rain...

...and the sound of igniting diesel fuel.

3

Karl saw Brick crawling over seats toward the open window.

"Is there anyone back there?" Karl asked.

Brick shook his head.

Karl looked down the length of the bus. The interior was already dark, quickly filling up with smoke.

There was a red glow on the windows as a fire burned somewhere behind the bus.

"Who's back there?"

Brick shook his head, and pushed past Karl. "It's on fire," he said. "Got to get out before it all goes up."

As the glow from the flames increased, the additional light allowed Karl to recognize the outline of a hand hanging limply over the edge of a seat.

It wasn't moving...

But that didn't mean it was too late.

Karl started toward the back of the bus.

The interior was clouded with smoke. He could smell the fire burning, and the diesel fuel that was just waiting to transform itself into a fireball.

Karl knew he had to get out, but there was a hand...someone still in the back of the bus.

He got past two more rows of seats. Just two or three more rows to go.

He thought about who he'd helped off the bus, and who would be left inside.

"Ronald!" he called out.

The fire was closer now. He could see the flames licking up against the back of the bus. There were supplies stored there. Food and clothes and sleeping bags...

And lanterns and propane cooking tanks.

The smoke was all around him now.

He couldn't breathe.

And the person in the bus probably couldn't either.

Fire had worked its way inside.

The whole thing was going to go up in seconds.

He reached for the hand.

And grabbed it.

Only to find that it was cold and lifeless, and bloody.

Dead.

The fire was on him. He could feel the heat eating into his skin, singeing his eyebrows.

Karl had to get out.

He turned, and scrambled back over the seats. He could feel the fire behind him now, hot against his feet, legs and back.

"Come on Karl!"

Through the thickening cloud of smoke Karl could see it was Brick, hanging down through the open emergency window.

Karl kept moving.

The smoke had moved up the bus, surrounding him again. Choking him.

He began to gag and cough.

"Give me your hand!"

Karl reached out.

Felt his hand touch another.

And then he was being pulled.

Up and out.

The air was moist, sweet and clean.

He took two, three, four steps...

Whumpf!

And felt a force slam into his back, throwing him to the ground.

4

"Are you all right?"

The voice seemed to echo through the air, as if Karl were listening to it in a cave or through some sort of tunnel.

There was an intense heat pushing against his side, as well as the cold tickle of rain coming from above. Something warm and wet was running down into his eyes and his head felt as if it had been hit with a hammer.

He drew a sleeve across his eyes and saw that the bus was burning.

A couple of people were scurrying around it, trying to put out the flames with the extinguishers they happened to have in their cars and trucks.

But the bus continued to burn.

For a moment he wondered what the hell had happened, but slowly it all came back to him.

He'd been driving the bus in the pouring rain when a car...a black car had crazily pulled out to pass him. There'd been a truck too...

"A car cut me off," he said to anyone who would listen. "It was a black car. I had to stop...no choice."

He could feel hands grabbing his arms, his body slowly rising off the ground.

"Never mind that now," said a voice. "Are *you* okay?" The voice belonged to Brick, who had managed to get a shoulder under one of Karl's arms, helping him stay on his feet.

"I'm all right," he said, slipping away from Brick, wanting to stand on his own. "But there was someone still on the bus." He turned and headed toward the fireball.

Brick grabbed Karl by the arm and held him back.

Searing pain tore through Karl's side, but he didn't care. There was someone still on the bus...Someone burning in the fire.

Karl's body slowed.

"He's already dead."

"Was it Ronald?"

Brick nodded.

Karl suddenly felt tired. Oh so tired.

Brick put an arm on Karl's shoulder to keep him steady.

Karl's knees felt incredibly weak.

His mind was reeling.

Brick put another hand on Karl to hold him up, but it didn't seem to help – he was going down.

Karl fell forward onto the highway and threw up what little breakfast he'd had onto the oily highway asphalt.

The blood began to run down his face again, the slick dark liquid flowing into his eyes and drawing the nightmare to a close.

Like a curtain.

PART TWO: MARTYRS

Others took refuge upon some frightful rocks that lay in the midst of a great Lake nearly four hundred leagues in circumference – choosing to find death in the waters, or from the cliffs, than by the fires of the enemy.

– The Jesuit Relations and Allied Documents

CHAPTER THIRTEEN

Constable Vincent Tremblay stared at the inside back page of *The Toronto Sun* and wondered how old the bikini clad girl staring back at him was. The copy under the photo claimed she was twenty-one, but she didn't look a day over eighteen.

He wouldn't be surprised if she wasn't.

When he was in high school, one of the girls in his class had been a Sunshine Girl, even though she wasn't even sixteen at the time. The girl had probably lied to the photographer and the photographer hadn't mentioned anything about the girl's age to his editor. When the picture appeared, no one in the school kicked up a fuss – even though it was a Catholic school run by Basilian Fathers – and the whole thing had been over with in a day. Nowadays, there'd be all sorts of politically correct people crying child abuse and who knows what else, maybe even a lawsuit against the photographer and everyone up the chain.

Constable Tremblay wondered which way was better as he flipped through the pages that carried news from across Canada, from across the province, and from Toronto, the editorials and columns, the world news, and finally ended up at the back of the tabloid, where they kept the sports section. Vince Carter supposedly had another big preseason game last night and people were beginning to talk MVP...

The phone rang.

Constable Tremblay put aside the newspaper and picked it up. "Abbotville Police. P.C. Tremblay speaking."

"Ah, constable, I'm glad I caught you in."

The voice had a sort of East Indian accent to it, although Constable Tremblay couldn't be sure. It could just as easily be

English, the sort of upper crust English you see in movies all the time.

"This is Doctor Moe Hussein calling from the Centre for Forensic Science in Toronto."

Constable Tremblay closed the newspaper and put it aside. He'd never had a call from the Centre for Forensic Science before and as far as he could remember the small Abbotville force had never made use of their services. Never had any need. "What can I do for you, doctor?"

"Nothing really, I'm calling on the advice of Detective Joe D'Allesandro of the Ontario Provincial Police."

"What about?"

"The O.P.P. brought in the body of the student who died in the bus fire that occurred just north of your jurisdiction. I believe the boy was from the college just outside of Abbotville."

"That would be Ronald Henschel," the constable nodded.

"Yes, I believe that's the name."

"That accident happened on a provincial highway so we're not investigating the incident," said the constable.

"Quite right. But when I gave my verbal report to Detective D'Allesandro, he asked that I call you since the boy was from your area and you might want to know."

"Know what?"

"Well, when the body came into the centre it had obviously been burned in the fire. It had been badly charred and most of the features had been burned away...As you no doubt know, the prime task here at the centre is to determine cause of death, and in a fire we check the lungs for smoke inhalation because the smoke often kills people before the fire ravages their body."

Constable Tremblay remembered reading up on this in one of the textbooks he flipped through on occasion whenever he gave some thought as to who might replaced the chief when he retires. "Okay," he said, letting the doctor know he was following.

"But the boy's lungs were clear..." The doctor paused, giving the constable time enough to reach his own conclusion. "...meaning that he died before the fire swept through the bus."

"I saw the photos, it was a pretty bad crash."

"Right, so our next course of action would have been to check for blunt force trauma to the head, which would have been consistent with such a crash..."

Another pause.

Constable Tremblay was getting a little annoyed with the doctor's method of delivery, but understood that the man probably had to explain such things all the time and couldn't be sure who was keeping up and who was not.

"But there was no evidence of that either," said the doctor at last. "Not to the head nor any of the vital organs."

"So how did he die?"

"A very good question."

"What's the answer?"

"A rather puzzling one, I'm afraid. Despite the damage done by the flames, there seems to be a throat wound on the body, a large rent in the flesh, the kind that might be made by a knife."

"You're saying someone cut his throat?"

"I can't say that for certain. As I said before the body was severely burned and it's possible that the fire itself played a part in splitting open the skin on the throat..." The doctor's voice trailed off, but it wasn't because he was waiting for Constable Tremblay to make a connection. This time it sounded as if there was another theory.

"And?" prodded the constable.

"Well, the bus did receive quite an impact. Seats came undone, windows were blown out, the young man could have been cut by any manner of flying debris."

"So what you're saying is that the student who died in the crash may or may not have been killed by a knife to the throat?"

"No, I'm not really willing to say that."

"What are you willing to say, then?"

"Of course I'll be sending you a copy of the full report, but for now all I can say with certainty is that the student's death is…well, curious."

Constable Tremblay wondered why they called it forensic *science* when all it seemed to be was *guess work*. "Is that all?"

"Yes, that's it. And again, I'm just calling because Detective D'Allesandro thought you should know."

"All right, then. Thanks."

"You're welcome." The doctor hung up.

Constable Tremblay cradled his own phone and glanced out the window of the storefront police office on Abbotville's main street. The wind was blowing down the street in an easterly direction, sweeping the town clean of leaves, cigarette butts and plastic bags.

Have I got a murder on my hands? the constable wondered, or just a mysteriously tragic accident?

Either way, he'd be paying a little more attention to Ste-Claire College in the future, maybe even ask a few questions just to see what he could come up with.

He glanced over at the newspaper on his desk and suddenly felt that reading it would be a waste of his valuable time.

CHAPTER FOURTEEN

1

Karl had been hoping the mission study would garner some media attention, but this wasn't what he'd had in mind.

Television reporters and cameramen, and all sorts of print journalists had strategically placed themselves throughout the courtyard between the church and the arena, each one trying to get the best possible photograph of Ronald Henschel's grieving family. For some the focus of the story was better highway safety, for others it was stricter vehicle maintenance, and still others were zeroing in on the Henschel family – an only son gone, and a mother and father with a huge hole punched through the fabric of their lives.

No one was there, it would seem, to ask about the mission study. That didn't bother Karl since a failed excavation paled in comparison to a young man's tragic death, but in all of the news items he'd read in newspapers, heard on the radio, and seen on television, none had even bothered to mention *why* the bus had been traveling on the highway that afternoon. If Karl didn't know better, he would have thought that the only reason he'd been driving the bus that day was in order to crash it.

Even Lucy and Diane had only spent a few paragraphs on the mission study in a splashy two-page spread they did in the *Ste-Claire Sentinel.* And while he was trying not to be too cynical about such things, Karl couldn't help but think that the two girls were using a fellow student's death to their advantage. They had each written first-person pieces for the *Globe and Mail* and *National Post* and while there had been more than a half-dozen people on the bus when it crashed, Lucy and Diane were the only ones who had wound up on all the evening newscasts. Even today, instead of mourning the death of a classmate, they were working the memorial service, covering it for a national student magazine and campus radio syndicate.

Karl shook his head at the thought. Those two might not do so well in the next life, but they sure were going to go far in this one.

On the makeshift stage that had been set up in the courtyard, Father Dionne stepped up to the microphone to introduce the next speaker, the president of Ste-Claire College's student union.

Father Dionne had asked Karl to say a few words at the funeral, and he had refused since it was inappropriate for anyone other than the priest celebrating the mass to speak of the dead and of dying. And besides that Karl felt responsible for Ronald's death and standing up before the young man's family, friends and fellow students to offer a few words of consolation seemed like such a hollow gesture.

But Father Dionne had insisted that Karl be involved, and ended up celebrating a private Mass of the Resurrection inside the church the night before for family and friends, then conducting a more public memorial service the next morning for the general school population, the people of Abbotville, and to a lesser extent the media.

And now Karl was tapping his foot, nervously awaiting his turn at the microphone so he could tell the world that it was Ronald's time, that God had called the young man to be by his side and all the other clichés that go over so well with such occasions.

That's what he would say when he got up there even though all he wanted to say was that he was...sorry.

Oh, God, he was so sorry...

Karl held his head in his hands and struggled to hold back the tears.

When he had recovered his composure and looked up, he saw that the clouds had parted enough to let the sun shine down onto the gathering. Even so, the sunshine did little to chase away the day's somber autumnal chill. The October wind continued to sweep hard across the courtyard, penetrating the Sunday-best clothing worn by the crowd and touching their flesh like cold fingers. The birch and maple trees skirting the circle had lost their leaves to the season, their naked white and grey branches providing an appropriately barren and desolate backdrop for the occasion.

Father Dionne had opted for the outdoor service because of a forecast of warm weather and to accommodate the large number of students and faculty expected to attend the memorial. But fewer than half the anticipated number had shown up to brave the cold, leaving the courtyard full of empty seats.

As the president of the Ste-Claire College Student Union droned on about how Ronald had been active in student politics, Karl did his best to compose and prepare himself for the moment he'd be called upon to speak. As he looked out from the makeshift platform at the scattered mourners – all of them dressed in black – he couldn't help but think that Ronald deserved better from his fellow students, and from his school.

At the far end of the circle from the platform were dozens of television cameras set up in a long ragged line. Other cameramen had set themselves up closer to the platform or on the roof of the administration building. There had been some jostling for position earlier in the day but the reporters and cameramen had quickly realized there was no point in fighting for a spot since there wasn't going to be any shortage of good ones.

Karl hoped the copies of the testimonials he and the others would be making available to the media would satisfy their need for quotes and sound bites because he dreaded the thought of going in front of the cameras again, just to go over what he will have already said on the stage. After all, what could he possibly say to convey the feeling of complete and utter loss pervading the campus that hadn't already been said by others a dozen times already?

"...And now Regent Karl Desbiens would like to say a few words," Father Dionne said over the public address system.

Karl could the feel the collective stare of the crowd shift over onto him. Although he'd lectured in front of large classes before, sometimes to as many as two hundred students at a time, he'd never been comfortable in front of people. As he got up from his chair a lump of dust seemed to form in his throat and his hand trembled as he fished inside his pocket for his speech.

How many of them would be looking up onto the stage, pointing their fingers at him and saying in whispered breaths,

"He's the one!" Or "It's his fault Ronald's dead!"

The thought made his knees go weak.

He struggled to make his way to the podium and grabbed hold of it as soon as he was able. As long as his nervousness didn't affect his eyes and he was able to read his speech without tripping over too many words he would be all right. He'd written his speech the night before and checked it with Father Dionne earlier in the day. The priest had changed a few of the words to make it sound a little more compassionate, having had a bit more experience with funerals than Karl.

At five-foot-ten Karl was somewhat taller than the petite student union president and he had to bend over sharply in order to speak into the microphone. He swallowed in an attempt to wet his parched throat, but it didn't seem to help.

"I've been teaching the same North American History class for several years now," Karl began, "and in that time I've seen a lot of students come through my class room. I've had students go on to become professional hockey players, actors and actresses, doctors and lawyers...I've even seen one of my students run for mayor in a big city – and get elected.

"The death of a young person is always a tragedy, even more so when the possible futures for that life had been limitless, and the reason for it being snuffed out so senseless," Karl paused to turn his paper over. The crowd remained silent. "Ronald Henschel saw the world differently from most, and judging by what he had already accomplished, the world is a poorer place for his passing."

He paused a beat, expecting someone to shout out, call him a "bastard," or a "reckless driver" or say "you killed my baby," but that didn't happen. Just silence, and the blowing of a chill wind.

"On behalf of myself and the rest of the faculty of Ste-Claire College I would like to extend my most sincere condolences to the Henschel family and to those students who called Ronald *friend*. We can only hope that he's in a better place and that God will make use of his talents."

Karl straightened himself up and stepped back from the microphone. There was just a polite amount of hand clapping as he walked back to his seat. As he sat down, Karl felt as if someone were watching him, staring at him with an unwavering gaze. He looked out at the crowd, and noticed a dark figure in the front row looking back at him. Although the man was dressed in black, he somehow managed to stand out amid all the other black-clad mourners. He was looking at Karl, looking him in the eye, and his gaze seemed to go right through him.

Karl wondered for a moment if this might be the darkly-dressed man who had so graciously funded the mission study.

And then Karl suddenly felt weak and dizzy. His clothes had become damp with sweat and the cold wind was now chilling him to the bone. He sat back in his chair, closed his eyes and hoped that whatever it was that had come over him – grief, nausea, despair – would pass as quickly as it came. He listened to Father Dionne resume the Mass, his voice sounding as if it were coming to him through some long echoing tunnel.

And then the service was over.

Karl felt better.

He opened his eyes and looked out into the crowd, searching for the dark figure he'd seen before, but the man was gone, an empty seat now in the place where he had been.

No matter.

Karl didn't know how or why, but he was sure he would be meeting up with the man at some point in the future.

2

Later that evening, Karl sat at his desk in his dorm room looking over the text of the lesson he'd be teaching in the morning. Father Dionne had wondered if it wasn't too soon for him to get back into the classroom and suggested that he take some time off, or perhaps do a thirty-day retreat of meditative silence at Regis College at the University of Toronto, but with the way Karl felt, he couldn't get back in soon enough. He wanted to forget all about the mission study for a while and filling his mind with work and getting back into a routine seemed like the best way to keep out the guilt and anguished thoughts that had been haunting him since the day of the accident.

Over the course of the last week, a few people had asked him what his plans for the mission study were, but his only answer had been that he didn't have any. How could he right now? One student was still in hospital and in danger of losing an eye, and another student was dead. Was he supposed to ignore these things and carry on? Act as if they'd never happened? Maybe in the spring he'd feel different about going back to the site, but for now he didn't want anything to do with the study.

After all, he was a Jesuit and a teacher.

Not an archeologist or historian.

Karl heard the rap of something hard against his door and immediately knew that it was Father Dionne knocking on it with his cane.

"Come in, it's open," Karl said, then realized such a casual response was inappropriate for a superior such as Father Dionne. He got up and opened the door just as the priest was reaching for the door handle.

"Father."

"Mind if I come in?" asked Father Dionne, already stepping into the room. "I want to talk."

"About what?"

"Well, you, for one." Father Dionne eased himself into a chair. "I was watching you during the memorial service. You looked sick there at the end."

"I was." Karl shivered at the recollection. "I don't know what came over me."

"You know the offer of time off and meditation still stands."

Karl nodded. "I know it does, and I appreciate it. But I don't feel like I deserve any time off."

Father Dionne sighed. "Guilt can be a devastating emotion, Karl. It can tear you up inside, hamper your judgment. Make you physically ill."

"I know, Father, but I can't help myself. I was the one who was driving the bus when it crashed. I was the one who decided to leave for home when we did. I was the one who organized the trip in the first place."

"And I was the one who approved the trip, and your patron was the one who financed it…How many people do you want to share in the blame?"

Karl remained silent.

"Well, if you really want to blame someone, you can start with the driver of the black car. The truck driver and a few of the students confirmed you were cut off. The provincial police are looking into the matter. They haven't caught anyone yet, but they haven't stopped looking either."

Karl shook his head, more in defeat than denial.

"We are both men of God," continued Father Dionne. "Both members of the Society of Jesus. We've been trained to believe in God's will, and that things happen that are beyond our control for reasons we may never understand. And although that reason isn't apparent to us right now, we *must* believe that God is at work shaping our lives and the lives of those around us – *especially* when we don't like the way things go."

"Yes Father," said Karl. He'd never really had any trouble with the concept of God's will. If you believed in God at all then you had to believe that things happened according to God's will. It was just that sometimes it was impossible to see meaning in life's more tragic events. In a way, it was like he was standing too close to a large canvas, looking at individual brush stroke and wondering what possible difference they could make to the entire, much bigger, picture. But then once you took a few steps back, the single strokes vanished from view as they took their place in the whole and no matter how hard you tried you were never able to see the individual brush strokes and the whole picture at the same time. And so, Karl was stuck being too close to the canvas, able to see the individual strokes, and having to trust that the larger canvas, the bigger picture, was a thing of infinite beauty.

Father Dionne looked at Karl closely, as if making an assessment. After several moments he gave a satisfied nod and said, "Now, what do you plan to do about the site and the mission study?"

"Nothing."

"Nothing at all?"

"Maybe in the spring I'll go back and take a look around, but I don't even want to think about it for a few months."

"I think that would be wise."

Karl looked up at Father Dionne, curious as to what he had meant by *wise*, but the elderly priest was done talking and already on his feet, heading for the door.

"I'll check in on you at meal time and at prayer, but I'd appreciate it if you dropped by my office to chat as well." He tapped his can against the door. "After all, you are a bit more mobile than I am."

"Of course, Father. I'll stop by daily if you like."

"No, that's all right. Once a week would be fine."

Karl nodded, and opened the door for the priest. "Next week, then."

In the doorway, Father Dionne hesitated. "Oh, I almost forgot. Mary Jane Mendes is returning to the college tomorrow."

Karl felt his heart leap into his throat at the news. "Is she all right? Will she be able to see?"

Father Dionne shook his head. "It's still too early to tell. Her doctor's decided it would be all right for her to travel back to the college and be under the care of the college nurse. That way she can listen to lectures on tape, maybe even attend a few classes while she recovers. Mary Jane doesn't want to lose the school year because of the accident and I trust you'll do everything you can to accommodate her."

"Oh, yes, of course, Father. I'll help her do all her assignments verbally if I have to." Karl was grateful for the chance to make amends in some small way, even if her accident and potential blindness had been "God's Will."

"Well, you just might have to do that, so be prepared."

"I will be."

"Good, see you at supper, then."

Karl watched Father Dionne leave, looking forward to seeing Mary Jane, even if she wouldn't be able to see him.

CHAPTER FIFTEEN

1

"Does everything check out all right with you?" Graham Thompson asked.

Diane Darby sat at a computer terminal in the office of the *Ste-Claire Sentinel*. On the screen in front of her was her latest article for the school's newspaper. It was a feature on the memorial service held earlier in the day and was peppered with call-out quotations and photos of the family and friends of Ronald Henschel coming to terms with their grief.

Graham, the *Sentinel's* editor, had held the paper back one day to include coverage of the event in that week's edition. If he hadn't, they would have had the memorial story a week later and by then it would have been old news. This way, they could all feel – at least for one issue – like a real daily newspaper competing for stories with the Toronto and national papers like the *Post, Globe and Mail, Star* and *Sun.*

"It looks good," Diane said, not taking her eyes away from the screen.

And it did look good.

There were all sorts of tear-jerking quotes in bold typeface on the page like "I can't believe my baby is dead!" from Ronald's mother and "The death of a young person is always a tragedy," from Karl Desbiens. In addition the two full pages, Diane had also convinced Graham to go for a full-color photo spread. Even though it would double the cost of that week's printing – and might put them over budget for the year – she had made a strong case for justifying the extravagance.

First of all, a student's death during the school year was big news and now was not the time to look cheap when so many of the country's media outlets would be looking over the *Sentinel's* shoulder. Also, she told him that Ronald was worth it since his graphic design work was known outside of the school's campus. Finally, if there was going to be a single issue on which the *Sentinel's* entire year would be judged this would be the one.

Graham had been unconvinced at first, always citing the bottom line, but then Diane had undone a few buttons down the front of her blouse and batted her eyes at the man, and he wound up agreeing to all of her demands.

He was such a pushover.

And now it was done.

Diane was pleased.

It was splashy and well designed.

It was gritty yet compassionate.

But most important of all were the words in the center of the pages in twenty-four point Arial Bold – *Stories and Photos by Diane Darby*. This feature was going to win her a couple of community newspaper awards, be a big part of her resume package, and probably open a lot of doors for her that would normally have been closed until she'd gained some real-world journalism experience. With this story under her belt, and a nose job scheduled for the Christmas break, she was sure she'd be filing reports for some television station in Toronto by the end of next July.

Graham looked at his watch. The printing window was closing rapidly and if they didn't put the paper to bed soon, they'd have to wait an extra day for delivery of the finished product.

"I wanted to read through my story one more time, but I guess I'll have to let it go," said Diane. "I've read it through enough times already, anyway."

"Oh, were you reading it? I thought you were just admiring your name."

She looked up at him then, giving him an ice cold glare.

"All kidding aside, Diane. I've read it through a couple of times myself and it's fine. Hell, it's better than fine, it's terrific. I think you really got a handle on what everyone's been going through the past week."

"Do you really mean that?" It still felt as if he were teasing her.

"Oh, I mean it." He paused a moment, looking directly into her eyes. "It's a really good piece of work and will probably get you a couple of award nominations…at least."

Diane felt slighted by the comment. Award *nominations*. "Don't you think it's good enough to win something?"

Graham shrugged. "I don't know. It's best to take these things one step at a time." He busied himself on his own computer terminal, sending the newspaper's files to the printer in Abbotville. "Besides, it's tough to know what the judges are looking for from year to year."

"Screw that," said Diane, getting up from her desk. "That award is mine."

"Well, I'm sure Ronald's family would find it heartwarming to know that the death of their son inspired you to do some award-caliber work."

Diane looked at Graham, stung by the jab he'd made. Maybe he wasn't as soft a touch as she'd made him out to be. What did it matter, anyway? She'd gotten what she wanted from him, and the paper, and that's all that was important.

After a few moments of awkward silence, Graham said, "The last file has cleared and I'm out of here. Can I give you a lift to the residences?"

"No," Diane said smiling, the feeling of satisfaction over a job well done washing over her in a wave. "It's a nice night out, I think I'll walk to the dorm."

"Are you sure? It's pretty late."

"I'll be fine. Really."

"Suit yourself," Graham said, tucking his scarf down into the front of his jacket. "See you around two tomorrow. I'm sure you'll want to be here to hear everyone say a lot of good things about your work."

"Of course."

The newspaper office door swung open and shut with a creek as Graham left, leaving Diane alone. She spent a few minutes straightening up her desk, picking bits and strips of paper up off the floor and cleaning mounds of butts and ashes out of the ashtrays. When she realized what she was doing she suddenly stopped and sat down in her chair. The room really didn't need cleaning, there were cleaners who came in every morning around four to straighten up. Diane was really cleaning up because she didn't want to go back to her dorm just yet. She was far too excited to go to sleep. She felt too good about herself, too strong a sense of accomplishment to leave the office and have the feeling go away. She wanted to stay, but she needed something to do while she was there. She rifled through one of the nearby desks, the one used by the entertainment editor, until she found a pack of cigarettes, and lit one up.

She coughed once. She wasn't much of a smoker, but somehow the act of smoking a single cigarette alone in the office seemed an appropriate act of celebration. She took her time, inhaling the smoke in long lazy drags until she felt just a little bit dizzy. As the affect of the cigarette smoke strengthened, and her head slowly began to feel as if it was filling with water, Diane knew it was time to call it a night.

She butted out the cigarette and quickly put on her coat. She left the lights on and locked the door behind her as she left. She walked down a short, dimly lit hallway and made a series of left and right turns until she found herself at the main doors of the college's administration building.

She stopped at the doors for a moment to do up her coat and wrap her scarf tightly around her neck. Through the glass of the doors in front of her, the early October night looked dark and promised that her walk to the residences would be a chilly one.

A sound echoed from the foyer behind her and she turned to see one of the night janitors mopping his way across the linoleum floor. "Good night," he said between slushy wet slaps of the mop against the slick hard floor.

"Good night," Diane said. She turned and opened the door, the cold night air tightened the skin on her face and immediately began to claw through her layers of clothing.

To her surprise, the cold didn't bother Diane all that much. She was aware of the icy little pin pricks working at her skin, but she was still too buoyed by her sense of accomplishment to care.

As she passed by "The Head", a fifteen-ton modern metal sculpture of fifteen tons of rusting metal that had been donated by an alumnus too famous for the school to turn down, Diane thought she heard someone coughing off in the distance. She kept walking but turned her head to scan the darkness.

There was no one there.

She picked up her pace slightly as she passed through the

well-lit walk between the Fine Arts building and the Centre for Theological Studies. At Masson Drive she crossed the street and headed south, keeping a brisk pace as she skirted along the edges of the Ste-Claire Arboretum, heading toward her dorm building. The Arboretum was nothing more than a patch of woodland that had once been part of the original farm endowed to the college so many, many years ago. It had been untouched by the construction of the school's original few buildings and had been preserved by various campus conservation groups ever since as the school's nod to the world's environmental concerns – that, and the fact they had no other use for the land at present.

From somewhere in the mottled growth of trees Diane heard a sound but she couldn't be sure if it was the *crick* of a twig snapping or the *crew* of a nightowl. Part of her was curious enough to want to stop and investigate the sound, but another part of her was frightened and wanted to run home as fast as her legs could carry her.

Just then she noticed movement in the woods to her right. Leaves parted and branches were pushed out of the way to reveal a dark figure standing among the trees.

She inhaled a gasp and stopped dead-still in her tracks.

And then she recognized the figure standing there. Even though the woods were set back from the walkway and the overhead lights barely illuminated the path, the figure in the trees was familiar to her.

How could she not recognize such a big man?

Although her heart was pounding against her chest like a sledgehammer, Diane smiled, relieved. "Hi Brick," she said. "You scared me, popping out of the woods like that."

He stepped out of the woods and moved toward her.

"What were you doing in there anyway?"

It seemed as if he was going to walk with her the rest of the way. Diane was glad for the company after receiving such a scare. She put her right foot forward to continue her walk home.

"So, how do you think the Cardinals will do this year?"

Brick didn't answer.

She turned to look at him.

And saw something shiny flash in a downward arc...

...and slam into her back with all the force of a railway spike.

2

The woman turned to run.

As she did, the hilt sticking out of her back came free of his hand. It twirled as she spun to get away, like a straw caught in a glass full of churning ice.

Kill her...

The voice whispered in his ear. The blood coursed through his head, roaring through his skull.

Kill her...

He grabbed her with his left hand, clamping his viselike hand down around her collarbone and slowly bringing his fingers together, her bones first bending, then snapping like kindling in his hands.

With his free right hand, he grabbed the protruding hilt of the dagger and pulled it out of the woman's back. Then he plunged it deeper into her body. After each stab, he gave the dagger a twist, then moved it in up-and-down and side-to-side motions that ripped through muscle, tore through veins, and scraped against bone.

In seconds there was a six-inch hole in her back and gory lines extending out from the holes across the rest of her body. His grip on her shoulder became necessary to keep the body upright.

Instinctively, he wiped the bloodied dagger off on the right shoulder of the woman's coat. As he ran the blade over the course wool, the rust on the end of it seemed to come away like dirt. When he was done, the blade seemed to shine like new, the last three inches of it glistening yellow-gold in the moonlight.

He held the dagger up above him until it caught the light of the moon and glinted like a jewel in a crown.

Voices then...on the path.

They were approaching.

Without another second's delay, he dragged the body of the woman into the woods, pulling the carcass roughly over bushes and stumps and fallen trees. In the center of the woods, he lay the body down and positioned a log over top of it. That done, he covered the body with fallen leaves and then used the dagger to break up the ground around her until he had enough loose dirt to scatter over the leaves to hold them down.

He took a final moment to inspect his work and then quietly pocketed the dagger.

Then he picked up a pile of leaves in both hands, carried them out of the woods, and dropped them onto the pool of blood that was slowly seeping into the ground at the side of the walkway.

He scattered the leaves with his shoe, then turned and silently headed home to his residence.

"Hey Brick!" someone shouted a short time later. "Think the Cardinals will beat U of T on Friday?"

He gave the caller the thumbs up.

"All right!"

CHAPTER SIXTEEN

1

They had wheeled Mary Jane into the nurse's office around ten that morning. The college's nurse, an elderly matron named Francis Bruneau, had spent the rest of the morning making sure her charge would be as comfortable as possible, going as far as to dust the crucifixes over the doors as well as the framed likenesses of Jesus, Mary and St. Ignatius that adorned the walls. After all, word had come down from none other than Father Dionne himself that she be treated as a V.I.P. and that she shouldn't be denied any reasonable request.

"Would you like me to draw the curtain?" the nurse asked, aware that the sun streaming in through the window might cause Mary Jane some discomfort.

"No, that's all right," she answered. "These bandages are so thick, I don't even know which side of the bed the window is on."

"It's on your right, if you'd like to know."

"Now that you mention it, that side of my body does feel a bit warmer."

"The doctor will be visiting this afternoon to take a peek at your eye. I hope he sees that you're making progress."

"I hope I *see something*, period," Mary Jane said with a laugh.

"We all do, love," Nurse Bruneau said, giving Mary Jane's left foot a squeeze through the sheets. "If you need me I'll be just outside in the hallway."

Mary Jane nodded and listened to the nurse's soft-soled shoes pad out of the room.

She was alone again, and that was the worst part of the

accident she'd had. She'd enjoyed those ten days at the site, not only because she'd had a chance to get closer to Karl, but because there hadn't been a moment she'd had to spend alone. There'd always been somebody close by, or at the very least, within shouting distance. After growing up an only child with a traveling salesman – pardon, account executive – for a father and an alcoholic for a mother, being around other people made her feel safe and secure.

She'd been looking forward to returning to Ste-Claire with a host of new friends. There was Karl of course, but she'd gotten along with the others well enough too, especially Ronald. He'd been the funniest and friendliest of all of them, mostly because he was lonely like her. They'd agreed to meet for coffee at least once a week when they got back on campus, but now he was dead.

She still couldn't believe it.

Ronald was dead and she was in the school nurse's office, which was basically a room with a bed that was lorded over by a full-time nurse who doubled as the school's health officer. It was like still being in hospital, only she was closer to her friends and she wouldn't have to miss too many classes. According to Nurse Bruneau, there were people instructed to bring her tapes of lectures so she could listen to them, and still others would be helping her with assignments.

Mary Jane appreciated the extra care, but she wondered if they would have made such a fuss if she'd hurt herself skydiving, or rollerblading, or anything else that might have happened outside of the school.

And, she wondered, which one of her new friends would be visiting her first.

Just then, as if on cue, the nurse came back into the room. "There's someone here to see you," she said, a wide grin on her face.

"Who?" Mary Jane said quickly. "Male or female?"

"Male. Most definitely male."

It's Karl, she thought. He would be the first to visit, to say hello, maybe even to tell her that he missed her.

"How do I look?" Mary Jane asked, sitting up slightly in her bed.

"Except for that wad of bandages wrapped around your eyes

and head like a turban, you look terrific," said the nurse.

Mary Jane imagined she was quite a sight, but it wouldn't hurt for Karl to see her this way. If he felt guilty enough, maybe she could convince him to take her out on a date when she recovered. "Your point's well taken," she said. "Send him in."

There was silence for a few moments then a faint, "You can go in now," sounded from out in the hall.

"Hey M.J., how ya doin'?"

Although it sounded familiar, the voice definitely did not belong to Karl.

"Who's there?"

"It's me."

"Me who?"

"Me, Brick."

Those last couple of words seemed to sum him up in a nutshell. "Me, Brick," he'd said. Mary Jane wondered if he was going to follow it up by saying, "You, Mary Jane."

But instead he said, "Surprised?"

"Uh, yeah." More than surprised actually. Of all of the people on campus, Chris Wahl was the last – *the very last* – person she'd expected to pay her a visit. He hadn't said more than two words to her at the site, and now here he was standing at her bedside. It was enough to give her the creeps. "What are you doing here?"

There was a moment of silence and she could picture the big hockey player shrugging. "Just came by to see how you were doing."

2

It had felt good to be back in the classroom again.

The first few minutes of class time had been taken up by talk of the trip, the funeral and memorial services and the wonderful story Diane Darby had written about the latter for the *Ste-Claire Sentinel*. Karl was particularly impressed with the piece in the paper, since it showed a side of Diane he hadn't been aware of. He had thought of her as simply an ambitious young journalist who wasn't going to let anyone get between her and her ultimate goal, which Karl suspected was to become one of the top female broadcasters in the country and mentioned in the same breath as Valerie Pringle, Pamela Wallin and Hanna Gartner. Who knew,

maybe she even had her eye on following Adrienne Clarkson into
the position of Governor General of Canada. But the piece in the
paper betrayed none of that ambition. It was a plainly written,
emotional and down-to-earth exploration of loss and recovery.
Reading the article, Karl learned more about Ronald than he'd
known after living with him for ten days in the bush.

When the class was done chatting, Karl got things underway,
making a mental note to drop by the *Sentinel* office afterward to
congratulate Diane on a job well done.

†

The Sentinel was a weekly community newspaper which
employed one full-time editor and was staffed by dozens of
volunteers, mostly students, who were trying to get some real-
world experience before heading out into that same real-world.
While the newspaper sold advertisements and printed exams and
other schedules for the school, it was mostly financed by a ten
dollar levy – as part of their tuition – paid by each student
attending the school. The newspaper office was tucked into a
couple of large rooms on the ground floor of the college's main
administrative building. It put *The Sentinel* in the middle of the
campus and accessible to every student at Ste-Claire.

After writing various columns for the paper over the years,
Karl knew the staff would be having a meeting to discuss the
latest issue. Diane would be there, receiving her kudos, and Karl
wanted to make sure he added his voice to the others.

When he entered the office, there was the usual crowd of
people gathered, everyone from reporters to photographers,
editors to layout and design people.

"Good afternoon, Karl," greeted Graham Thompson.

Karl smiled. "Hi Graham, good issue."

"Thanks."

"Where's Diane? I want to congratulate her on the piece she
did on Ronald's memorial service. It was really well done."

"I'll pass along the information when I see her."

"She's not here?" It wasn't like Diane not to be around to
receive people's praise. It was what she lived for.

"Has she been in class?"

Graham shook his head.

"Have you tried her in her dorm?"

"Nobody's seen her there either," said one of the girls in the room.

Karl turned and realized it was Diane's best friend Lucy Bartolo. There were deep worry lines on the woman's face.

"Hi Lucy," he said, trying to sound cheerful.

"The girls on her floor aren't even sure she slept there last night." Lucy crossed her arms and chewed at a thumb nail.

Karl forced a reassuring smile. "Maybe she was out celebrating and stayed out all night."

"Maybe." Lucy seemed unconvinced. "But that's not like her."

"Or perhaps she's just trying to make an entrance. That would be her style, wouldn't it?"

Graham nodded in agreement. "Yeah, that sounds more like it."

"Well, I'm sure she'll show up. And when she does, give her my best, okay."

"I'll do that."

"And congratulations to you too, Graham."

"For what?"

"I know you had a hand in Diane's article, even if your name isn't on it."

Graham smiled, but the smile didn't last long. "Thanks."

3

If it wasn't for the old bitch out in the hall he'd have done it by now.

He had hoped to slip in unnoticed, cut up the one on the bed, and then stroll out of the room whistling a tune…but that was pretty tough to do now.

Almost impossible.

Correction, it wouldn't be all that tough to do, but it would be difficult to get away with it after it was done.

Still, it *could* be done.

"So, how are you doing?" Brick asked, reaching into his Cardinals team jacket and feeling the dagger in his hand.

"I've been better."

"Yeah, I bet." Brick took the dagger out from inside his jacket and traced the tip of it gently across the sheets. "Once I got hit by a puck just over my left eye. Fourteen stitches."

"Ouch!" said Mary Jane.

"It was okay, I mean, they sewed me up and I finished the

game...I know it's not as bad as what happened to you, but even so it hurt like fucking hell."

"What?"

"Oh, I'm sorry. I mean it hurt a lot." Brick held the dagger in the air over Mary Jane's throat, toying with the idea of bringing it down hard against the soft white flesh of her neck and watching the blade cut into and through the skin and muscles there.

That would be sweet.

Not now...came the voice inside his head.

Just then there were footsteps in the hallway.

It was Nurse Bruneau again.

Brick hid the dagger.

"A pot of flowers," she said, carrying a basket of mixed flowers into the room and setting it on the window sill. "And they're beautiful."

"Who are they from?" Mary Jane asked.

"The student union."

"That's nice. Another thing I have to look forward to seeing..." She let out a little sigh. "...as if I don't have enough reasons to want to see again already."

"They are a sight for sore eyes," the nurse said as she left the room.

After several seconds of silence Mary Jane said, "You were telling me how you got hit by the puck."

"Yeah, it hurt something awful." The dagger was out again, its slightly-rounded point level with a spot just behind Mary Jane's left ear.

Oh, how he wanted to thrust it forward into her brain.

He pressed the tip against her skin, and watched as a tiny bead of blood bubbled up onto the blade.

A split second later, she jerked her head to the side as if she'd been pinched by a needle.

"Ow!"

Not now...the voice whispered in his head, stronger this time.

"Sorry, that was the zipper of my jacket," said Brick. "Must have got caught or something."

It's not safe...

Brick wiped the blade clean on his pants.

There will be another time, another place.

Then he slipped the dagger inside his jacket.

There were voices in the hallway.

Female voices.

Several of them.

"I guess I better be going," Brick said.

"All right," Mary Jane answered, a hand over the tiny puncture in her neck. "Thanks for dropping by."

"No problem. I'll probably see you again soon anyway."

He turned to leave, and passed the girls in the hallway.

"Hi Brick," a few of them said, the words long and drawn out as if their mouths were full of sugar and honey.

"Hi girls," Brick said. "What's up?"

As Brick kept the girls busy out in the hall, a dark figure swept into the room, his feet seeming to glide over the floor tiles without a sound.

God had too much of a presence in this place, and too many people came and went at random for his liking. In order for her to be sacrificed, she needed to be out among the rest of the students, alone and vulnerable.

And for that she needed to be well.

Mary Jane lifted her head slightly. "Who's there?"

The dark figure didn't answer. Instead he moved to the side of Mary Jane's bed and raised his right hand. Then while he mouthed out words and syllables in silence, he waved his right hand over Mary Jane's eyes, as if he were wiping an invisible sheet of glass that was suspended in the air just inches above her eyes.

For a moment it seemed as if Mary Jane would speak, but she failed to get a word out, falling back on the bed and into a deep, deep sleep.

The dark figure left the room moments later, as silently as he'd entered.

"Bye Brick," said one of the girls in the hall.

"See you girls around."

They laughed and giggled like school girls as they entered the room to visit with Mary Jane.

4

Karl had just finished changing his shirt – a clean light-blue denim shirt with the Ste-Claire emblem on the left breast pocket – when there was a knock at the door of his dorm room.

He opened the door slightly, then stepped back in surprise

when he saw a town constable standing in his doorway. "Yes?" he said.

"Are you Brother Karl Desbiens?" the officer asked.

"I'm not a brother," Karl answered. "I'm a regent."

"Okay, then," the constable seemed irritated. "Are you *Regent* Karl Desbiens?"

"Yes."

"I'm Constable Vince Tremblay with the Abbotville Police Department–"

"I've seen you around."

"Well, I was on campus answering a report of a missing person–"

"Yes, Diane Darby."

"That's right, but we can't really consider her officially missing for another twelve hours."

"It is strange that she didn't show up for the newspaper meeting today."

"That's what the editor there told me...So, I don't think I'll be waiting that long to start unofficially looking into her whereabouts."

"And that's why you've come to see me?"

"Not exactly. Since I was here, I thought I'd kill two birds with one stone and talk to you about another matter."

"Please come in." Karl moved away from the door to let the officer into the room. He offered the man his chair, and sat himself down on the edge of his bed, doing up the buttons of his shirt as they talked.

"Before I came out to the college, I received the final forensic report on Ronald Henschel from the Center of Forensic Science in Toronto."

Karl sat in silence, listening.

"And according to the report, he didn't die in the fire that swept through the bus."

"No," Karl said flatly. "He was dead before the fire."

The officer's eyebrows arched in surprise. "How do you know that?"

"As I told the O.P.P. officers investigating the accident, I saw a hand sticking out into the aisle. I reached out and felt it. It wasn't exactly cold, but it didn't feel right to me. There wasn't any pulse, for one thing."

"You knew the body was there, but you didn't try to get it out of the bus?"

Karl lowered his head, regretting that he'd been unable to do more to help Ronald, even if he had already been dead. "The fire was right there, and there were all sorts of kerosene lanterns and propane tanks at the back of the bus."

The officer nodded. "Are you sure you didn't do more than just leave the body there?"

"What are you getting at?"

"According to the forensic report, Ronald Henschel's throat was slit."

"What?"

"There was a deep gash across the front of his neck about four inches long, and another cut on the left side of the throat intersecting the first."

"How could that happen in an accident like that?"

"I don't know. Neither did the doctor I spoke to at the center. So, I thought I would ask you about it, Regent...Karl."

"Me?"

"You *were* the last one out of the bus."

Karl felt his stomach turn as he began to understand the full implication of what the officer was saying. "You think I *murdered* Ronald?"

The officer took a breath. "Let me tell you what I think. You were the last one out of the bus. You knew there was a fire coming and that the whole thing might go up in a fireball at any moment. You see Ronald, and he's not quite dead yet, but he might as well be because of what happened to him in the accident. You're a compassionate man, a good man, and you can't bear to see someone suffer like that. So instead of allowing Ronald to die horribly in the fire, you slit his throat so he dies more quickly, before the smoke and flames choke him to death or burn him alive."

Karl was stunned, not only by the constable's insinuation, but by the very thought that someone might have *killed* Ronald, that there might be a killer on the Ste-Claire campus at that very moment.

He took a few seconds to compose himself, and then addressed the officer in as calm a voice as he could manage under the circumstances. "You're right about a few things, Constable

Tremblay. I am a compassionate man and under the exact circumstances as you've outlined, who knows, perhaps I would show a dying man some mercy. But that's not the way it happened on the bus. And I swear to you as God is my witness, Ronald Henschel was already dead when I went to check on him."

The constable nodded, seemingly satisfied with Karl's version of events. "I guess swearing to God's got to mean something coming from you, being a Jesuit and all."

Karl wasn't about to lighten the moment with a smile.

The constable paused, then got back to business. "Did you notice any blood on the floor of the bus, or I guess that would be on the windows since the bus was on its side?"

"There was debris and supplies everywhere. If Ronald bled to death his blood might have been absorbed by someone's duffel bag, but then the bag would have been incinerated by the fire."

The officer nodded. "Yeah, that's about the way it happened. And from what I'm told, they're still looking for blood traces inside the bus."

Karl waited for the police officer to say something, but he continued to make notes in silence.

Finally, Karl asked, "Are we done now? I'd like to visit one of my student's who's just returned to the college from hospital."

The officer nodded. "I'm sorry to interrupt your day, Reg– uh, Karl, but when something's not right, it has to be checked out."

"I understand you have a job to do, and I'm happy to see that you're covering all the bases."

"There's only two possibilities on this one. Ronald Henschel was either mortally injured by some sharp object in the crash or someone cut his throat after the accident. And if that's the case then the question is–"

"Who did it?" said Karl.

"Exactly."

5

The Ste-Claire campus didn't have a florist shop so Karl had to improvise by picking a few hardy flowers from the beds that lined the walkways and courtyards around the main administration building. By the time he was done, he had a handful of flowers that didn't look like much. And although Mary Jane still couldn't see, he realized he'd seem more thoughtful if he bought her a box of chocolates at the tuck shop housed in the basement of the admin building.

A half-box of Turtles was all he could afford.

He'd only been to the nurse's office once before. One afternoon a few summers ago, he'd slipped out of his sandals to join in on a pick-up soccer game being played on one of the fields adjacent to the courtyard and he'd cut his foot on a shard of glass from a broken bottle. The nurse at the time had cleaned up his foot well enough for him to avoid infection, but he had to use a pair of crutches to get around for two weeks afterward. Since then, he'd never taken his shoes off outdoors again.

"Ah, Mr. Desbiens," Nurse Bruneau said in recognition as he approached her station. "It's good to see you."

"Is Mary Jane here?"

"The room is on the right."

"I remember, thanks."

"But I warn you that the doctor will be dropping by to check on her in a few minutes and I'll be changing her bandages, so you might not have a lot of time to visit."

"I understand." Karl walked down the hall and slowed as he approached the open door on the right. He stopped in the doorway and marveled at how much brighter the room was in comparison to what he'd remembered it to be. They'd either given the room a coat of paint since he'd been there, or his outlook had been rather gloomy as he'd contemplated the deep gash on the bottom of his foot. He hoped Mary Jane's outlook on things was as bright as the room around her, for her sake...and maybe for his too.

"Who's there?" she said.

"Give you three hints and one guess. It's not the Father, the Son, or the Holy Ghost."

"Karl?"

"Hi, M.J. how're you doing?"

"Better, now that you're here."

Karl smiled. She was still positive and upbeat, which probably wouldn't be true for most people in her situation. Not only could she wind up blind, or lose an eye, there was also the possibility that her face might not heal all that well, and she'd be disfigured for life. Karl had tried not to think too much about that part of her situation, but it continued to weigh heavily on his mind.

"It's good to see you," he said, putting a hand on hers.

"I wish I could say the same thing."

Karl was silent, wondering what more he could say. What could someone say in this sort of situation? "I brought you some chocolates."

"Pot of Gold?"

"No, Turtles."

"Oh, they're good too."

Just then the nurse came in pushing a cart that carried gauze, tape and scissors, among other things. "If you'll excuse me, Mr. Desbiens."

"No, that's all right," said Mary Jane. "He can stay."

"But your scars will not have healed yet."

Karl looked at Mary Jane, unsure if he wanted to see the raw scars around her eyes and the eyeballs that were probably still swollen with blood. But of course, he would do whatever she wished.

"That's okay, I don't mind." She tightened her grip on Karl's hand.

He looked to the nurse. "Fine by me."

The nurse began cutting away at the bandages. Although Mary Jane had injured her left eye, the doctors in North Bay had covered both her eyes to prevent her from moving the left one in tandem with the right.

Watching the bandages come off, Karl felt his heart rate begin to quicken. He steeled himself against reacting to Mary Jane's injuries in a way that might hurt the woman's feelings. He would smile, or remain impassive, but he would not under any circumstances cringe or act surprised by what he saw.

Before the nurse was done, the college's physician, Doctor Sheldon Katz, came into the room. It always struck Karl as odd that a Jesuit College would employ a Jewish doctor, but Dr. Katz was the only one in Abbotville who agreed to spend one day a week on campus and to be on-call the rest of the week on an "as needed" basis. Besides that, Dr. Katz enjoyed being the team physician for the Ste-Claire Cardinals and never missed a game.

"Right on time," said Nurse Bruneau.

"I would have been here earlier, but I stopped by the arena to check on a few players. There's a flu bug going around and Coach Chambers is worried about his line-up for Friday night in

Toronto against U of T."

"Did you prescribe them all chicken soup?"

"No, mostly rest, fluid and vitamin C."

The nurse continued pulling at the bandages, but slowed when she got to the final few that would leave Mary Jane's face uncovered.

"Are you ready?" she asked.

Mary Jane nodded.

Karl swallowed, held his breath.

The nurse removed the last bandage from Mary Jane's eyes and to Karl's amazement, two perfectly clear and beautiful blue eyes stared back at him.

"Wow," said Dr. Katz.

Wow, indeed, thought Karl.

Although there were stitches and scars on the side of her head and under her eyes, the skin didn't look disfigured at all. And although Karl knew little about cuts and how they healed, it appeared to him as if the scars that were left behind would be small, tiny in fact.

Mary Jane looked around the room, first at the doctor, then at the nurse, and finally at Karl. There could be no mistaking that they were making eye contact. He was looking straight into her eyes and she was seeing him.

Seeing him.

"Hi there," she waved.

"Can you see me?" asked the doctor.

"I can see all of you."

He held up three fingers. "How many fingers?"

"Three."

The doctor glanced to his right. "What color is the shirt Karl here is wearing."

"Light blue," she said. "Denim in fact. And there's the Ste-Claire emblem on the pocket."

The doctor looked over at Karl to check his shirt.

"I can see perfectly, can't I?" said Mary Jane, on the verge of tears.

"I still want to conduct a few tests," said the doctor, "but it would appear that way, yes."

"That's wonderful," exclaimed Nurse Brunea.

"It's a miracle, is what it is," Karl whispered under his breath.

CHAPTER SEVENTEEN

1

Karl stayed at the nurse's office while Mary Jane collected her things, then escorted her back to her dorm room. Despite the injury she'd suffered, she seemed her old self, making jokes and eager to get back to her studies.

"So what will you be doing now?" Karl asked her. Mary Jane had often talked about becoming a teacher or librarian, and he wondered if that was still the plan.

"Well, I haven't given up on becoming librarian," she said smiling. "But these days I'm interested in getting into a missionary position..." Her smiled broke into a laugh. "You know, teaching health and English to the natives in some African school."

Karl laughed. "You might want to think about stand-up comedy with material like that."

"Don't think I haven't. It's just that missionaries make so much more money than stand-up comedians." She gave a little shrug. "I do have to look out for my future, after all."

"Absolutely."

"What about you?" she asked, taking hold of his arm. "What are you going to do with your life, Karl?"

Karl sighed. It wasn't as bad as being asked by Father Dionne, but it was pretty close to it. "I'm not really sure. I had wanted to stay at the college and teach while I worked to uncover the history of the Ste-Claire Mission, but that doesn't seem like such a good idea at the moment."

"No, but it will be again in say, six months."

"That's what Father Dionne thinks too."

"What about a life outside of the order?"

Karl could feel himself getting warm all over. It wasn't as if he hadn't thought about it before, but hearing Mary Jane ask it in so many words put the question front and center, and unavoidable. Did he even want to be a Jesuit priest? Was the life of a Jesuit for him? "You're not one to beat around the bush, are you?"

"Hey, things worked out okay for me, but with what happened to me and with Ronald dying, I've realized that time's not something to be wasted in our lives."

That was true enough.

"I'm not sure of what I want in this life, but I know what I don't want and that's to be in some dead-end high school five years from now wishing I had taken a chance with you."

Karl felt his heart leap up into his throat. God, she was moving fast.

They stopped walking then, and turned to look into each other's eyes.

Mary Jane's scar had healed even further and it seemed as if the stitches were getting in the way, rather than helping her to heal. But more than that, Karl realized – perhaps for the first time – that she was pretty, and that he liked the way her eyebrows arched expectantly as she waited for his answer. It also occurred to him that she was ten years his junior and there was something about catching the attention of a younger woman that gave Karl a thrill.

"I don't want that either," he said.

He could picture himself teaching Theology 101 five or ten years down the road and wondering what Mary Jane was doing with her life, and imagining an ache in his heart over not knowing.

"Maybe we could spend some time together?" she said.

"Time together, that would be nice," said Karl. Time together was good and non-committal. Like a trial, to see if they were a good fit. "I'd like that, very much."

"Good. I've got to catch up on my school work tonight, but maybe we could do something together on Friday."

"I was thinking of catching a ride into Toronto to watch the Cardinals beat the Blues."

"We could go together."

"You mean, like on a date?"

"Yes, exactly like on a date."

"I'll meet you in the arena lot. I think one of the Fathers is going to be taking a car down to the game."

"I'll be there," she said.

"Then I'll be waiting."

They parted, but only after Mary Jane gave Karl a quick kiss on the cheek.

It felt good.

He wondered if he might get another on Friday night.

2

Geoff Willett and Charlotte Harriette-Reid stepped out from the back door of the Regent's Theatre, a 150-seat theatre located at the south end of the Ste-Claire campus, on the other side of Heritage Creek. Most thought that the theatre's name stemmed from something to do with the Regencies of England and France between 1811-1820, but the name actually came from the three Jesuits who founded and constructed the theatre at the turn of the last century. All three of the brothers had been in the "Regency" period of their training as Jesuits in which they were required to teach at a Jesuit school for a period of three years. The regents who built the theatre wanted to add drama to the school's curriculum and the Rector at the time named the theatre in honor of the three young men.

Geoff and Charlotte had been rehearsing for the annual Ste-Claire College Christmas pageant, which had become a tradition at the school in recent years. People would come in from Abbotville and the surrounding counties, even as far as Toronto, to take in the play. As a result the show ran for two weeks each December and was the main reason why the Regent's Theatre itself was in such good condition, and why other less-commercial shows could be put on in the theatre throughout the rest of the year.

Charlotte was the best actress in the school's history and people were expecting great things from her when she graduated. She had, of course, taken the part of the Virgin Mary for herself in this year's pageant, and although the casting had drawn snickers from those in the theatre program who knew Charlotte well, she had the angelic face and slight build that made for an ideal virgin. Geoff on the other hand, had a decent voice, but little skill as an actor. He had been conscripted by Charlotte to play the part of Joseph, although he seemed more comfortable with the administrative and technical side of the pageant's production. His goal was to act as Charlotte's manager after graduation, with the hopes of pitching her as host of a new young people's show on one of the family-oriented networks. With him working for her behind the scenes and her in front of the camera, there was a good chance they'd be set for life in less than five years.

"Oh, shit!" Charlotte said, as they stepped up onto the bridge that spanned Heritage Creek and connected the Regent's Theatre to the rest of the campus.

"What is it?" Geoff asked.

"I forgot my purse back stage."

That was typical of Charlotte. While every other female on campus carried around a backpack, Charlotte toted a purse, which she left behind more often than not, just so she could remind people how different she was.

Geoff stood there, saying nothing.

"Well?"

"Well, what?"

"Aren't you going to go back and get it for me?"

Geoff remained motionless, looking as if he might answer her back or raise his voice to her, but in the end he let out a sigh and said nothing. "I'll be right back."

"Thanks, hon," she said.

As she watched Geoff head back to the theatre, she couldn't help but think how well she had the boy trained. She knew there wasn't anything he wouldn't do for her, and she'd used that to her advantage every chance she got. It served him right, thought Charlotte. She knew that one of the reasons he did all that she asked was that the sex with her was better than anything he'd ever had in his life, and probably better than anything he could ever hope for with another woman. She also knew that he thought of her not just as a girlfriend, but as his meal ticket. He had plans for her career and if they all worked out, he had as much to gain from her success as she did. But Geoff was from Minden, a small town in the Haliburton Highlands of Ontario, and all of his dreams had that small-town feel to them. He kept talking about a show on a family network. Well, fuck that! That was only a starting point for Charlotte. She was going to ride her good looks all the way to the top. She'd be as rich and as famous as Kathy Lee Gifford, but without the old fart of a husband who dared to sleep with another woman. She was going to be–

"Hey Charlotte!"

"Huh." She had been staring down into the creek, watching the moon ripple and roll over the surface of the water. The voice had startled her, especially since it hadn't sounded like Geoff. She turned to see who it was and was surprised to find it was…"Brick?"

"The one and only."

"What are *you* doing here?"

"Come to see a show."

"I'm surprised you even know where the theatre is."

"I wouldn't mind seeing you up on stage."

Charlotte laughed.

"I bet you'd look hot in heels and a thong."

Charlotte felt herself getting warm. She did look good in heels and a thong, and Geoff was always appreciative when she dressed like that, but having Brick – the student athlete on campus that every girl wanted – talk to her in such a way, well, that was a real turn on.

"Wouldn't you like to know."

"Oh, I know all right. I know all about you."

"Really?" she said coyly, flinging her hair over her shoulder. "What do you know?"

"I know you like cock–"

Charlotte knew she was supposed to be shocked by Brick's words, but she couldn't help herself from getting more turned on by them. God, there was even a bulge in his pants. She'd heard he was big, but she'd had no idea.

"–I know you like sucking it, fucking it, even having it crammed up your ass."

She desperately wanted to say something, but she couldn't. How could she when he was right on all counts?

"Charlotte?" came a voice from the other direction. It was Geoff, who had returned with her purse. "Are you okay?"

"Well, if it isn't her man-servant, carrying her purse for her like the good little boy he is."

"Yeah, very funny Brick." Geoff gave Charlotte her purse and put his arm around her, leading them along the bridge heading in Brick's direction.

Brick looked directly into Charlotte's eyes, and she could feel herself melting inside. There was real heat coming from his gaze, as if there were desires and passions coming from something more than just his loins. If she went to Brick, he'd not only take her in his arms, he would take her completely, consuming her in his lust, enveloping her in a primal passion that would leave her spent and sore for days.

"Are you gonna spend the night with the boy?" said Brick. "Or do you want to try something that's more than a man?"

It was a tempting offer. Charlotte felt a flame of desire flare up inside her. It needed to be quenched, and somehow she felt that Brick was the only one who could satisfy her.

"What the hell are you doing, Wahl?"

"Just giving the slut an option."

Charlotte gasped. Geoff obviously thought she was insulted, but it wasn't like that at all. Brick was stirring up Charlotte's darker side, and she was liking it.

Liking it a lot.

"That's it Brick," said Geoff. "I don't care who you are on campus, there's no way I'm going to let you talk about Charlotte like that."

"What are you going to do about it, Geoffie-boy?"

Geoff stepped forward, putting himself between Brick and Charlotte. He got Charlotte past Brick and gave her a slight push. "Go to your dorm room," he told her. "I'll be there in a few minutes after I teach this blockhead some manners."

Brick was laughing.

Charlotte hesitated, not wanting to go anywhere. The prospect of watching two men fight over her was too wild to let go.

"I said go!"

Reluctantly, Charlotte stepped off the bridge and began walking toward her dormitory. Behind her she could hear the two men talking.

Their voices were rising in anger.

Charlotte began to run.

She couldn't wait to slide into bed and get some relief from the ache that throbbed between her legs. Then, by the time Geoff came by, she would be ready for a long and slow lovemaking session that would stretch long into the night.

3

"Look Brick," said Geoff. "I don't know what's gotten into you lately, but whatever it is I'm willing to let it slide tonight."

Brick stood there, impassive.

"I can't imagine you said those things to hurt Charlotte, so let's just forget about it. C'mon, we'll go to the Friar's Lounge and I'll buy you a draft."

"Charlotte's a slut, and everyone on campus knows it."

Geoff took a deep breath to calm himself. "Okay, all right. I see what you're doing. You're trying to provoke me…Well, I'm a good Catholic and I'm going to turn the other cheek. Good night, Brick." Geoff stepped forward, trying to walk past Brick, but the big hockey player wouldn't let him by.

He put his hands on Geoff's shoulders. "You're not going anywhere, asshole."

"C'mon, Brick. I'm sure you know that if you're caught fighting with a fellow student you could be pulled from the Cardinals' roster. And no NHL scout is going to be impressed by the way you play with yourself in the press box."

Brick's head jerked slightly as if what Geoff had said had made sense to him for a moment before being discarded in favor of the anger that seemed to be seething within him, just below the surface.

"Now let me go!" Geoff said.

Brick gave Geoff a hard push, sending him reeling backward. He landed on his ass, and then rolled head over heels until he stopped in a kneeling position. "I don't know what this is all about, Brick, but if you want to fight, then I'm happy to oblige you."

Brick smiled, began to laugh.

"But I must warn you I'm a red belt in Taekwondo," Geoff said, turning his body slightly to the side, bending his legs and putting his fists out in from of him in a *joon-bi* position.

Brick took a step forward…

Geoff gave a yell, *"Ki-up!"* and thrust out his right leg in a front kick. The sole of his foot connected solidly with Brick's mid-section, but it didn't slow the big man down. Instead, Geoff was pushed backward, struggling to regain his feet.

Brick took another step forward.

This time Geoff tried a series of middle and high punches. *"Ki-up!"* he cried again, connecting solidly with his right hand, and managing a glancing blow on Brick's right cheek with the follow-up left.

But again, the big man didn't slow down.

Geoff tried yet another strategy, this time a hard side kick to Brick's left knee. If he hit it right, the knee would snap backward and Brick would be immobilized. His hockey season would be over, maybe even his career, but Geoff was out of ideas as Brick continued to attack him like a man possessed.

Geoff pivoted to the side, lifted his leg slightly and drove a hard kick directly at Brick's kneecap.

The blow never connected.

There was a knife in Brick's hand. No, more than a knife, it was a dagger, a gleaming golden dagger.

As Geoff kicked, Brick brought the dagger down in a swinging motion – like that of a pendulum – to block Geoff's kick. The dagger caught Geoff's leg midway between the knee and ankle, easily cutting through his pant leg, leg muscle and shin bone. It also effectively blocked the kick, sending Geoff spinning against one of the handrails on the side of the bridge.

"Ah," he screamed, grabbing his now bleeding leg. "Jesus Christ, you cut me!"

"No," said Brick. "Not Jesus Christ – *Astaroth!*"

"What?"

Brick laughed, raised the knife over his head.

It seemed to hover there for a long, long time, and Geoff marveled at how shiny it looked, as if it were made out of pure gold. The handle looked like an erect phallus and the blade had to be eight inches long. Looking at the blade lengthwise from the tip, it seemed to have a diamond-shape to it, or perhaps that of a cross.

And as he watched the dagger streaking down toward him, the only thought Geoff could manage was what sort of wound would a dagger like that make in a human body.

A split second later the dagger punched a hole deep into Geoff's chest cavity. He looked down at it, and in the few seconds before his blood began gushing out of the rent in his chest, he had his answer – the hole was shaped like a cross, only it was upside down.

And then the blood came, slowly at first, but increasing in volume with each passing moment until it began to stream from his body in a torrent.

Just as the blood was about to run off his body and onto the wooden cross pieces surfacing the bridge, Geoff felt a heavy boot slam into his back, rolling him over, off the bridge and into the water of the creek below.

Geoff remained alive long enough to hear the splash his body made as it hit the water.

He tried to scream after that, to cry for help, but all he managed to do was swallow several mouthfuls of water, speeding his descent down…

down…

down…

To the bottom.

4

Charlotte lay on her stomach, naked under the covers, her body humming in the afterglow of an intense orgasm. When she'd arrived at her dorm room, she'd quickly got undressed, put on her bathrobe and went down the hall for a hot shower.

She'd spent a bit of time on herself in the shower, letting her soapy hands roam her taut body as the thought of Brick and Geoff fighting over her continued to thrill her. Her hands eventually found their way to her sex, but she decided to forego the shower for the more comfortable confines of her bed.

Back in her dorm room, she made herself comfortable and let her fingers do as her body pleased, allowing them to go to work relieving the ache she felt down there before it wound up driving her mad. But just because she allowed herself the indulgence didn't mean it had to be done quickly. She toyed with her body's own desire, teasing it relentlessly by bringing herself to the edge of pleasure's threshold, only to let herself slide back down again so she could make yet another delicious assault at orgasm. When she finally gave in to her body's urgent demand to release all of that pent-up sexual tension, she came in a shuddering climax, wetting the sheets and bed with a gush of ejaculate.

And now she lay still, a smile on her face and every part of her body luxuriating in a feeling of utter satisfaction.

But it wasn't enough.

She wanted more.

She could hardly wait for Geoff to arrive, to tell her how he beat up Brick and sent him running, all in defense of her honor. The thought of it brought a new tingle to her sex. They would make love slowly, talking the whole time, so Geoff could tell her exactly what it felt like to go up against Brick Wahl.

She could almost see the two men's muscles straining against one another as they wrestled and fought.

Charlotte slipped a hand down between her legs and rubbed her fingers against the wetness there.

And that's when the door opened.

A slice of light shone briefly into the room from the hallway, and then it was gone.

The door closed, its lock *snicking* into place.

"Geoff, is that you?"

No answer.

He was breathing hard, fresh from his defense of her honor. She could smell the sweat on his body and yearned to have it closer to her.

She reached over with her right hand and slowly pulled the sheets aside, leaving herself naked on the bed. She bent her knees and spread her legs, lifting her ass into the air like an open invitation.

He let out an approving grunt. It wasn't like Geoff to make such primal sounds, but it was understandable – even appropriate – under the circumstances. Charlotte wanted to be ravaged, and from the sounds of it, he wanted to ravage her as well.

She heard him slipping out of his clothes.

Charlotte adjusted herself on the bed, lifting her ass even higher. Her entire body was coursing with electricity, as if it were one big sexual receptacle just waiting to receive a man.

She didn't have to wait long.

Seconds after he was undressed, he placed his cock against the swollen lips of her sex. It felt bigger and hotter than Geoff had ever been before.

"Happy to see me, baby?"

He grunted and pushed himself inside her.

She almost screamed as she felt herself being stretched wide open. God, she felt so full. He was just so big tonight!

She began to grind her body against him, but a pair of strong hands grabbed her and held her in place.

He wants to be in control, she thought. Well, that was fine with her. Charlotte was more than happy to leave the driving to someone else tonight so she could just lie back and enjoy the ride.

And then she felt something, maybe Geoff's fingers, pressing against her anus.

"What are you doing?"

Another grunt.

There was something pushing hard against her, something spreading her sphincter open, straining to get inside. She and Geoff had talked about doing this before, but they'd both agreed – or at least Geoff had been of the opinion – that Sodomy was a sin.

Now Charlotte knew why people thought that way. It felt so good, it had to be a sin.

She reached back with her hands and spread her ass cheeks for him.

And suddenly he pushed his way inside.

"Oh God!" she cried.

That's when he slapped her on the back of the head.

"Hey!"

"Not that name," he said.

The voice was deep and throaty and not very much like Geoff's...

"Who's there?"

Laughter.

She turned to look behind her and in the darkness and shadows she saw that it wasn't Geoff behind her.

"Brick?" she said in disbelief.

He pushed harder now, stretching her so wide she felt as if she were going to be torn apart.

"You're hurting me!"

But that didn't stop him. He kept thrusting, pushing deeper into both her vagina and anus.

"Stop, please!" she cried softly.

He pulled out of her vagina and she fell to her stomach in relief.

But there was still something pressing into her anus.

What the hell could it be?

There were hands on her now, strong hands holding her down on the bed, constricting her movements. Still, she was able to turn her head far enough to see that there was some sort of gold phallus sticking out of her ass.

"Take it out please, it's hurting me."

He put his hand on the dagger's handle and forced it up the length of her back, splitting open her spinal cord along the way.

She was about to scream, but he grabbed a pillow off the bed and pressed it down over her head before she had the chance to make a sound.

After cutting a line into her body, he made a second incision horizontally across the small of her back just above the buttocks, completing an upside down cross on a canvas of unblemished flesh.

In time her body stilled.

He wiped the dagger clean on the bed sheets, most of the blade's surface was golden and gleaming. There were a few dark spots yet to be transformed, but more blood would take care of that easily.

With the dagger clean he got dressed, and locked the door behind him on the way out.

CHAPTER EIGHTEEN

1

Alexandre Sauve went straight from the drama lab to Charlotte Harriotte-Reid's dormitory. She'd missed that morning's acting class and as a result Alexandre hadn't been able to act out their scene from *A Man for All Seasons*.

But that wasn't the only reason he wanted to visit her in her room. He also happened to have a crush on her and jumped at the chance at seeing her outside of a classroom situation. She had a killer body and if he was lucky, he might catch her hung over and still in her night clothes. That had to be some sight, Charlotte Harriotte-Reid in a skimpy nightgown that left little to the imagination. If he was lucky, maybe he'd even be able to catch a peek at her nipples. He'd seen them before, through blouses and sweaters, and knew for a fact that they were very wide and very dark. And when they got stiff, they poked out a good half-inch from the breast, almost like the tip of his thumb. If he was able to catch a glimpse of those puppies now, his day – no, his week – would be made. Another reason he wanted to see her was that he wanted her to star in the student film he would be making for his major communications project this term. It would be a short subject about a sexy female vampire cruising bars in search of a drink. It would be shot on video with no budget, and there was no reason why Charlotte would want to do it, but she did want a career in front of the camera and this would be good experience for her. And, if it worked out well, she could use clips from it on her resume.

That, and Alexandre wanted to put Charlotte into black stockings, black leather and blood-red lipstick.

He took the stairs two at a time to the third floor of the dorm building then counted off the numbers on the doors as he passed students on the way to Charlotte's room.

When he got there he knocked on the door, then waited.

He nodded hello to a couple of students as they wandered the halls, then tried the door again, this time knocking even harder.

When there was no answer, he tried the door knob.

It was locked.

Again, he knocked on the door.

"She's not there," said a voice.

Alexandre looked up and saw that it was Brick.

"Where is she?"

Brick looked at him for several moments, then said, "She's down in the common room waiting for you."

"What?"

"She said if I saw you I should tell you she was there."

Alexandre didn't quite understand. While it was possible that Charlotte was in the dorm's common room where most of the students hung out, watched television, and did homework, there was no way that Charlotte would know he'd be coming by her dorm room after class. But even if she'd known he'd be coming to see her, she didn't normally hang out with Brick so there was no reason why she'd tell him to pass on the message about where she was. And besides all that, Brick Wahl was basically an asshole and there was no way in hell he would ever take this much interest in anyone's life other than his own.

"She's down there waiting for me?"

"Yeah," Brick nodded. "She said she wanted to talk to you about something."

"She wanted to talk to me?" he repeated in disbelief.

"That's right."

"About what?"

"I don't know."

"Where is the common room?"

"In the basement. C'mon, I'll show you."

Alexandre had been preyed upon by enough bullies in his time to be certain that something was not right here. Brick was being way too nice, and hadn't even called him "freak" once during their conversation, even though he'd gooped his hair into an especially stiff set of spikes this morning. While it was possible that Charlotte wasn't around, there was no way Brick was serving as her errand boy. Much more likely was that Brick was messing with Alexandre so he could get him in a stairwell and give him an atomic wedgie, or who knew what else. Alexandre decided it was best to forget about Charlotte for today and get out of the situation as best he could.

"No, that's okay," said Alexandre. "I'm sure I'll see her around later."

"C'mon, I'll take you to her."

"I don't think so."

Brick put his hands on Alexandre's shoulders and pressed him up against the wall, bending the spikes at the back of his head. "It's no problem."

Alexandre knew he had to act fast or Brick might just forcibly take him down to the basement. He looked up and down the hallway, and luckily saw Jean Dupont, one of his *Dungeons and Dragons* role-playing gamer friends, approaching.

"Hey Jean," said Alexandre. "Where you going?"

Jean Dupont, dressed in black like Alexandre – but without any make-up or dyed hair – stopped just behind Brick. "Monique's got a new sourcebook for *Vampire: The Masquerade*. We're going to the pub to check it out."

"Sounds great. I'll go with you."

After a moment, Alexandre said, "He's waiting for me."

Brick's grip on Alexandre's shoulder slowly relaxed.

When Brick's hands were off him Alexandre took a step away from the wall, straightened his coat and the shoulder strap to his bag, then looked over at Brick. "See you around, Brick. Say hello to Charlotte for me if you see her."

Brick said nothing.

Alexandre hurried down the hall with his friend Jean, not once looking back at Brick.

2

Karl entered the rectory dining hall looking for Father Dionne.

He found him at the long table in the middle of the hall, sitting across from Constable Tremblay. Karl wasn't sure if he should intrude on the two men's conversation, but Father

Dionne settled the matter by waving to Karl and calling him over to join them.

"Join us, Karl. Join us," said Father Dionne as Karl neared. Father Dionne had finished his lunch of cooked ham and mashed potatoes, but the constable was still working on a steaming cup of coffee.

Karl sat down, sliding his tray onto the table next to Father Dionne.

"I believe you know Constable Tremblay."

Karl forced a smile. "We've met."

"He's been looking into the disappearance of Diane Darby, but so far—"

"I checked with her parents," the constable cut in, "but they haven't heard from her either and they're worried. Apparently she calls them every day...Or had been, until she went missing."

"Constable Tremblay would like our help," said Father Dionne.

"Of course," Karl said. "Whatever you need."

"Abbotville is a small police department with just three full-time officers..."

Karl nodded, unsure why the constable was telling him this.

"...We'd like to do a complete search of the campus, but we don't have the manpower for it."

"You think she might be on campus..." Karl's voice trailed off as he considered the implications of what the constable was saying. Basically, he was strongly considering the possibility that she was somewhere in the tall grass and woods that spotted the campus.

Dead.

"Constable Tremblay needs someone to organize a search, and I suggested you for the job."

"Of course," Karl said immediately. "I'll get started on it right away. But it's late in the day...I don't think I can get much of a search started before dark. It might have to begin first thing tomorrow morning."

"That would be fine." The constable shook Karl's hand. "Thank you."

"And between you and me," said Karl. "I hope we don't find her."

"I understand."

3

After lunch, Father Dionne returned to the rectory to call faculty and department heads and ask them to direct their staff to the Lecture Hall where Karl was already getting students together to post flyers with Diane Darby's picture and the phone number for the Abbotville police on them. He would inform the other priests and brothers at the evening meal and all of them would makes themselves available for the search in the morning.

In the meantime they would pray that some news might turn up by the end of the day.

"There's a package for you, Father," Martine Ayres said when she realized that he'd returned from lunch.

"Where's my copy of the campus directory?" he said, ignoring Martine as he rifled through his desk drawers. "It's always either in the way or nowhere to be found."

Martine stepped into Father Dionne's office, holding the directory in her hand. "I keep one on my desk since you're always asking me for phone numbers."

"Ah, good." He took it from her.

"I said, there's a package for you." She pointed to the small table opposite the couch in one corner of the office.

"I haven't got time now." He began dialing a number.

"But it's from Rome," she said. "It came UPS."

"Diane Darby is missing. The Abbotville police have asked us to help organize a search of the campus. They think she might be…" his voice trailed off. "I need to get in touch with faculty and staff and send them to the Lecture Hall. Karl is handling things there."

Martine nodded. "I'll call the dorms and grad students."

"Good," he told her. Then someone picked up on the other end of the line. "Ah, Professor Raymond, I'm glad I caught you in…"

Martine left Father Dionne's office, sat down at her desk and began making calls.

4

By late afternoon Karl, with Mary Jane's help, had organized five teams that would begin searching the wooded areas just beyond the campus borders as well as the woods between the two western dormitories and on either side of the Regent's Theatre.

He'd also made up a flyer with Diane's picture on it and managed to get it posted in the lobbies and on the bulletin boards of every building on campus. The flyers might not produce Diane, but they just might jog someone's memory, or convince them to come forward with information that might help the police figure out what might have happened to her.

"Would you like another coffee?" Mary Jane asked as she cleared away the empty paper cups from the table they were working on.

"No thanks," answered Karl. "I've had too many already. Another cup and I'll have to take up permanent residence in the men's bathroom."

Mary Jane smiled at him. "I guess we won't be going to the game tonight."

Karl looked at her strangely a moment. "What game?"

"The Cardinals game against the University of Toronto Varsity Blues. You forgot about it, didn't you?"

Karl sighed. "I guess it did slip my mind. I'm sorry."

Mary Jane put a comforting hand on Karl's shoulder. "Don't worry about it, it's understandable. Besides, I think what we're doing here is a bit more important than watching a Cardinals game."

"Yeah, it's just that I was hoping to slip over to the museum to see Doctor Bos before the game. You know the ROM is just a half a block from Varsity Arena where the Blues play."

"I would have liked to see him too, and thank him for the ride to the hospital, but there'll be other games. We're needed here tonight."

"Absolutely," said Karl, straightening a sheaf of flyers. "I can always pay him a visit next time."

5

Doctor Cornelius Bos shuffled the papers on his desk and wondered what he had done with his pen. It had been there on top of the pile just a minute before and now it seemed to have vanished.

He looked to either side of the desk, and then to the floor.

There was his pen, right next to his left foot. He picked it up and began looking through the papers again, struggling to make his grant application as good as he knew how.

Some of his colleagues at the Royal Ontario Museum were very, very good at writing grant applications. In fact, in some cases that seemed to be the only writing they ever did. While Doctor Bos had published articles in dozens of scientific journals over the years, even a few pieces of short fiction concerning the exploits of George "Jackrabbit" Hunt – a fictional archeologist working out of the ROM and exploring the uncharted northern territory of the province at the turn of the century – none of that seemed to impress the institution's administrators.

Research grants were the thing. Government grants, Big Oil Company grants, even private donations, were all held in high regard by those who pulled the strings, especially now that the Tory government was once again cutting and trimming the museum's annual funding like it was fat on a T-bone. Whenever one of the ROM's staff received a grant or endowment there were always plenty of press conferences and media releases, but no one ever inquired about what the grant money got them after all was said and done. Doctor Bos wasn't one to point fingers, but Elisa Freeman in the Botany Department had vacationed in the Bahamas the year she received her grant after spending the previous six years' worth of vacations visiting relatives in Philadelphia. And Georges Polikarpov in Medieval History seemed to do a lot of research in Florida whenever he received a grant, as opposed to the cold damp moors of northern Scotland.

And so, mindful of keeping his job at the museum and pulling his weight in relation to the rest of the museum's staff, Doctor Bos was now writing proposals and filling out applications so that he might receive an exploration grant for the museum's Archeology Department. He was proposing a project at the site of the old Ste-Claire Mission in the northern part of the province. Sure, they hadn't found anything on their rain-shortened survey of the area, but there was no denying that chances were good that something would eventually turn up at the site. In his application he cited the thousand year-old walking stick Karl Desbiens had brought him, and the written accounts, as scant as they were, of the site's existence and the Jesuits' interaction with the native Huron Indians. And, there was the strong belief of the Jesuits at Ste-Claire that the mission had really existed and would eventually produce artifacts in the two to three-hundred year range.

From what he'd heard from the more prominent grant writers at the ROM, his application was a slam dunk. First of all, it had the Jesuit angle, and the exploration and reclamation of a holy site. What administrator could turn down an application that proposed a search for the existence of God in Canada in the 18th Century? But more than that, it also had a native Canadian element to it, and the built-in guilt factor associated with it. Who could say no to a plan that would try to track the history of one of the country's indigenous people, especially ones that had been literally wiped out by the meddling of white Europeans? Finally, there was simply a piece of the province's history that had yet to be explored. The Ste-Claire Mission site was a Pandora's Box, and with a little help from Big Oil and maybe the provincial government, he would open that box for the greater glory of himself and the Royal Ontario Museum.

If he succeeded, his job would become bullet-proof against any big-R Recession, big-D Downsizing, and big-L layoffs. If he failed it would be fifteen more years to retirement, and daily glances over his shoulder at administrators who were just itching to designate him "redundant."

Doctor Bos let out a sigh. It was almost enough to make him want to find a position at some community college teaching Archeology 101.

He tried his pen out on a scrap of paper and when the ink was rolling out in an thick even line, he picked up the form on the top of the pile and read the section listed as 1A: *Please provide a brief description of the project.* They had to be kidding, he thought. There was only three lines on the paper under 1A and that was only room for a hundred, a hundred and twenty-five words, tops. He'd need a few thousand to explain the importance of the project in terms of Ontario's history and that of the Society of Jesus.

Doctor Bos laughed under his breath. "If I get this grant, it'll be a miracle."

At that moment he heard the sound of footsteps out in the hall. He glanced at his watch and saw that it was after six and as far as he knew there was no one in the ROM's offices at this time of the day, especially on a Friday. Even the cleaners had already gone through the offices and wouldn't be back until Monday afternoon.

"Hello!" he said.

No answer.

It was possible that something had fallen over in an office down the hall, or a breeze from an open door or window somewhere else in the building had swept through the hallway. Doctor Bos gave a little shrug and tried to get back to the task at hand.

Please provide a brief description of the project

Doctor Bos began to write.

"There is little known about the Jesuit Mission of Ste-Claire and a properly funded excavation of the Mission site would piece together not only a piece of Ontario's history, but also that of the Society of Jesus and the early introduction of the Catholic religion to an infant nation destined to become one of the greatest in the world."

Doctor Bos put down his pen and read what he'd written. It was all crap of course, but it was the type of language granting officers loved. In other parts of the application he would sprinkle phrases like "explore religious heritage" and "unlock the mysteries of the sudden demise of our indigenous people." And the word "vibrant," he would use that a lot. Serge Roy in the Armory had told him that he'd been awarded a grant every time he'd used the word "vibrant" in an application. Doctor Bos didn't believe there was such a thing as a magic word that ensured the approval of grant applications, but it was worth a try.

Again he heard a sound out in the hallway, this time like a door closing and footsteps approaching.

Who could it be? he wondered.

He got up from his chair and walked around his desk. When he reached his office door, he turned the handle slowly so as to not make a sound, and then pulled the door back slightly so he could look out into the hall unnoticed. You could never tell when you might catch the administrators talking in confidence and be privy to information that might save your job or that of a co-worker.

But there were no voices.

No more sounds for that matter.

He opened the door fully to glance out into the hall...

And saw a man standing in the doorway, filling every corner of it like a giant.

"Oh, hey!" the doctor said.

The young man in the doorway said nothing.

"You scared the hell out of me," the doctor said, breathless. "I didn't know you were there."

Silence.

It was then that Doctor Bos recognized the man's red jacket. There was a crest over the left breast that read *Cardinals*. He looked at the man's face and something about it was familiar. "Do I know you?" he asked.

The man nodded.

Doctor Bos thought about it for a moment and then it came to him. "Yes, you were one of the students from Ste-Claire who was at the mission site."

Again the man nodded.

"Well, isn't that curious. I was just filling out a grant application for an archeological project on that very same site. I thought Karl Desbiens could use all the help he can get."

The young man put his hands inside his jacket pockets.

"What are you doing here?"

"Ste-Claire has got a game tonight against the Varsity Blues."

"Oh, really, well, good luck…but what are *you* doing *here* in the museum? This area is restricted to *employees only*." He said the last two words loudly and clearly, hoping the young man would get the hint.

Apparently he didn't.

He just stood there, looking at Doctor Bos in silence.

He had work to do and all this cement-headed hockey player was doing was wasting his valuable time.

"Why *did* you come here?" Doctor Bos asked again.

"To kill you."

"Wha–"

Before he could finish the word, something sharp and shiny was pulled from the man's right jacket pocket. It arched around in a semi-circle and pierced the left side of the doctor's head through the temple.

A bright shooting star of pain flashed across the inside of Doctor Bos's eyes, and then it seemed as if someone turned out the lights…

For good.

CHAPTER NINETEEN

1

A crowd of about thirty-five students and faculty, and citizens of Abbotville gathered at the lecture hall by eight Saturday morning. It was a clear day, a bit on the cold side, but there was a good chance things would warm up with the sun shining down throughout the day. One of the on-campus caterers had donated a couple of urns of hot coffee and a few dozen donuts. Judging by the number of steaming cups in the hands of volunteers, the gesture was very much appreciated.

Constable Tremblay glanced at his watch and stood up on a chair to address the crowd.

"First of all I want to thank you all for coming out today," he said, "I just wish it were under better circumstances."

A slight rumble coursed through the crowd.

"As you all know we're looking for Diane Darby. She may or may not be on campus, and if she's not, then we're looking for anything out of the ordinary, evidence of a struggle of some kind – you know, the contents of a purse strewn on the sidewalk or a stairwell, things like that. If you're not sure about something, contact myself or one of the other constables and we'll come take a look."

A few latecomers joined the crowd, bringing the number of volunteers to almost fifty.

"And it's not a race," the constable continued. "We want to cover as much ground as we can, properly rather than quickly." He gestured to Karl. "Regent...Karl Desbiens will be assigning areas of the campus to you searchers. If you know one area of the campus better than another, let him know and that's where he'll send you...Any questions?"

There were none. Everyone seemed to be anxious to get started.

"All right, then, good luck!"

†

After dissecting the campus into grids and assigning the volunteers to sectors, Karl decided to assign himself to the search of the Ste-Claire Arboretum. It wasn't exactly his favorite part of campus, and at this time of year there would be wet leaves covering an already slick and muddy ground, but it did seem to be the place where the police needed the most searchers.

Mary Jane joined him on the search even though he would have understood if she'd decided to pass. She was still recovering from her injuries and it might not be a good idea to strain her eye searching the shadows of the Arboretum before it had the chance to heal properly.

But she'd insisted, and in the end Karl was happy to have the company.

They walked northward along Masson Drive with the Arboretum on their left. Mary Jane kept close to Karl, bumping up against him several time as if she wanted to be in contact with him while they walked. Karl appreciated the sentiment, and at times felt himself wanting to curl his arm through hers, but such a thing would be inappropriate for him to do, particularly under the circumstances.

"Where do you want to start into the woods?" she asked.

They had been walking for a while and were now halfway between the dorms and the maintenance yard.

"The others are starting from the north end by the yard. I guess we should enter at the southeast corner and work our way toward them."

And so they headed into the woods.

There were leaves everywhere, much of them freshly fallen now that they were into October and green was giving way to yellow and red and orange. The new leaves made walking over the muddy ground a little easier, but didn't do much for finding tracks, or any other evidence of someone having passed through here on anything more than a leisurely walk.

Karl and Mary Jane had been walking back and forth in a

east-west pattern for about half an hour before they could hear the voices of the other searchers approaching from the north.

"You think we'll find anything?" Mary Jane asked.

Karl shook his head. "It doesn't look like it."

"With the leaves, everything looks the same."

"I know." Karl let out a sigh and stopped to sit on a stump. Mary Jane joined him and together they sat there, resting their feet and legs for their final assault on the woods.

"The leaves are everywhere, they've even covered that entire log over there."

Karl said nothing in response. Instead he just stared at the log, marveling at how *many* leaves had fallen on top of it. It looked unnatural somehow, as if the leaves hadn't just fallen, but had been heaped up on top of the log...

The realization hit him hard, like a punch to the gut from an iron fist.

"I don't think that's a log," he said.

"Then what is—"

Karl got up and started to run. When he reached the pile of leaves, he dropped to his knees and began brushing them aside with his hands. After the third swipe he had uncovered the body.

It was lying face down on the ground, its back was bare and the exposed flesh was a pale and pallid shade of grey. There was a huge rent in the middle of the back and lines had been ripped into the flesh by what had likely been a very jagged blade. The lines looked like a cross, only upside down.

Karl held off the urge to retch.

Mary Jane came up behind him, and screamed.

2

Within an hour the Arboretum had been taped off and all the searchers had been moved out of the area. A provincial coroner was called in and while the police waited for her to arrive, the entire crime scene was photographed and videotaped.

A mobile broadcast truck from the New VR was the first to pull to a stop on Masson Drive next to the Arboretum. A CHEX truck followed, and in a few more hours there would be trucks and cars from the CBC, CanWest, CTV and who knew where else?

But while the search for Diane Darby was called off, questions began to arise about the whereabouts of Charlotte

Harriette-Reid and Geoff Willett. While it had been thought that the couple had gone home for the weekend, a call to the dormitory from Mrs. Harriette-Reid suddenly made Charlotte an official missing person.

"Is this her room?" Constable Tremblay asked Karl after they'd travelled to Charlotte's dorm and hiked up the three flights of stairs to her floor.

Karl nodded, as did the students that had tagged along, curious about what all the commotion was about.

The constable sniffed at the air. "Smell that?"

Karl took a few sniffs of his own and felt his stomach churning again. It smelled bad, like the time he'd left a package of hamburger meat in the trunk of Father Dionne's car for a few days following a trip to the supermarket last July.

But of course, that wasn't the problem here.

"Oh my God," Karl said.

Constable Tremblay took a few steps back and threw himself against the door to Charlotte's room. There was a sound of wood giving way, but neither the door nor the jamb broke free. He tried it again and this time the door gave way.

The smell was suddenly unbearable.

The body was lying naked on the bed. A trough had been dug down its back starting at the anus and ending between the shoulder blades. There was a second trough across the top of the buttocks, making the wounds look like an upside down cross.

Both the constable and Karl put their hands over their mouths, and the students that had been hanging around in the hallway started moving backwards away from the door.

Karl took a quick look about the rest of the room.

There was no one else there.

"Where's Geoff?" he shouted.

3

Karl and Constable Tremblay stood outside the front doors of the dormitory waiting for the coroner and her staff to make their way over from the Arboretum so they could come and retrieve Charlotte Harriotte-Reid's body from the dorm room.

After a check of Geoff Willett's room found it to be empty and without any signs of foul play, only the third floor of the building had been cordoned off. Even so, most of the dormitory had emptied out since most of the students who lived there had decided that a dead body in the building was a pretty good reason to visit the library or spend some time with friends elsewhere on campus.

"You think the two deaths are connected?" Karl asked the constable.

The constable seemed annoyed by the question. "You saw the wounds on both bodies yourself and you're asking me?"

"Well, you're the professional here. I was just wondering what your experience tells you."

"Handing out traffic violations, settling domestic disputes and locking up drunken students didn't exactly prepare me for anything like this."

"Okay then, how about just your thoughts on the two deaths."

"Three!" said the constable. "Three of them, and they're more than deaths, they're *murders*."

"What?"

"There have been three of them so far, Ronald Henschel – his throat was slit, remember – and the two found on campus today."

"So you think we've got a serial–"

The constable turned sharply to face Karl. "You want to know what I think, *Regent*. I've got three dead kids so far, maybe even a fourth. They're all pretty much disconnected from each other in terms of who they were and what they did on this campus, except for one thing…You!" He emphasized the last word by stabbing his finger into Karl's chest.

"Me?"

"Yes, you. So far, the only thing the dead students have in common is that they were all on that field trip with you."

"But I–"

"You gathered them together, you took them to the mission site, and after you brought them back, they've started dying one by one. So, if you're asking me what I think about the murders, I think that you're connected to them somehow and either you don't know it, or you're not about to tell me. And since you're supposed to be a Man of God and a Jesuit, I'm willing to give you the benefit of the doubt and consider it to be the former. But if I find out you're somehow involved and you're holding out on me, I swear to God I'll personally make the cross they'll use to crucify you on."

Karl was left speechless, not by the constable's threats, but by the realization that what the man had said was true.

The mission study, *his* mission study, was the only thing that connected each of the victims.

The thought that he might have played a part in the student's deaths made Karl ill.

4

Father Dionne stepped slowly through the reception area of the rectory and continued on past Martine's empty desk and into his office. The reception phone began to ring, but he let it go. He had called Martine at home and asked her to come into the office to handle calls from the press until he was ready to answer questions, which would probably be sometime in the afternoon. Right now, he had more important things to do.

Although the Abbotville police would be calling the families of Diane Darby and Charlotte Harriette-Reid, he had asked that they let him be the first to contact them with the news. Although Father Dionne didn't relish the task, it might be best if the families first heard the news from a priest rather than a policeman, or even worse, a reporter.

But before he could make the calls, Father Dionne needed a few moments to relax and collect his thoughts. The morning had been filled with more excitement than he'd had in years and his heart was feeling the strain. He needed to be the voice of calm on the phone, and that would take some time.

As he sat down at his desk, Father Dionne thought about checking his emails to pass the time, but there was a good chance there would be messages from news organizations asking what was going on at Ste-Claire and he wasn't ready to deal with that yet.

On the corner of his desk, he noticed the box that had arrived from the Vatican the day before. Although he wouldn't have time to deal with whatever might be inside, he did have a few minutes to open up the box and see what it was. In fact, it was just the sort of distraction he could use at the moment.

And so after rifling through his desk for a knife, but settling for a pair of scissors, he stabbed at the box and sliced it open.

The box was filled with Styrofoam peanuts. He pushed his

hand inside and felt around. There was a number 10 envelope in there, presumably with a letter inside, as well as some sort of oblong object. He pulled the object out and saw that it was about the shape and size of a coffee-table book, shrouded in enough layers of bubble wrap to make the markings on the cover illegible.

Father Dionne decided to read the letter first and used the scissors to cut the envelope open at one end.

The letter slid out onto his desk. It was printed on heavy cream-colored stock, and crisply folded into thirds.

He unfolded the paper and began to read.

October 3, 2001

Father Gilbert Dionne, S.J.
Ste-Claire College
Abottville, Ontario
CANADA H7N 2G7

Dear Father Dionne:

I was surprised that you asked me to reconsider my decision concerning the excavation of the Ste-Claire Mission site. Since only a madman would want to unearth the secrets that are buried there, I could only deduce that you had no idea about what you were asking me to do.

A check of the Society's library confirmed this belief.

I have enclosed the diary of one of the Ste-Claire martyrs, Father Jean-Louis Trudel. It isn't as extensive a history as those written by the others, but it is both the most detailed and concisely written of all the martyrs' diaries.

If you're wondering, the martyrs' diaries were brought to Rome in 1850 so that the works could be copied and included in our library. However, Father Marcel Gagne died before completing the task, and it would appear that the task died with him. With no one else to take over, the originals were simply cataloged and placed on our shelves.

I apologize for the oversight, which we are now working to remedy. Father Trudel's diary has been photocopied and scanned and is now stored in our library in a hard copy format, as well as several different electronic formats. Other original volumes in the Ste-Claire diaries will be sent to you as the copying process of each volume is completed.

Again, we are sorry for the oversight committed by our predecessors, but glad it is a wrong that can so easily be righted.

Yours sincerely,

General Barthelme Rousseve, S.J.
Society of Jesus Headquarters
Vatican City, ROME

Diaries? wondered Father Dionne.

There had been some writings attributed to the Ste-Claire martyrs, but he'd never known there were actual diaries.

He took his scissors and carefully began cutting the bubble-wrap to get to the book beneath it. There were four layers of wrap around the book, but at last he managed to remove them all. The book was actually about the size of a hardcover, but its front and back covers were made out of elaborately tooled leather with a design of crosses – oriented both correctly *and* upside down – framing its borders. There was a picture inside the frame which depicted the sun shining up from the ground illuminating a battle between mortal men and angels, all of which was going on under the watchful eye of some higher being – presumably God.

Simply looking at the cover image sent a shiver down Father Dionne's spine. He was almost afraid to read what was inside.

The telephone that had been ringing off and on since Father Dionne entered his office suddenly stopped.

"Ste-Claire Rectory, Father Dionne's office," said the voice of Martine. "No, he'll have a statement for the media this afternoon."

The moment she hung up the telephone, it rang again.

Father Dionne took the diary in his hand and went to the reception area.

"Afternoon, Father," said Martine.

"Good afternoon, I'm sorry–"

Martine put up her hand to cut him off. "If you can't call me in to help at a time like this, what kind of employee would I be?"

Father Dionne smiled and nodded his thanks. "I'm going to my room for a while," he said. "If Karl comes by, send him to see me, otherwise I'm not to be disturbed."

"Yes, Father."

Father Dionne left reception and headed up the stairs at the end of the hall that led to his bedroom. When he got there, he switched on an upright brass lamp, sat in his reading chair and rested the heavy tome on his lap. Then he pulled a pair of wire-rimmed reading glasses from his shirt pocket and set them gently onto the bridge of his nose.

He settled himself back into the chair, adjusted his glasses and blew a little dust off the cover. Then he opened the book to page one and began reading.

CHAPTER TWENTY

1

When the coroner's van pulled up in front of the dormitory, Karl left Constable Tremblay and headed back to the Lecture Hall to see if anything had turned up in the search for Geoff Willett. He was also looking forward to seeing Mary Jane since she was also at risk now, having been part of the mission study.

"Hi M.J." he said, entering the hall. "Anything new?"

She shook her head. "Most of our searchers lost interest when we found Diane, and the rest just up and went home when they heard about Charlotte."

Karl nodded. "How are you doing?"

"I'm tired…and not ashamed to admit that I'm a little freaked out."

"I think we all are."

"I mean, first Ronald, then Diane and now Charlotte…" She wrapped her arms around herself as if to stave off a chill. "They were all at the mission site – just like I was."

"The constable pointed out the very same thing…" Karl's voice trailed off as he considered it. "Which is why I want you to go to your dorm."

"But that's where they found Charlotte, in her dorm room."

"Right, so I want you to stay with other people, and if you do go to your room, I want you to lock the door and not open it for anybody."

"Do you think it'll be okay?"

"The killer…" He paused to let the word he'd just said sink in. "If there is a killer, he'd be crazy to try anything right now. There are police all over campus and I've heard that there are more provincial police officers on the way."

"Can't you stay with me," said Mary Jane, lowering her head slightly and arching her eyebrows. "To protect me."

"Believe me, there's nothing I'd rather do than spend time with you, acting like none of this ever happened, but Father Dionne is going to have the press on his back later today and he might need some help explaining what's going on."

Mary Jane nodded.

"I'll be by to see you as soon as I can, okay?"

"You promise?"

"Yeah, I promise."

"Will you at least walk me to my dorm?'

"Sure, no problem."

2

After leaving Mary Jane safely with a few friends in the common room of her dorm, Karl crossed the campus to see Father Dionne, who was probably up to his collar in media inquiries by now.

As he entered the rectory, Karl could hear the phone ringing in the reception area followed by the decidedly haggard voice of Martine. She sounded both tired and annoyed all at the same time.

"Father Dionne will have a statement this afternoon...If you need something right now, try calling the school paper." She gave the number of the *Sentinel*.

"Hi Martine," Karl said. "Is Father Dionne in?"

She hung up the phone with an exaggerated gesture, as if putting it down emphatically would stop it from ringing. "He's in his room. He wanted to see you as soon as you got here."

Karl nodded and headed up the stairs to the priest's quarters where Father Dionne occupied the largest of the six bedrooms on the floor, which had historically been reserved for the Rector of the college.

At the end of the hall, Karl knocked on the door.

"Come in!"

Karl opened the door and found Father Dionne sitting in the reading chair off in one corner of the room. He looked older than Karl remembered, but considering what had been going on at Ste-Claire of late, it was understandable.

"Sit down!"

Karl looked for a chair, but the urgency in Father Dionne's voice made him settle for the edge of the bed.

"What is it?"

Father Dionne put a bookmark in the ancient-looking text he'd been reading and put it onto the table next to his chair. Then he took a deep breath and let out a long, long sigh. "I'm afraid we've made a terrible mistake."

"What do you mean?"

Father Dionne took another deep breath, but this time instead of sighing, he began to speak.

"When you first approached me about doing a survey of the mission site I wondered why anyone would want to waste their time digging holes in the ground. Not very scholarly of me, I know, but I'm an old man and the thought of taking on any project that may take ten or twenty years to complete just doesn't excite me as it might have in my younger days." He gestured toward Karl with an open hand. "But you, you're young and full of life and energy, you wanted to do it, felt a real need to do it, you had the passion for it, and I wanted you to stay at the college in the hopes that you might take over for me some day, and so I gave you permission to go up there and start poking around."

Karl didn't understand, but had too much respect for Father Dionne to interrupt him with questions. He would get to the point in his own time.

"I'm able to console myself, at least in part, because I didn't know what was up there. Neither did you..." He shrugged. "How could we?" He paused a moment and seemed on the verge of tears. "We had nothing but the best intentions..."

Father Dionne's voice trailed off again, only this time it didn't sound like he was going to say anything more. "I'm sorry Father, but I really don't understand what you're talking about."

"There was never any Indian massacre of the Jesuit priests of Ste-Claire."

"What?"

"That was simply a story concocted by the Society of Jesus to cover-up the real reason the mission had been built."

"So there *was* a mission."

"Yes, and from the account I've just read, it was an entirely successful mission at that."

For a moment Karl had thought he'd understood, but now he was more confused than ever. "I don't understand. If the mission was a success, then where is it?"

Father Dionne pointed to the leatherbound text on the table next to him. "I've been reading the diary of Father Jean-Louis Trudel."

"One of the martyrs?"

"Yes, it came today...from Rome."

Karl reached over and ran his hand over the leather-tooled cover of the book.

"And according to its entries, the three Jesuits didn't build Ste-Claire to convert savages to Christianity, but rather to battle the demon Astaroth who was attempting to establish a foothold in the New World."

Karl shook his head in disbelief.

"I know it sounds crazy," said Father Dionne. "But it's all starting to make sense now. The mission, Ste-Claire College, the murders...You can read it for yourself if you like."

Karl looked at Father Dionne curiously, wondering if he'd gone mad, but the man seemed convinced that whatever he'd read was true. And he was an academic, a scholar, even a bit of a skeptic, so if he believed the fantastic things he was saying, there had to be some merit to them. But, Jesus Christ – taking the Lord's name in vain seemed somehow appropriate for Karl at the moment – a battle against a demon...

"Around the middle of the eighteenth century, reports started coming in from Christian settlers in Huronia that a terrible evil was pervading the area. There were murders within families, stories of human sacrifice, torture and rape in the forests, or as Father Trudel call them in his diary, 'all manner of heinous and despicable acts.'

"The General and the rest of the European Jesuits all believed that the stories of torture and debauchery occurring in Huronia were simply the acts of savages...savages who had already had their chance at salvation at Ste-Marie Among the Hurons, but had done the devil's work against it. The opinion at the time was that the Jesuits had already given up too many martyrs in the attempt to bring God to the heathens. These new reports of evil acts only strengthened their conviction on the matter. In the end, the General and the Society decided to simply ignore the problem, concentrating instead on places like China and the Far East where there was at least some semblance of civilization."

"But, what does this—"

Father Dionne put up his hand to cut Karl off. "Patience," he said. "This is not a simple story and it needs to be told in its entirety."

Karl nodded, vowing to remain silent until Father Dionne was done.

"But the General's opinion didn't sit well with all the Jesuits in Rome. Nor was it popular with the government of France at the time. They had barely a hundred families in Huronia in the mid-Eighteenth Century and any more deaths would wipe out the settlement and send the survivors south to the newly-formed United States. And so a group of merchant traders with a vested interest in the fur trade approached the Society of Jesus in secret, seeking spiritual help for their troubled colony.

"The traders were eventually put in touch with these three brave young priests – much like you in many ways – who weren't afraid to voice their objections to the supposed wisdom of the General. They had openly questioned the Order's turning a blind eye to the problems in Huronia, even so far as accusing the Order of invading a society they knew nothing about and destroying its very fabric by arrogantly imposing themselves and their beliefs on those native to these foreign lands."

Karl laughed under his breath. The three priests might have realized trying to convert the Indians had been a mistake, but it would take hundreds of years for the rest of the Order to admit to it, if they did at all. There was a reason *Star Trek's* Captain Kirk had a *prime directive* to follow, and it was a shame the Jesuits hadn't had a similar edict when they boldly went where no Christian man had gone before.

"The three Jesuits came to Huronia to investigate the accounts of otherworldly evil without either the help or blessing of the Order. As you can imagine, few in the Society were sorry to see them leave Rome, and they were probably counting on the trio never returning."

Father Dionne smiled. "That's why they named their mission after Ste-Claire. It was a gesture meant to further infuriate the General and the other Jesuits."

The priest paused a moment. Karl waited patiently for him to continue, but when the pause lengthened into a very long moment of silence, Karl was compelled to ask questions. "Did they live? Did they return to Rome? Is that why there is nothing written about the Ste-Claire Martyrs?"

"No, they died here, but not at the hands of the savages like the martyrs at Ste-Marie Among the Hurons."

"Then how?"

"They came to Huronia and found the demon Astaroth."

"Found him?" It seemed impossible, ridiculous, yet here was Father Dionne, explaining it all to him without any hint of skepticism or disbelief. He was telling the story of the Martyrs and the demon as if it were fact. "Found him doing what?"

"Trying to open up a portal into hell."

"And they stopped him?"

"Yes. They confronted him, and vanquished him, silencing the demon forever…"

Karl looked at Father Dionne with a sense of dread building inside of him. Although he'd seen some pretty horrid things on campus, there had been no evidence of any supernatural forces at work. However, if a demon was to blame for the recent string of deaths, then Karl had a good idea about what Father Dionne was going to say next and the mere thought of it made Karl sick to his stomach.

"…or at least until now."

CHAPTER TWENTY-ONE

1

Constable Tremblay pulled his cruiser into an open spot next to Chief Dunbarton's car in the parking lot between the arena and sports fields. The chief was sitting in his car, waiting for the constable to show up. They hadn't had a lot of time to talk in the past couple of days and the chief wanted to be brought up to speed on how the investigation was going. The constable didn't have much in the way of good news, but there was still plenty to talk about.

He picked up the cardboard tray with two Tim Hortons coffee cups in it and got out of the car. The chief opened the door to his car and Constable Tremblay slid into the passenger seat next to him.

"Two kids in one day, eh?"

"That we know of, anyway." The constable handed the chief his coffee, a medium black with sugar.

"Jesus Effing Christ!" the chief said under his breath. He wasn't much of a churchgoer and didn't like visiting the college campus much.

Constable Tremblay couldn't be sure, but he suspected that the chief didn't like the Jesuits much either. The constable had to admit that some of the priests at the college had an air of superiority about them, like they were living on some higher plane of existence than the rest of the population. That sort of thing unnerved the chief, which wasn't all that hard to do with the set of ulcers he'd earned working twenty years on the Toronto police force. Constable Tremblay couldn't fault the chief for his feelings toward the Jesuits, since their we'll-handle-this-situation-ourselves-officer attitude got on his nerves too from time to time. But the constable was always able to console himself with the knowledge that at least he got laid every once in a while. With prostrate trouble the past four years, he couldn't say the same for the chief.

"So you're saying you expect to find more dead bodies?"

"There's another student missing, but today's search didn't find a trace of him."

"Shit." The chief took a sip of his coffee.

"Murder weapon?"

"At least that's consistent. The killer's probably using a long knife or dagger. The blade's a strange shape, so we'll know it when we find it."

"Any other clues?"

The constable shook his head. "A few, but most important is that all the victims had been on a field trip to the site of the old Ste-Claire mission last week."

"What the hell happened up there?"

"They dug around in the mud for about ten days, then came back when we got that storm."

"The one where the kid died in the bus crash?"

"Yeah."

"Oh, shit." The chief shook his head.

Constable Tremblay said nothing. The chief's assessment of the situation had pretty much summed it up.

"Any suspects?"

"There's somebody I like for a couple of the murders. He had opportunity, but I can't seem to figure out any motive."

"Well you stay hard on him. I've got all sorts of police forces calling me offering help, from the R.C.M.P. to the god damn University of Toronto Police, can you believe that?"

"They have their own police force?"

"They sure do, and it's bigger than ours."

"We could use some help," said the constable.

"I know that. There's some provincial police coming in today from Barrie. They'll be here working with us for as long as we need them."

"Am I still leading the case?"

"For now," said the chief. "But I don't have to tell you we're a little bit over our heads with this...okay maybe a lot. And not only are other police forces watching us, so is every newspaper, and radio and television station in the country." The chief let out a sigh, and shifted in his seat as if his ulcers had suddenly acted up at the thought of the press looking over their shoulder. "So if we don't come up with something soon, there'll be O.P.P. homicide detectives here by Sunday night going through all your work and looking for a reason to take over, since by then they'll have more men working the case than we will."

Constable Tremblay felt his stomach spasm, and suddenly understood a little bit more about the chief's condition than he had five minutes previously.

"Got it?" asked the chief.

"Yeah, I got it."

2

Karl struggled with the suggestion that his disturbance of the mission site had unearthed a centuries old evil. He had only wanted to do something meaningful with his life, something good for the college. How could he have known his actions would lead to this? He looked at the face of Father Dionne for an answer, but of course there was none there.

And so he asked.

"How did digging around the mission site unearth the evil? We didn't find anything."

"According to the diary, Astaroth wielded a long, golden dagger, which he used to commit his murderous acts, or rather, which he put into the hands of the Christian settlers so that they could commit the acts on his behalf...But the murders and torture were just a prelude. You see, the dagger's blade has a distinct shape to it. Along its length it is diamond-shaped, or as Trudel described, "like a cross that had turned hell to heaven, and heaven to hell."

"An upside down cross?" said Karl. "Like on all the bodies we've found so far."

Father Dionne nodded. "But the dagger's use as a murder weapon is actually of little importance."

"What do you mean?"

"The killings are only a means to an end. With each murder, the blood of the victims rejuvenate and restore the dagger, so that it will eventually work as a key."

"A key?"

"To unlock a gateway into hell."

Karl was dumbfounded. It was all too incredible to be believed, yet somehow he did believe it. Why? He thought about it for several moments and then a piece of the puzzle fit into place. "I think I've seen the lock. Yes, I'm sure of it. It was at the mission site, a strange hollowed-out hole inside a rock in the middle of an outcropping. We didn't know what to make of it at the time, but I asked Lucy Bartolo to take pictures of it."

"Good," said Father Dionne. "At least it will give us some idea about what we're looking for."

"But we didn't find anything on the site. We certainly didn't find any dagger. I think I would have noticed a golden dagger lying around."

"*You* didn't find anything, but what about the rest of the crew?"

"They would have told me about it. I mean, we were excited about finding beer bottles in the mud..."

"Perhaps, but if the demon wanted the dagger to be found, he wouldn't let everyone know about it, just his designate."

"His designate? You mean the one he's chosen to kill for him?"

"That's right."

"But why would a demon need someone to do his killing...and why wait for the dagger to be excavated, why not just dig it up himself?"

"He can't...the dagger's empowered by evil done by basically good people. The killer, probably one of the students who'd been with you at the mission site, is doing the demon's work for him."

"But there's only four of them left – Mary Jane, Lucy, Alexandre and Brick."

"And Geoff Willett," said Father Dionne. "I understand he's missing as well."

"That's right, do you think that maybe he's the killer?"

"One of them is either the killer, or his next victim...and that list would include you, I'm afraid."

"Me?" Karl said. "Father, you can't possibly–"

"You were on the trip, organized it in fact, and so far, all the victims were students who were with you. I don't think you've killed anyone, but you can't be ruled out yet."

Karl was silent.

"Now, I haven't found a reference to such in the diary, but I suspect the demon is targeting everyone who was on your trip."

"Everyone?"

Father Dionne nodded.

"My God!" exclaimed Karl. "That's almost a dozen people."

"I know," answered Father Dionne, suddenly sounding very weary.

"How do we stop the killing?"

"That, I don't know…I haven't read that far in the text yet."

"Then maybe you should get reading."

Without another word Father Dionne picked up the diary, opened it up to the page where he'd left off, and resumed reading.

3

Karl left Father Dionne's room and headed back down to the rectory reception area where Martine was still gamely answering the phone and either instructing callers to wait until the afternoon, or redirecting them to the school paper.

"Or you can just drive out here and see for yourself," she said, hanging up the phone.

"Problems?"

"Just pushy reporters wanting me to write their stories for them."

"That bad, huh?"

"Not really, some of them just want directions to the college. I imagine most of them had never heard of Ste-Claire College before this morning…At least the ones who aren't hockey fans."

Karl hesitated, then said, "I need to make a few phone calls."

"Help yourself." Martine moved the phone on her desk so that it was directly in front of Karl.

"And the college phone directory?"

"If Father Dionne had returned the one I'd lent him, it would be right here on the desk. Luckily I keep a spare for just such circumstances." She pulled open a drawer on her right and pulled out a small, red three-ring binder.

"Thanks."

"Are you going to be here for a while?"

Karl nodded.

"Good, because I could use a coffee."

"Double, double for me, thanks," said Karl.

When Martine was gone, Karl dialed Mary Jane's number. There was a chance she wouldn't be in her room, but he had to try. After three rings, she answered the phone. "Hello?"

"Ah, M.J.," said Karl. "You're in your room."

"Of course I am, what's wrong?"

"Is there anyone there with you?"

"Don't tell me you're jealous…" There was a coyness to her voice.

"Dammit, Mary Jane is there anyone there with you?"

"No. Why?" All the fun was suddenly gone.

"I want you to find some other people on your floor and stay with them. The more the better…and don't let them out of your sight."

"What is it?"

"Just trust me for now, and I'll explain later."

"Okay."

"I've got to make a few more calls right now, but I'll be by later. Okay?"

"Sure."

"Bye."

"Bye." He hung up the phone, searched the directory and found the number for Alexandre Sauve.

"Hello?"

"Alexandre, this is Karl Desbiens."

"Hello Karl, how are you?"

"I've been better, listen, are you alone in your room?"

Alexandre was hesitant. "Y-yes."

"I want you to go somewhere where there are other people. A group of friends would be best."

"Well, I was on my way to my *Forgotten Realms* role-playing game group. We're meeting in the Coffee Shop."

"Those games go on for a long time, right?"

"We play for a few hours, but the game never really ends."

"Good. I want you to stay with your friends for as long as you can, even spend the night in someone else's room if you can."

"Well, we were thinking about getting some refreshments and pulling an all-nighter."

"You do that."

"Does this have anything to do with finding Diane and Charlotte's bodies?"

"Yes."

The line was silent for several seconds. "Okay, I understand."

"Good. I'll check on you later."

Karl next dialed the number for the *Sentinel* hoping to find Lucy Bartolo there. With all that had happened on campus there was a good chance she'd be in the newspaper office working on the story.

"*Ste-Claire Sentinel*," said the voice on the other end. It was a male's voice, but not an entirely familiar one.

"Graham?" he said. "Is that you?"

"Yeah."

"You sound terrible."

"I caught a cold walking through the woods today. I don't feel all that bad, but it sure screwed up my voice."

"I'll say…Listen, I'm calling to speak to Lucy Bartolo, is she there?"

"Yeah, but she's processing some photos. If you wait five minutes or so, I can put her on for you."

"No, that's okay. I guess she'll be working at the paper pretty much all night."

"Oh yeah, we've got a lot of news to cover."

"Good, because I thought I'd drop by later and get some photos of the mission site from her."

"We'll be here."

"Great, see you later."

Graham hung up quickly without saying good-bye.

They must be working hard, thought Karl, putting down the phone again and checking the directory for Chris Wahl's room. When he had the right page it was easy to find the number since Martine had scrawled "Brick" next to his name in tiny letters. Karl dialed the number, but there was no answer. He waited a minute, tried again, but still nothing.

Checking the directory again, Karl called Coach Chambers' office inside the arena. The coach picked up the phone after just a single ring.

"Hockey Office."

"Coach Chambers, this is Karl Desbiens."

"You can't use the bus."

"What? No, that's not why I'm calling."

"Just kidding. You know you actually did me a favor. The new bus rides like a dream. Last night the guys were so well rested by the time they got into Toronto, they had U of T singing the blues all night long, ha!"

"So you won, then?"

"Five two."

"Great, congratulations."

"It was a big win—"

"Listen, the reason I'm calling is because I'm trying to get in touch with Brick, but he's not in his room. I thought he might be at the arena, or else you might know where he is."

"He's not here at the arena."

"No?"

"Nope, but I do know where he is."

"Where?"

"He decided to stay in Toronto for the weekend, talk some things over with his agent. Said he'd be back on campus Sunday night, Monday morning."

"Okay, great, thanks."

Karl hung up the phone before Coach Chambers had the chance to ask what was going on. If Brick was in Toronto then at least he was out of danger for another day and Karl had one fewer possible victim to worry about."

It looked as if the killer was Geoff Willett, although he sure didn't seem the type to kill anybody. In fact, he seemed more likely to take someone's wallet than take someone's life. But that's the way it always went in these sorts of things, the one who ended up being the killer was the one who seemed least likely to hurt a fly.

Karl went down the list of people who had been on the field trip, just to make sure he hadn't missed anyone. Ronald, Diane and Charlotte were all dead, he'd called Mary Jane, Alexandre, Lucy Bartolo and Brick. That left himself, Geoff – who was still missing – and…Doctor Bos.

Martine returned then with his coffee. "Just in time," said Karl. "Do you have a Toronto phone book?"

Martine handed Karl his coffee cup and went to a file cabinet and picked one of the big telephone directories off the top of it.

With the Toronto listing gone, the other books fell over, hitting the cabinet with a big *boom*.

"What number do you need?" Martine asked, noticing Karl was busy trying to tear the plastic lid to his coffee and fold the little tab out of the way, and failing at the task badly.

"The Royal Ontario Museum."

Martine started flipping pages. When she found the number she dialed it for Karl and handed him the receiver.

It rang several times before the bilingual tape recorded message kicked in.

Karl dialed the extension number for Doctor Bos.

The line was silent for a moment, and then someone answered, "Hello?"

"Yes, I'm calling for Doctor Bos, please?"

"Who are you?"

Karl thought it was an odd question to ask, and that it was asked very rudely. Nevertheless, he felt compelled to answer. "My name is Karl Desbiens. Doctor Bos joined me and my students on a field trip to the Ste-Claire mission site a couple of weeks ago and–"

"Oh, I'm sorry..."

"Sorry, for what?"

"This is Detective Morelli of the Toronto Police Department...I'm afraid Doctor Bos was murdered last night."

"Oh, my God. How did it happen?"

"As far as we can tell, someone broke into the offices after business hours and Doctor Bos, working late, was in the wrong place at the wrong time."

Karl felt his heart fall into the pit of his stomach. He didn't feel like talking anymore, to anyone, but there were a few questions he needed to know the answers to. "How did he die?"

"I don't know if that's–"

"Please, I need to know."

"Knife wound to the head, most likely."

"What did the wound look like?"

"What do you mean?"

"Did it look like a...like an upside-down cross?"

"Now that you mention it, the wounds did sort of look like that."

Karl hung up, and for a moment he imagined Detective

Morelli stupidly saying "Hello?" over and over again into the dead phone.

Doctor Bos was killed last night, thought Karl. Friday night. And the ROM is just a half-block from Varsity Arena where the Ste-Claire Cardinals played the Varsity Blues...

And Brick had been the last one on the mission site...And he'd been at the back of the bus just before Karl got there, and he'd been the one who told Karl that Ronald was dead.

Told Karl, because he was the one who had *killed him.*

"My God, it's Brick!" he said out loud.

"What?" asked Martine. "Where?"

But Karl was gone, running back up the stairs to tell Father Dionne.

CHAPTER TWENTY-TWO

1

Six Ontario Provincial Police cruisers approached the Ste-Claire campus, heading east out of Abbotville. They turned left at Masson Drive and then made a right onto Dominicus Circle.

A dark figure stood at the curb of Masson Drive and Dominicus Circle, watching the procession of gleaming white police cars pass him by. The figure was smiling broadly, knowing that six, twelve, a hundred more police officers weren't going to make a bit of difference.

It was almost too easy...

2

"It's Brick!" shouted Karl before he got to Father Dionne's door. "What's Brick?"

"It's Brick, he's the killer."

"Are you sure?"

Karl nodded. "He's the only one with the strength to wield the dagger the way it's been used in the murders...He had the best and last chance to find the dagger alone...He was the one on the bus who told me Ronald was already dead..."

"All of that is hardly proof," said Father Dionne.

"Maybe, but last night the doctor who joined us on the mission study was murdered in his office at the ROM. His wounds were similar to those found on the bodies here. And last night the Cardinals played in Toronto against the Blues..."

"Could be a coincidence."

"The arena is half a block from the museum."

"Oh," said Father Dionne, his head lowering slightly. "Do you think we should tell the police?"

"No!" said Karl. "Police deal in facts, and I doubt we'll be able to convince them that this string of murders is ultimately being committed by a demon who is thousands of years old."

"You're probably right, but we can't just sit back and let the killings continue."

"No we can't," said Karl. "That's why I have to stop him."

"You?"

"Yes, me. If I hadn't had doubts about my faith, if I hadn't questioned the order's handling of the mission site, if I hadn't needed some glorious cause to keep me at this college…none of this would have happened."

"Please, Karl," said Father Dionne. "You can't blame yourself for this. It's not your fault, it's nobody's fault. It's simply–"

"God's will?" Karl sneered. "Please, Father, you know as well as I do that God doesn't *will* the apocalypse to happen."

"No, I wasn't speaking about God." The priest paused, then let out a sigh. "I was going to suggest that it's the will of the demon."

Karl was caught off guard by Father Dionne's assertion.

"The demon is immortal, and he was no doubt the one searching around in my office for his walking stick."

Karl's eyes open wide at the realization that Astaroth was the likely owner of the walking stick and not one of the Ste-Claire martyrs.

"After he was defeated by the three martyrs, he set the wheels in motion for this series of events to eventually occur, so what if it took more than two-hundred years to finally come about. Think about it…How often do you think Jesuits misplace diaries and journals having to do with the end of the world as we know it. And now, thinking back on the circumstances of my arrival at this school, I wonder what the chances are of the previous rector dying in his sleep while I'm on my way to take over from him."

"I didn't know that."

"I thought it nothing more than an unfortunate coincidence at the time. But not now. There are other things too."

"Like what?"

"Like an anonymous donor suddenly appearing to fund the mission study with cash when all your own efforts to raise money had failed."

Karl gasped.

"And like the time I called you during the first week of your field trip to tell you to stop digging – by order of the General himself. Your cell phone was out of range, or inaccessible for some reason. At the time I thought it was God's will, but now I know better."

"Doctor Bos was making calls all the time on that phone."

Father Dionne extended his hands, palm up, as if to say, "You see."

Karl shook his head. "This might be the work of the demon, but it was my crisis of faith that got the ball rolling, and I was having doubts long before I thought about searching for the Ste-Claire Mission."

"All right, if you prefer, you're partly to blame for what's happened. Now do you feel better?"

"Yes."

"So what are you going to do about it?"

"This is a fight between good and evil, between God and Satan. Satan has sent the demon Astaroth. And since it doesn't look as if God has sent anybody to battle on his behalf, I guess I'll have to do."

Father Dionne gave a reluctant nod. "Well, it wouldn't be the first time a Jesuit found himself in such a position."

"Have you found anything new in the diary that might help?"

"Not yet, but I have plenty more reading to do."

"Father Dionne?" It was Martine calling from down the hall.

Karl went to the bedroom door. "What is it?"

"It's Constable Tremblay on the phone. The police have scheduled a press conference in twenty minutes, they want to know if you'll say something on behalf of the school."

"I'll do it if you like," Karl told the priest.

"No," said Father Dionne. "Your time can be better spent doing other things. I'll say a few comforting words, and then I'll return to finish reading the diary."

Karl nodded and turned to face Martine. "Tell him Father Dionne will be there."

Martine disappeared down the stairs.

"Wish me luck," said Karl, preparing to leave.

Father Dionne shook his head. "Luck will have nothing to do with this."

Karl just looked at him.

"Have faith!"

CHAPTER TWENTY-THREE

1

If Karl was going to stop the killings, he had to find Brick and take the dagger from him. If that wasn't possible, he might be able to warn the others to stay away from Brick until Father Dionne discovered how the three Jesuits managed to defeat the demon.

Since Brick wouldn't be returning to the campus until Sunday night, it gave Karl some much needed time to prepare, and to put together the pieces of the puzzle so that at the end of it all he might be able to convince laymen about the demon's reign of terror. First up were the photographs of the "lock" that Geoff had discovered in the rock formations at the mission site.

The main administration building was unusually empty, even for a Saturday afternoon. Campus life was such that no matter what time of the day or night it was, there was always someone hanging around, or passing through on their way to somewhere else.

But not today.

The place looked deserted.

As he neared the *Sentinel* office, things began to look even more desolate.

Abandoned.

He opened the door to the newspaper office and stood in the doorway listening for the sounds of people.

There were none.

But there was sound. It was a *drip, drip, drip* sort of sound, the kind that a leaky bathroom faucet can make in the middle of the night.

"Hello?" he said. "Anybody here?"

No answer.

Karl stepped inside and let the door slowly close behind him.

"Graham?" he said. "Lucy?"

Where could everybody be? he wondered. And then he saw a note on the bulletin board about a police press conference being held – he checked his watch – in less than five minutes. Well, that made sense, he thought. They wouldn't be very good reporters if they weren't there to find out what was going on.

He decided to leave a note on Graham Thompson's desk, telling the editor he'd be by later, and asking if he could take a look at any photos Lucy might have printed up of the mission site. He signed the note and placed it on the top of a cluttered pile of papers in the center of Graham's desk, and was about to leave when he became aware of the dripping sound again. It seemed to be coming from the dark room where there was a sink and chemicals for developing film and the old-style black and white photos the newspaper still used. Karl decided to be a good Samaritan and turn off the drip before gallons of water ended up going down the drain.

He opened the door to the dark room…

And found Lucy Bartolo.

"Oh, no…no…no…" Karl cried.

She was lying on her side across the countertop, naked from the waist up. Her throat had been slit vertically, the cut beginning just under her chin and continuing down between her breasts and over her abdomen. The blood from her neck had pooled on the countertop and was dripping off it onto the lid of a plastic chemical container. Inside the darkroom, the dripping sound had turned into the thump of a drum.

There was a second slash across her belly, deep enough to allow much of her entrails to empty their contents onto the counter.

Another upside down cross.

The clotheslines hanging around the room were full of large black and white photos. There were a few photos of the strange lock – and Karl pulled those down and slipped them inside his jacket – but most of them seemed to be blow-ups of certain areas of much smaller pictures. In one, the edge of a tent could be seen on the left, and on the right a dark figure standing in the middle of the forest, looking in. In another, the heads of several students gathered together for a group photo peeked up from the bottom of the picture, the rest of which was filled up by the excavation site. In one corner of the site, the dark figure was crouched down, as if curious to see what was going on, but still trying to remain hidden from view.

The rest of the photos were the same, barely discernible portions of people and things, and a grainy dark figure, looming constantly in the background.

Obviously Lucy had noticed something unusual about the photographs, something not right, and was in the process of trying to figure out what the hell the dark spot was – just like any good reporter would.

Karl took a few of those photos as well, and then went into the newsroom to use the phone to call the Abbotville police.

He picked up the telephone, then quickly put it down again. Constable Tremblay wasn't going to like the fact that *he* had been the one who'd discovered Lucy's body. The constable was already looking at him with suspicion, and this wasn't going to do anything to dissuade the man. Still, Karl had done nothing wrong, and therefore had nothing to fear from the police. Besides that, he needed their help to stop Brick from killing again. If he could just convince them to question the rest of the students who'd been on the trip again, then surely they would become suspicious of the only one in the group who had an opportunity to get to Doctor Bos on Friday night.

He picked up the phone and dialed the number for the Abbotville police.

2

"So you just happened to wander into the newspaper office when everyone else on campus is attending the press conference?" said Constable Tremblay. He had ushered Karl into Graham Thompson's office and put him into the comfortable office chair behind the editor's desk. Then he'd started asking Karl questions about where he'd been and what he'd been doing the last few days.

If Karl had been a suspect before, the discovery of this most recent murder victim had put him at the top of the constable's list.

"Father Dionne didn't need me at the press conference, and I know everything you would be telling the press, so..." His voice faded, leaving the rest of the words unsaid.

"So you thought that maybe you'd slip in and take care of Lucy Bartolo while everyone was out of the office."

"No, that's not it at all."

"But you did call the *Sentinel* editor to see if Lucy was here about a half hour before everyone left for the press conference."

"Yes, but–"

"So you knew she would be here."

"I was coming by to see her, yes."

"To see her, or to kill her?"

"I wanted to speak to her about the mission. I wanted to look at some of the photographs she took at the mission site."

"The ones hanging up in the darkroom?"

"Yes."

"What for?"

Karl hesitated. "I believe they show the killer."

"The killer?" said the constable, suddenly more interested in what Karl had to say. "Where?"

Karl had not wanted to get the police involved with the demon Astaroth since enough innocent people had already died and if the police got in the demon's way, they'd probably be wiped out, stepped on, or cast aside, just like any other obstacle it had come up against. But Karl was a prime suspect in a string of vicious murders – which he didn't blame Constable Tremblay for thinking, since he was actually partly responsible for the deaths – and if sharing what he knew with the police would free him up to find Brick and defeat the demon, then he had no choice in the matter.

He had to tell the constable what was going on.

"Do you see the black spot in the enlarged sections of the photos?"

"Yes."

"That's the demon Astaroth. Our excavation of the mission site has uncovered a dagger that belongs to the demon. It's in Brick's hand right now and he's killing all of us who were on the mission study so that the dagger can be transformed into a key...a key which will unlock a gateway between our world and hell."

Karl spoke the words slowly, clearly and evenly, without much emotion, and with as much conviction as he could muster. When he'd finished, the constable simply stared at him, probably trying to make sense of what he'd just said.

"Are you crazy?" he said at last.

"No, I assure you, I am not."

"I know you Jesuits are into some strange things, but you don't expect me to believe that crap you just laid down, do you?"

"I do expect you to believe it, because it happens to be the truth."

"If you think this is the work of some demon, why aren't you out looking for the little devil, instead of stumbling over all these dead bodies?"

"I was on my way to warn Lucy."

"Warn her about the demon?"

"Yes."

For the second time in just a few minutes, the constable stared at Karl. His gaze was ice cold, and penetrating, as if he wanted to jump across the desk and beat the truth out of Karl so he could be done with this whole mess. But the constable didn't move. Instead he made himself comfortable sitting at the edge of the desk, getting closer to Karl.

"I've been reading up on the Society of Jesus," said the constable, smiling as if he knew some dirty little secret. "You guys have done plenty of killing in the name of God over the years, right? Anybody who gets in your way, anyone who goes against your wishes, anyone who might hurt the Order."

"Those were extreme Jesuits who lived five-hundred years ago."

The constable continued, ignoring what Karl had said. "I remember reading about one Jesuit asking if it would be morally justifiable to murder Queen Elizabeth because she had done a lot of things to hurt the Catholic faith. Now, you tell me, if a member of your Order thought that killing the Queen of England would be justifiable homicide in the eyes of God, what's to stop you from killing off a few students?"

Karl looked at the constable through narrowed eyes. "And because some cops are corrupt and on the take, why not you? Right, constable?"

Constable Tremblay's face darkened and he shook his head as

if Karl had made a point he was unwilling to concede. "You had the opportunity in at least two of the murders, and I'm sure a check on your whereabouts at the time of the other killings will prove to be very interesting."

"And what might my motive be?"

"I haven't figured that out yet, but I wouldn't be surprised if you have one."

"And the murder weapon?"

"We'll find it."

"Any blood on my clothes?"

The constable pointed to Karl's jacket and pants. "Black is perfect for hiding blood. When I get a court order to search your room, maybe the lab will come up with something when they test your clothes with luminous."

Just then the door to the office opened up. Another policeman stuck his head through the opening and said, "Vince."

"Don't move," said Constable Tremblay, slipping through the doorway and standing out in the hall with his back to the slightly opened door.

He returned to the office a moment later, with a slight grin on his face. "You're under arrest for the murder of Lucy Bartolo," he said.

"But I didn't—"

"Yeah, well a secretary working across the hall whose too sick over what's happened to attend the press conference, says you were the only one to enter the newspaper office after all the students left it."

"That proves nothing," said Karl.

"Maybe, but it's enough to stop the killing by getting you off campus for a while."

Karl felt his hands pulled roughly behind his back. "No, it's not me," he said in desperation. "It's Brick, he's the one you want."

"It's Brick now, is it? A minute ago you were saying it was a demon named...Astagas."

"Astaroth," said Karl. "It's possessed Brick, making him do the demon's will."

Karl felt the cold bite of steel on his wrists.

"Did it will him to score two goals Friday night in the Cardinals' win over U of T?"

"No," said Karl. "I don't know...I'm not sure how the possession works twenty-four hours a day, I just know it's commanding him to kill when it wants him to."

Constable Tremblay pushed Karl toward the door and the few photos he'd hidden inside his jacket fell to the floor.

The constable stopped and looked at the photos.

"I needed to know what the demon looked like," Karl explained. "So I'd know him when I saw him."

"You know, it's not my place to say this, but you might not want to say anything more until you've talked to a lawyer."

Karl knew a lawyer wasn't going to do him any good, but talking to the constable without one wasn't helping matters either.

And why would the constable even suggest he get a lawyer?

It was as if the constable was also under the demon's power.

The thought sent a chill down Karl's spine.

"All right, let's go."

Karl walked out of the office, his arms cuffed behind his back, and saying nothing.

CHAPTER TWENTY-FOUR

1

By the time they reached the small police station in downtown Abbotville, a television crew from the New VR was already set up outside waiting for them.

Constable Tremblay hurried around the block and pulled up behind the station building, escorting Karl inside before a cameraman could get around the building to catch him on tape.

Once inside, the constable put Karl in the station's one holding cell and removed the handcuffs.

"I do hope I get a phone call," said Karl, rubbing his suddenly tender wrists.

"Sure." The constable picked up a portable phone and passed it to Karl through the bars.

Karl immediately dialed Father Dionne's office...and got a busy signal. He tried again, but with the same result. He continued to dial, hoping the line would be free, but it never was. He was about to try again, for what would have been the twelfth time, but the constable reached in to the cell and pulled the phone from his hands.

"But I didn't make my call."

"You could have tried another number."

"I wanted to speak with Father Dionne, his line's busy with media and concerned parents and who knows what else."

"Maybe you can try again later."

"Vince," came a woman's voice from across the room, most likely that of the small force's civilian secretary.

"Yeah."

"A call came in for you from a student named–" She checked

her note pad. "–Alexandre Sauve. He says he wants to talk to you about one of the murders. He says he thinks he knows who the killer is."

"It's Brick," said Karl. "Chris 'Brick' Wahl. And Alexandre is in great danger!"

Constable Tremblay stared at Karl. "You know, I've had just about enough of you!"

Karl pursed his lips tightly together and turned his head to one side out of frustration.

"For your information, I've checked on Brick. Coach Chambers told me he's staying in Toronto for the weekend. I'll be talking to him when he gets back tomorrow night, but until then I've got other important things to do."

Karl wanted to tell the constable about Doctor Bos, but knew it wouldn't get him anywhere with the man.

The constable turned back around to face the secretary. "Did he leave a number?"

"No, just a place where you could meet him on campus."

"Thanks, Gina." The constable took a slip of paper from the secretary and headed out of the station.

As he watched the man leave the building, Karl was certain that Constable Tremblay was somehow being manipulated by the demon. How else could you explain why Karl – a man of God – had been locked up in a jail cell without a hint of evidence, while the killer – a minion of the demon – was still free to roam the campus without anyone even thinking to look for him for another twenty-four hours?

It had to be the work of the demon.

And, as much as Karl hated to admit it, the demon was very good at being bad.

2

The killer had to be Brick, thought Alexandre as he sat idly at the table in the Coffee Shop waiting for his turn to play.

It just had to be him.

When the thought first came to Alexandre, he'd looked up from the table and said the word, "Brick!" For a few moments, Alexandre's fellow players thought it was some sort of code intended for the *Forgotten Realms* role-playing game they'd been into for the past four hours, but when they asked about it,

Alexandre just answered, "It's Brick, he's the one!"

After that he took a break from the game and called the Abbotville Police Department. Constable Tremblay, the one that had questioned him before about Ronald's death, wasn't in, but he'd left a message for him to meet him in the Coffee Shop. That had been almost an hour ago, and while several police officers had passed through the halls and cruisers had driven by outside, Constable Tremblay still hadn't shown.

And now, after three cups of coffee and a long wait, his bladder felt as if it was going to burst.

"If the constable comes looking for me, tell him I've just gone to the bathroom and I'll be right back."

"No problem," said one of the players, waving a hand in the air but not bothering to look up from the sourcebook on the table.

Alexandre hurried out of the Coffee Shop, made a right and headed toward the west end of the building. The men's bathroom was tucked into the corner at the very end of the hallway, past the door leading out into the eastern end of the courtyard. It was a small bathroom with one urinal and one toilet, and had a single door with a lock that entered from the hallway. That all combined to make the bathroom fairly secluded...a good spot to smoke a joint, or pour a little Alcool into your coffee.

When he entered the bathroom, Alexandre made sure to lock the door behind him. He couldn't afford to be too careful these days...especially with Brick still on the loose.

It had to be Brick, he thought again, as he unzipped his pants and began relieving himself in the urinal. Why else had Brick been so interested in Charlotte when he'd knocked on the door of her dorm room? Why had he tried to be so helpful, when in reality, Brick detested him for being different? Why hadn't he called him "Freak!" that time, when that's what he seemed to think his name was?

The answer was simple.

Brick wanted Alexandre away from Charlotte's room. He didn't want him to keep prying into her whereabouts, because if he had, he would have found out she was dead.

And Brick had even offered to take him to where he'd said Charlotte was so he could...

So he could kill him.

The thought sent a shiver up Alexandre's spine.

Brick was the killer.

Had to be.

Alexandre finished up at the urinal, shook, then zipped up his pants.

At the sink, he checked the points of his hair spikes in the wall-width mirror in front of him – perfect. Then he ran the water and pumped some soap into his palms.

Hopefully the constable would be in the Coffee Shop when he got back and he could get everything off his chest. The sooner Brick was in custody, or at least checked out by the police, the better it would be for everyone.

At that moment, the door to the toilet stall opened.

Alexandre's heart leapt into his throat.

He looked over to see who was there, but whoever it was hadn't stepped out of the stall yet.

Alexandre rinsed off his hands as quickly as he could. Then he turned off the water, and looked up into the mirror in front of him.

There was someone behind him.

"Brick!" said Alexandre, feeling a few drops of urine dribble down the inside of his right leg. "How's it going, buddy?"

Brick didn't answer.

Alexandre stared into the mirror, eyes wide with fear.

He saw a flash of gold behind him...

Felt a sharp burst of white-hot pain in the back of his skull...

And then saw his head being split in two as something sharp and golden pierced his brain and opened up an exit hole in the middle of his forehead.

At first Alexandre thought the wound looked like a third eye, but it was really more like a cross, only upside down.

And before everything went black, Alexandre managed one last thought.

I was right. Brick is *the killer!*

3

Constable Tremblay was outside the Coffee Shop on the Ste-Claire campus twenty minutes later. He entered the shop casually and took a quick look around. There were about a dozen people inside, about half of them scattered about a few small tables and the other half sitting at a single, larger table playing some sort of game.

He had interviewed this Alexandre kid before. Dressed in black with two-inch spikes of hair sticking out of his head, the goth punk would be easy to spot in a crowd, but Constable Tremblay didn't recognize him among the students in the shop.

"Are you looking for Alexandre?" asked one of the students. The constable nodded.

"He just went to the can. He'll be right back."

"Thanks," he said, turning to order a coffee. The smell of toasted bagels filled the little shop, and he decided to have one of those too. He gave the woman behind the counter a five-dollar bill. She opened up the cash and gave him his change, a toonie, two loonies and four quarters – five dollars worth of coins. It wasn't the first time he'd received free coffee while on duty, and he appreciated that the woman at least made it look like he'd paid rather than make a big scene about how his money was no good here. "Thanks," he said.

"No problem," she answered with a smile.

At the condiments stand, he added cream and sugar to his coffee, and spread butter on his bagel. There was a copy of the *Ste-Claire Sentinel* on one of the empty tables, so he sat down and read it while he ate. The news was old, since the paper only came out once a week, but the stories and pictures in it were pretty well done. One thing was for sure, the entire campus was reeling under the strain of the murders and a killer still on the loose.

At the gaming table, one of the players gave a shout and the rest chimed in with a series of howls and whistles.

The constable amended his thoughts on the effect the murders were having on the campus population. *Most* of the campus seemed to have been placed under a pall of gloom and fear, all except for these gamers. They were joking and having fun, oblivious to the fact that several of their classmates had been brutally murdered and there was a good chance that more of them would suffer the same fate.

Maybe that was the appeal of these kinds of games, he thought. To escape the real world for a while, forgetting all your troubles while you pretended to be somewhere else, living a life completely different from your own. Thinking about it further,

Constable Tremblay concluded that maybe it wasn't such a bad thing after all. He could sure do with some time living someone else's life…

The constable finished eating his bagel and sipped the last of his coffee, wondering what was taking Alexandre so long to get back from the bathroom.

"Has he come back yet?" he asked the gamer who'd spoken to him before.

"No. I haven't seen him."

"Where's the washroom?"

"There's one down the hall to the right."

Constable Tremblay walked down the hall, wondering if Alexandre might be the next victim. It wasn't likely since Brother Karl was in custody, but it was still a good idea to check it out.

When he reached the end of the hall, he knocked on the door. "Anyone in there?"

No answer.

"Alexandre?"

Again, no answer.

He tried the door handle and found it was unlocked. He opened the door slowly, but the light was off in the room and everything was dark. He reached a hand over to switch on the light…

And saw that the room was empty.

He pushed the door open fully, checked behind it, and then pushed open the toilet stall.

Nothing.

The room was clean.

In fact, it looked as if the counter and mirror had just been given a wipe.

Constable Tremblay left the bathroom and looked down the hall, then outside into the courtyard.

There was nobody around.

He went back to the Coffee Shop. "Did he come back here?"

"Who?"

"Alexandre."

"No, we figured he was with you out in the hall."

Constable Tremblay shook his head. "When you do see him, tell him I want to have a talk with him. I don't think jokes like this are very funny."

"Yes, sir," said the gamer.

The others had stopped playing for the moment and were staring at him.

He looked at them all in turn and was about to say something, give them all a stern lecture, but there didn't seem to be much point to it.

"Just tell him to call me," he said.

"Will do."

As he left the Coffee Shop, he could hear laughter behind him.

4

Back in his cruiser, Constable Tremblay radioed in to see if there'd been any calls for him.

"Plenty," said Gina, the Abbotville Police's receptionist. "CBC Newsworld, Global, CityTV, a bunch of radio stations, even an Internet site about serial killers that's based in Germany."

"You're kidding me."

"The guy was wondering if pictures of the victims were available on-line."

"Jesus."

"That's what I said."

"Have there been any calls from a student named Alexandre Sauve?"

"Hold on." There was a brief pause as she was likely sorting through the stack of messages in front of her. "No, sorry."

"Okay, I'm coming back to the station."

"10-4."

5

Karl had been pacing back and forth in his tiny cell since Constable Tremblay had left the station. By estimating how long it took to drive from the station to the campus and back, and how long it would take Alexandre to explain that Brick was the killer, Karl figured that the constable would be walking through the doors any minute now.

The way Karl imagined it, he would walk through the doors, head down, doing his best not to look Karl directly in the eye. He would unlock the door to the cell, and while he was doing that he would apologize for suspecting him, and then the two of them would figure out the best way to find Brick and bring him in.

That was, of course, the best-case scenario. Another scenario, not as good, but acceptable, had the constable returning to the station and questioning Karl in light of what Alexandre had told him. Over the course of say an hour or two, it would become obvious to the constable that Karl was innocent of the murders and he would have no other choice but to release him. That would cost Karl time, and would put more students at risk, but it would be worth it to get out from under the shroud of the constable's suspicion.

Karl continued to pace in his cell. He glanced at his watch and wondered where the constable could be. And then, as if on cue, the door to the police station opened up and Constable Tremblay strolled in.

His head was held high, and he didn't seem to have any problem making eye contact with Karl. In fact, there was a bit of an angry scowl on his face.

"Did Alexandre tell you who the killer is?" Karl said, trying to get the constable's attention from across the room. "It's Brick, right? He said it was Brick."

The constable strolled over, shaking his head. "No he didn't tell me."

"But he had to. That's who the killer is. If he knows, that's who he had to say it was."

"I thought you said it was a demon."

"Yes, and the demon is controlling Brick."

"Well, Alexandre didn't tell me that, either."

"What did he say?"

"Nothing. He didn't show."

Karl's heart sank, somehow knowing that something bad, something very bad, had happened to Alexandre.

"Does that mean you won't be releasing me?"

"That's right, in fact, I think it would be a good idea if you spent the night right there in that cell."

"But I can't, *you* can't–"

"We're processing your paperwork. But you can see how busy we are in here at the moment, so it might take some time."

Karl opened his mouth to speak but the constable put a hand up to silence him. "It's not going to hurt you to spend a night here. And I'll be sure to check out Brick tomorrow, as soon as he gets back on campus. How would that be?"

At least it was a start, thought Karl. If the police just took a closer look at Brick they'd see how everything fell into place. "He's already on campus," Karl said, unable to keep the sense of defeat from creeping into his voice. "But if that's the best you can do, I suppose it will have to be all right."

The constable shook his head in disgust.

Karl wondered how in God's name the man could be so sure of himself. Students were dying and he wasn't even close to catching the killer. The only thing he'd been right about was how it wouldn't hurt Karl to spend the night in jail. Karl wouldn't be hurt by it, but others would be.

They'd be hurt.

Or killed.

And the constable would have done nothing to stop it.

"What do you want for supper?" asked the constable.

"Nothing," said Karl.

How could he eat?

Instead, he got down on his knees, and prayed.

CHAPTER TWENTY-FIVE

1

Egidio DeAngelis saw the shriveled up condom lying in the dirt by the bushes and shook his head. He should have been shocked, but it took a lot more than something like that to impress him these days.

He swept the condom into his dustpan and lifted it off the ground so it would fall into the attached white nylon garbage bag.

As a child growing up in the small Italian town of Cesena, he hadn't even heard the word "sex" until he'd turned sixteen, and even then it was in a Sophia Loren movie playing in the town cinema. His wife Elisa had been the only woman he'd ever kissed and after that first kiss, he knew he had to marry her. The first he learned about condoms was working as a cleaner in downtown bars in Toronto, his first job after crossing the Atlantic to be with his brother in Canada.

After a few years in Toronto he'd moved his wife and two girls north of the city to get away from all the bad influences that would soil his daughters' upbringing. When he'd gotten a job as a custodian at Ste-Claire College more than twenty years ago, he thought he had finally reached paradise. It was a Catholic school with priests and brothers, and it was far enough away from the big city that his daughters could grow up safe and happy, without a care in the world.

But now, there were condoms here too, and murders.

Lots of murders.

Young girls, studying at the school just like his daughters, stabbed and killed by some beast, some animal.

In the old country whenever something like this happened, they said it was the work of the devil. After all, what *man* would be capable of doing such a thing? It was one thing to kill someone in a fight, or during an argument, but this...*creature* had killed three or four people – the police weren't even sure how many – and he was going to kill again.

The police said they had somebody in jail, but they wouldn't say who. Egidio figured it was because they weren't sure if they had the killer.

They didn't.

Egidio knew it, he could feel it in his bones, almost taste it in the air. There was something evil at work at the school, and it wasn't finished its job.

He took a few steps and swept a candy bar wrapper and an empty potato chip bag from the concrete walkway that snaked between the picnic and patio tables scattered about the courtyard.

Just then the wind picked up and a sheet of notepaper drifted across the yard. Egidio was happy to see it go, since it was one less piece of garbage he'd have to sweep up. But as he watched it glide over the concrete pad as if on a cushion of air, it suddenly stopped. It had gotten stuck on a dark spot on the courtyard floor. Someone had split their coffee, or a milkshake or who knew what, and had left it there for Egidio to clean up in the morning.

"*Disgraziato!*" he muttered under his breath. These kids today had no manners, no respect.

He walked over to the stain on the concrete and swept the paper into his bag...

And jumped back in fear.

His broom had left a dark red smear on the concrete, like a brush pushed through a half-dried puddle of paint.

But it wasn't paint.

It was...

"*Oh, Dio!,*" he said, realizing it was blood.

And then he looked up...

Where the body of Alexandre Sauve was hanging upside down from a flagpole, his hair mangled, his feet bound at the ankles, his body stripped naked except for a pair of bloody underwear, and his arms stretched out perpendicularly from his body – like he'd been crucified, only upside down.

His body had been punched full of holes, the ones clear of blood looking like tiny crosses, and the others simply looking like a mess.

Egidio dropped his broom and bag, made the sign of the cross, and ran away, screaming.

2

The cold autumn wind continued to blow hard across the courtyard, sending leaves and scraps of paper tumbling out onto Dominicus Circle.

At the southeast end of the campus, tiny whitecaps began to appear on the surface of Heritage Pond where a big black Labrador was noisily lapping up a few mouthfuls of cold, cold, water.

The dog's owner, a grey-haired gentleman named Sam Dutton, walked along the south side of Dominicus Circle, along Heritage Creek heading toward the pond where his dog Black would be waiting for him. Sam knew the college campus probably wasn't all that safe a place to be walking around alone, but it was Sunday morning for crying out loud, and he was far too old to be worried about being killed by some knife-wielding maniac. He'd flown Hurricanes on patrol of Canada's east coast in 1941 and then moved up to Spitfires in England where he'd flown fighter sweeps over France and Germany from D-Day until the end of the war. He'd been shot up and wounded enough times during the war to know that God could take him whenever He damn well pleased and there wasn't a damn thing he could do about it. And so, if the killer was lurking at the south end of the campus this Sunday morning, well it just meant that God had finally made up his mind about the life of old Sam Dutton.

As he passed the theatre he walked over the bridge, crossing Heritage Creek and joining Black at the southern edge of the pond. But long before he met up with the dog, Black began to bark. That was nothing new since the dog was always barking on their walks. Usually it was just a "Hello" and "How'd you do?" to the birds in the trees, or to some wild animal he saw in the fields. But those were usually half-hearted barks, like Black knew he wasn't impressing anybody. These barks however, were sharp and purposeful, and they weren't stopping.

Black had either found something, or someone was standing over him with a stick held high in a threatening manner.

Sam started running, but his knees weren't the best and his artificial left hip dictated that he settle for a quick hobble. He skirted the edge of the woods, hearing but not seeing Black. At last the row of trees on his right ended, and he could see Black taking a step into the water, and then two steps back onto dry land, as if he wanted to jump in but wasn't sure if it were the right thing to do.

"What is it, boy?" Sam said, out of breath after the short jog from the bridge.

Black continued barking, only now he was raising his snout toward the middle of the pond in time with each bark.

Sam squinted his eyes – not as good as they used to be, just like everything else on his body – and saw a bloated shape floating in the water. He'd seen a few airmen's bodies that had washed up on shore during the war and this one was no different. The flesh was bloated with gases, but not as severely as ones he'd seen in the past. The numerous holes on the body would probably account for that, letting out the gases and keeping the body under water for a little longer than usual. As the wind rolled the body over, Sam could see that there was some hair on the face and that it was obviously a young man.

A young, dead man.

Sam let out a sigh, and felt a tear well up in his right eye. You expected young men to die during wartime, but this college, this was a place of higher learning…it was supposed to be the place where young people got their start on life's path, not reach the end of it.

"C'mon, Black," he said, turning back and heading toward the bridge in front of the theatre in the hopes of flagging down a cop.

3

Karl extended his fingers and raised his arms over his head in a long, uncomfortable stretch. The night had been fitful and he'd been unable to sleep for more than a few minutes at a time. The cot didn't help much either and he woke up sore and stiff all over. But the night was behind him now and the day, a new day, Sunday, was stretched out before him.

Beckoning.

But he couldn't take part in the day if he were still stuck behind bars, and it was obvious that the constable wasn't interested in his theories about the demon Astaroth and its hold on Brick. It was time to try another tack.

"Constable," said Karl, his hands clenched tight enough on the bars of his cell to turn his knuckles a pale white.

Constable Tremblay put down the telephone and took a sip from a paper Tim Hortons coffee cup. He looked tired, worn out, and his uniform was badly wrinkled, as if he'd spent the night in it, or perhaps more than one. He turned his head and looked at Karl for a long, long time. "What is it?"

"Seeing as this is Sunday, and I haven't been formally charged with anyone's murder, I thought you might let me out, even for just a few hours, so that I could celebrate mass this morning with Father Dionne."

The constable got up from his desk and began to slowly walk toward Karl's cell. He appeared even more fatigued now that he was standing, his feet dragging behind him as he walked.

"You see, it's been a trying time for Father Dionne, and even though he's been strong these past few days, I'm sure he would appreciate my presence at his side."

"You want to get out," said the constable. "To celebrate mass."

"That's right."

"Sure, okay."

"You're letting me go?"

"Yes."

"And you no longer believe that I am the killer."

"I still have some reservations, but no." He shook his head.

Karl breathed a sigh. He was free...free to stop Brick and pursue the demon. "What changed your mind?"

The constable let out a sigh. "They found Alexandre Sauve's body this morning..."

"Oh God, no!" Karl took several steps back into the cell and sat down on the cot.

"...hanging upside down from a flagpole in the courtyard. The person who called it in said he sort of looked like Jesus on the cross, only the wrong way up."

Karl shook his head several times, trying to shake away the

feelings of guilt that were crawling over his mind and body like so many spiders. He'd been powerless to do anything to help, Astaroth had made sure of that. But if the demon knew he was a threat and had manipulated the officer to lock him up, why would he now allow the constable to release him when Geoff was still missing and Mary Jane–

"I need to use the phone!" Karl said, getting up from the cot and charging past Constable Tremblay to get to a telephone.

"What is it?" asked the constable.

Karl ignored the question. He picked up the phone on the nearest desk and dialed Mary Jane's dorm room.

"Hello?" she said after just two rings.

"Mary Jane, thank God."

"Where have you been?" she asked. "Father Dionne's been looking for you…and it would have been nice to hear from you last night."

"I spent the night in jail."

"What?"

"Never mind that now, are you alone?"

"You're not going to ask me what I'm wearing, are you?"

"Dammit, Mary Jane, this is serious. Alexandre was murdered last night…"

"Sorry. I heard about Alexandre…I was just trying to lighten things up…I'm sorry."

"And I want to know if you're safe. Is there someone there with you?"

"Yes. You told me not to be alone."

Karl breathed a sigh of relief. "Right, great…Who's there with you?"

"Brick."

The word hit Karl like a large calibre bullet.

"He came by to see how I'm doing. With Alexandre dead and Geoff missing, we're the only two left from the mission study and he thought we should stick together."

"No, run away. Brick's the–"

The line suddenly went dead.

Karl turned to the constable, who had been listening intently to Karl's half of the conversation. "Brick's with Mary Jane right now."

"What room and what building?"

Karl told him.

The constable radioed the provincial police officers on campus and told them about a possible assault going on at the location.

That done, he turned to Karl and said, "Let's go!"

The two men hurried out of the station.

4

With the siren blaring and the lights flashing, it took them less than ten minutes to get to the campus and the front door of Mary Jane's dorm building. There were three O.P.P. cruisers parked out front, and a single car from the Abbotville force already on the scene.

About a dozen students and Abbotville residents on their way to Sunday morning service were loitering outside the dorm building wondering what was going on, and probably fearing the worst.

Karl was first out of the cruiser, running up the front steps to the building as fast as his under-exercised legs could take him. Inside, he opted for the stairs, taking them two at a time until he reached the second floor firedoor, which had been propped open with a chair.

As he neared Mary Jane's room, he could feel a sort of tension in the air. The police officers already on the scene were quiet, and one of them, a young provincial officer was wiping his mouth with a handkerchief.

Karl stopped dead in the doorway. There was a coppery smell wafting out of the room, like fresh blood.

And then Karl saw her...

Saw it.

And felt his legs suddenly become too weak to hold himself upright.

Mary Jane's body was lying face up on the bed. Her arms and legs were strewn at awkward angles, as if she'd put up a fight, only to have her limbs broken by her attacker.

But that wasn't the worst of it.

In addition to the puncture wounds all over her body, both her eyes had been gouged out, probably with the same weapon that had put all the cross-shaped holes in her chest, stomach, arms and legs.

Karl felt as if his insides had been blown apart. His entire body was wracked with grief, not just for Mary Jane, but for every one of the students who had died because of his utterly foolish notion. In his entire time as a member of the Society of Jesus, Karl had never seen a Jesuit cry – not even tears of joy. For a split second he tried to hold back the tears that were welling up behind his eyes, but they were too much, too strong, too...

His body went limp.

He began to sob.

To wail.

Two police officers came up behind him and caught him by his arms to keep him from falling to the floor.

They took him out into the hall and escorted him to another room where he could sit or lie down. As he reached the room, Karl could hear Constable Tremblay telling the other officers about Brick.

Finally...

But too little, too late.

What would it matter now? Karl would be next on the demon's list, and the way he felt, a violent death just might be appropriate considering the evil he'd unleashed on the campus.

On the world.

5

Father Dionne appeared in the doorway still wearing his collar and vest from the mass beneath his black nylon jacket.

Karl looked up at the elderly priest for just a moment, too ashamed to make eye contact with him for more than a instant. "Mary Jane's dead," he said, his head down and cradled in his hands.

"I know," said Father Dionne. "They also found Geoff."

Karl had thought that it was impossible for his heart to sink any further into the black pit it had fallen into, but the news of Geoff's death – or rather the confirmation of his demise – managed to push Karl even deeper into despair.

"That's all of them, then," he said.

"Not all."

Karl looked up.

"There's one more...you."

"He can take me for all I care–"

Karl suddenly felt the hard slap of Father Dionne's hand across his face. It had happened so fast, he hadn't seen it coming, and wasn't sure about just what had happened. "What sort of talk is that for a Jesuit?"

Karl looked up at Father Dionne and was startled to see that the man's hand was raised and ready to strike another blow. He tried to speak, wanting to explain how hopeless it all was, but somehow he couldn't bring himself to say the words to the priest.

"This isn't over," said Father Dionne. "It's just the start."

Karl was silent.

"The demon's dagger is just two victims away from unlocking the gates of hell and unleashing an even more fearsome evil onto – not only this campus – but all mankind."

"And who can stop that from happening?"

"You can…" Father Dionne's voice trailed off.

Karl sighed and shook his head. He'd tried to stop the killings, but the demon Astaroth was too strong, too powerful, too cunning, to stop. If he were going to save the Earth from Hell's fury, he would need nothing short of a miracle.

"…with my help."

Karl looked up at Father Dionne, a needle of hope piercing his heart.

CHAPTER TWENTY-SIX

1

Father Dionne escorted Karl across the campus and toward the rectory. Karl leaned on Father Dionne's shoulder almost as much as Father Dionne leaned on his cane. There were television crews all over the place and several of them seemed to think that pictures of the two men walking across campus – Father Dionne in his collar and using a cane, no less – might be a useful, perhaps even a poignant image to broadcast on the evening news. Karl was eager to ask Father Dionne about what he'd read as they walked across the moist grass and damp asphalt, but there was no way they could discuss such things anywhere near the television cameras.

When they arrived at the rectory, Martine was there at the reception desk, casually leafing through the Saturday issue of *The National Post.*

"Any calls?" asked Father Dionne.

"No," she said, a hint of surprise in her voice. "It's been pretty quiet. I don't know if news of this morning's discoveries hasn't been broadcast yet or people are just tuning into CBC Newsworld to find out what's going on?"

"Well, whatever the reason, I'm sure you appreciate the respite."

"I do," said Martine. "But I know it won't last. This thing, whatever it is, isn't over yet."

"Why do you say that?"

"I don't know, I can just…feel it."

Father Dionne nodded silently, then said, "We'll be in my room."

They left reception and headed up the stairs.

Karl was tempted to ask Father Dionne now about what he'd read, but knew the man would want to wait until they were safely behind closed doors and in the privacy of his room before they discussed anything.

Karl opened the door and stood back to let the elderly priest by. Father Dionne took his usual chair and Karl sat down on the edge of the bed.

Father Dionne seemed hesitant.

"Well?" Karl said, prodding him. "What more have you learned, and how do we stop anyone else from being...from losing their life?"

"There will be at least two more deaths."

"Two?" Karl's mind was racing. "Myself and Brick?"

"Perhaps."

"You're not sure?"

Father Dionne shook his head. "According to Father Trudel's diary, before the dagger can be used as a key, it must kill all who had a hand or were present for its unearthing. In the mid-eighteenth century that meant all the Christian settlers in Huronia..."

"And now?" Karl held his breath.

"Everyone who was working with you at the mission site."

"And Brick is the one with the dagger..."

"That's right."

"Why does the demon need a designate anyway?"

Father Dionne gave a little shrug. "Father Trudel wasn't sure. He suspected it gave the demon pleasure to see humans doing his bidding, or that he didn't want to soil his hands doing something so mundane as murdering mere mortals...It doesn't really matter?"

Karl thought about that for a moment and remembered that Father Dionne had said there were to be at least two more deaths. "Well, if Brick kills me next, does that mean he'll have to kill himself as well?"

"No," answered Father Dionne. "After he kills you, Brick will turn the dagger over to Astaroth. Then, Astaroth, the demon, will lower himself to the level of mortals to commit the last murder, the one that will finally and fully transform the dagger into a key."

"What can we do to stop that from happening?" Karl said, his voice more confident and self-assured than it had been for days.

"Get the dagger from Brick," said Father Dionne.

Karl could feel his knees getting weak again. Brick was over six feet tall and weighed more than two-hundred and twenty pounds. Karl was five-foot-ten and weighed one-sixty with a pocket full of rocks. How on earth was he supposed to wrestle a dagger out of the hand of a big, muscular demon-possessed killer?

Father Dionne must have noticed Karl's unease. He got up from his chair, stepped over to the bed and placed a hand on Karl's shoulder. "There's a reason why you're the last," he said. "You're a man of God, a Jesuit. You have a power the others didn't. The demon can't manipulate you, can't bend you to its will. And you're also young, more than a match for the demon's designate."

Faith, thought Karl. It was the only strength he had, and although it hadn't been very strong of late, he was more than willing to test it now. For whatever reason, God had chosen him to be his soldier in the battle against the demon. And if it was God's will, then he would not let Him down.

Father Dionne went over to his dresser and picked something up off the top of it. "Here," he said, handing a large brass crucifix to Karl.

"What's this for?" Karl asked as he took it from Father Dionne.

"It might come in handy against the demon and his designate."

It was a heavy piece, probably weighed close to five pounds. He hefted the crucifix in his hand a moment, then held it out in front of him like a shield. "What am I supposed to do with this, show it to the demon and send him running away in terror?"

"You could try that, and if it doesn't work maybe you can hit him over the head with it."

Karl smiled and slipped the crucifix into his jacket pocket. "And after I take the dagger from Brick, what then?"

"One thing at a time," said the priest.

2

Coach Chambers was taking a break from marking quiz answers by reading through the latest issue of *The Hockey News.* From the sounds of it, the coach of the Pittsburgh Penguins was on thin ice with the team's ownership, and there were rumblings in San Jose about the Sharks being unable to keep up with last year's pathetic points pace. If he was reading things right, there would be at least two big league coaching positions open by mid-season. A strong start by the Cardinals might be just the thing he needed to make his life's dream of coaching in the National Hockey League a reality.

As he turned the page of the tabloid, he noticed the movement of a familiar shadow in the hallway to his left.

He got up to investigate.

"Hey, who's there?" he called, seeing a figure in the darkened hallway heading toward the Cardinals' dressing room.

Brick turned and stood in the doorway to the room, waiting for the coach to make his way over from the office.

"Where have you been?" asked the coach. "The cops are looking for you all over the place. What did you do?"

Brick shrugged. "I don't know, coach."

"You know, there's some people saying you're involved with the killings."

Brick sneered as he let out a lungful of air. "No way. I just got back onto campus."

"So why'd you come here?"

"My dorm room's crawling with cops. I thought I could spend the night on the cot in the trainer's room...you know, just til this thing blows over...til they find the killer and I'm cleared."

Coach Chambers considered it, struggling with the idea of hiding someone from the police. If he obstructed their investigation, he could get into a lot of hot water, maybe even ruin his chances for an NHL job.

"You know," said Brick. "If they take me in, I might end up missing Wednesday's game in Windsor."

"Right," Coach Chambers nodded slowly. Without Brick, the Cardinals wouldn't have a chance against the Lancers. "Okay, you can stay here tonight, but if the police know you played in Windsor, they'll be waiting for you when we get back."

"That'll be okay, I'm sure all this will all be over by then."

"Well, let's hope so, for everybody's sake."

"Night coach."

"G'night."

Just then the phone rang in Coach Chambers office. He hurried over to answer it.

"Chambers," he said.

He listened carefully to the man on the other end of the line.

"No, haven't seen him, but I'll let you know when I do."

He hung up the phone and returned to the pages of *The Hockey News* thinking San Jose was so much more warmer than Pittsburgh at this time of year.

3

Karl got up off the edge of the bed.

"Where are you going?" asked Father Dionne.

"To find Brick, of course."

Father Dionne held Karl back and shook his head. "No, no, two deaths on this campus are quite enough for one day. Besides, I suspect you needn't bother looking for him…Brick will be the one searching for you."

"Then he'll be coming here."

"I doubt that. For one thing, the police are finally looking for him in earnest, and even those who don't suspect him, will take notice of his appearance on campus, being the last surviving student from the mission study. No, I'm sure he's lying low somewhere on campus and will seek you out when the demon decides the time is right. And besides, the rectory is a holy edifice, a professed house which he can not enter, you'll be safe here for as long as you like."

"So I just sit here, doing nothing."

"No, stay here, but pray and meditate. Gather your strength and your wits, because you're going to need them when the time comes."

Karl let out a sigh, realizing that Father Dionne was right. He was exhausted by the events of the past few days and if he were going to have a chance against a dagger-wielding star hockey player, he'd need some rest. He could also use the extra time to pray, affirm his beliefs and restore some of his lost faith in God.

Maybe this way, he'd have a chance.

Karl sat back down on the edge of Father Dionne's bed and

stretched out on top of the covers. He closed his eyes for a moment, and quickly fell into a deep, but fitful sleep.

4

Karl awoke hours later to the sounds of Father Dionne asleep in his reading chair, his snores seemed loud enough to ripple the surface of the water in a glass on the night table.

He adjusted himself on the bed, tried to fall back asleep, but Father Dionne's incessant rumbling made it impossible for him to do anything but stare at the ceiling and think about all the other things he could be doing with his time.

Like searching for Brick.

Like standing in an open field and bringing on the confrontation once and for all.

Like going to the church and asking God to give him the strength he would need to battle the demon...

Karl got up from the bed, careful not to make a sound. One of the bedsprings *twanged*, momentarily throwing off Father Dionne's rhythm, but after a few snorts he was soon back sawing wood like a champion lumberjack.

Glancing out the window, Karl saw that it was raining outside. He grabbed Father Dionne's raincoat, put it over top of his jacket, and left the room. He stepped quietly down the hall, down the stairs past reception and out the front doors of the rectory.

The night was cold.

Judging by the moisture on the ground, the light mist had been falling for a few hours. Karl avoided walking over the strip of wet grass between the rectory and the church, and stayed to the lighted walkway that took a more circuitous, but safer, route between the two buildings.

Several times along the way, Karl felt a presence behind him, in front of him, and all around him, but never saw anything in the darkness. At one point he stopped on the walkway under a light, letting the mist swirl around himself like a shroud as he searched the shadows for his adversary.

But there was nothing there.

Nothing he could see, anyway.

Of course, this wouldn't be the way he would finally meet Brick. He was *looking* for Brick, and there was no way the demon would allow Karl any advantage. He'd probably come across Brick quite by surprise, or even by accident, at the moment he least expected it.

And how could he possibly know when that would be?

Of course, he couldn't.

He had to be wary, and aware, every moment of the day.

And he had to be ready.

Always.

Karl resumed walking, allowing his shoes to click out a sharp staccato rhythm against the walkway.

Across the campus in the distance, a police car slowly cruised along Dominicus Circle, the beam of the car's alley light shining off the top of the car's roof into the shadows between buildings.

A useless search, although the sight of the police patrolling the campus probably gave more than a few of the students and faculty a sense of security. Karl wondered how many at the college had turned to God for protection at this dark, dark hour?

He headed to the church and tried the front door. It was locked. Karl took a key from his pocket, slid it into the lock and gave it a turn. Then he pulled and the heavy wooden door swung slowly open on its heavy black hinges.

Once inside, Karl switched on a few lights and took off Father Dionne's raincoat to make himself comfortable. Then he took a deep, deep breath and smelled the rich aroma of wood oil, the pungent sting of burnt incense lingering in the air, and the dusty taint of recently snuffed candles. They were all familiar scents and they gave Karl comfort.

Karl remained at the rear of the church, standing in the middle of the aisle and looking at his surroundings.

Just looking.

Ste-Claire Church reminded Karl a lot of St. Philip Neri Church where he'd spent every Sunday morning growing up in Downsview, a suburb in the northern part of Toronto. The pews here were made of wood and shined as if they'd just been polished. There was stained glass on the walls, only here the stained glass was actually colored glass joined by leading, while at St. Philip Neri the glass was merely painted to give the effect of being stained. There was a pipe organ in the church that put the electric organ in the church of his youth to shame. Still, the altars of the two churches were very similar. They were raised up from the floor by a series of steps and behind them there were three chairs. In his youth, the big center chair was for the priest and the ones on either side of him were for his altar boys. Here at Ste-Claire, those chairs were taken up by a second priest or brother who was assisting with the mass.

But while Karl had sat in the chairs as an altar boy in his youth, that had never been the thing that had made him want to become a priest. No, his father had done that to him...showed him the way.

It was a Saturday and Karl had wanted to do nothing but sit in front of the television and watch cartoons. All three of the American networks in Buffalo ran cartoons from seven in the morning until noon, and then there was a half-hour of The Three Stooges that made the morning complete. Outside a storm was really starting to kick up. There were four inches of snow on the ground and another six predicted by the end of the day.

And right in the middle of the animated *Star Trek* his father had told him to put on his coat because they were going out. Karl had known better than to complain or question his father, but he'd still stomped around as noisily as he could just to let his father know where he stood on the matter.

They pulled out of the driveway and drove up the street at just a few miles per hour. Wherever they were going, thought Karl, it was going to take all day before they came home again.

He was right.

At eleven Karl's father pulled up to a loading dock of a food distributor, Lanzarotta Wholesale Grocers. Four men were waiting there for them, eager to load up the back of the Desbiens family car so they could go home for the day. The men started stuffing food boxes into the car. Each box had canned goods, pastas, dried fruit, rice and just about everything else that didn't need to be fresh or refrigerated. They put eighteen boxes into the car and closed it up with a smile.

And then Karl and his father went driving.

Karl had always known his father had done work for the church, but he never knew what exactly the man did.

That day he found out.

There was a list of eighteen addresses on the dashboard of the car. With the snow continuously falling and the roads getting worse and worse to drive on, Karl and his father went to each address on the list to deliver a box of food. At each home, Karl's father introduced himself, saying he was from the St. Vincent de Paul Society, then handed the person at the door a box of food.

And that was it.

It had made Karl feel good to help someone in need, a feeling that was way better than watching any cartoons. But while his father must have been feeling the same thing, he didn't wait around to have people say thank you, didn't gloat or make people feel bad about receiving charity, he didn't even have an air of superiority about him as he handed over the food. He just gave them what he had, then headed for the next home.

And when the day was done, he bought a coffee for himself and a chocolate milk and a donut for Karl at the Country Style across the street from the church. Later, when they got home, Karl's mother had dinner on the table waiting for them, and they ate. But even then Karl's father didn't gloat on his good deed, and was in fact more interested in the hockey game on television that night than talking about his day.

Karl had never been prouder of his father than he'd been on that day. He'd enjoyed the feeling that helping people had brought him and he wanted to experience the feeling again.

And that's when he first thought about possibly becoming a priest. And when he learned that one of the precepts of the Society of Jesus is to serve God wherever there was a need, he knew that the Order was the right one for him.

And here he was on the campus of Ste-Claire College and God was never in greater need of his services than right now.

Karl was ready to serve.

To do whatever it took to vanquish the demon…to restore order…to join his fellow Martyrs in defense of…

Of what?

The answer made Karl's heart skip a beat.

All of Christianity, perhaps even the entire world.

Karl was up to the challenge.

He was ready to face anything the demon could throw at him now…he was even ready to fight back.

He got up from the pew and went to the rear doors of the church. He wasn't sure why, but he felt as if there was something there waiting for him.

He opened the door…

And saw Brick standing directly under a light, about fifty yards from the church door. It was raining harder now, but the water didn't seem to bother him. Brick was standing there in a pair of jeans and a Cardinals T-shirt, which left his arms bare and did nothing to hide the foot long dagger he was holding in his right hand.

"C'mon," shouted Karl, standing in the doorway. "I'm right here waiting for you."

Brick didn't move.

Karl remained where he was, hoping that Brick would come to him, closer to the church and what had to be a source of power for Karl. He reached inside his jacket pocket and took out the crucifix, just so he'd have it in his hand. "I know you want to kill me, so let's get it over with."

Brick took a tentative step forward, then stopped.

Since confronting him didn't seem to be working, Karl decided on another tact. "C'mon Brick," he said. "I'm not going to hurt you...Nobody gets hurt in the house of God."

No response.

"I know you're not a killer. You're a good man, with a bright future. Let's end it here, and start putting God's house back in order. Come and pray with me, Brick. We'll ask God for forgiveness together, and try and put this all behind us."

Another tentative step, but then Brick stopped, turned and began walking away.

Karl watched him step out from under the light and vanish into the darkness. Karl stepped out of the church and was pelted by the rain that was coming down harder now – almost as hard as it had on the day he drove back from the mission site.

He needed Father Dionne's raincoat if he was going to go chasing Brick across the campus.

Karl went back into the church, put on the coat and headed back outside.

When he opened the door, Karl found Father Dionne standing beneath the light now, his face partially obscured by shadows cast by the black umbrella he was holding over his head.

Karl ran over to where Father Dionne was standing.

"He was here," said Karl.

"I know," Father Dionne said. "I was watching from the steps of the rectory."

"Where did he go?"

Father Dionne pointed with his cane toward the Administration Building. "That way, I believe."

Karl ran toward the Admin Building, but there was no sign of Brick, no sign of anyone.

An O.P.P. cruiser pulled up then, and the passenger side window rolled down. "Evening," said the officer.

"Good evening," said Karl.

"What are you doing out at this time of night?"

Karl ignored the question. "Did you see anyone running this way?"

The officer shook his head, then said. "I asked you my question first."

"Oh, just out for a walk. Father Dionne and I couldn't sleep, so we thought we'd get some fresh air."

"It's raining."

"So it is."

The officer looked at Karl closely. "I've seen you before. You're a Jesuit, aren't you? Father Desbiens, right?"

"Not exactly, I'm not a priest, yet."

The officer nodded. "Okay, well, priest or not, I don't think it's a good idea for you to be out walking the campus after dark."

"I suppose you're right, officer."

The officer nodded, satisfied he'd made his point. "Would you like a lift?"

Karl looked over to his right. Father Dionne was still there waiting for him. "No thanks. We'll walk, since we're already wet."

"Suit yourself."

Karl returned to Father Dionne's side. "The policeman didn't see Brick…hasn't seen anyone all night."

"I'm not surprised."

"Damn," said Karl. "I thought for a moment there I might have been able to reason with him."

Father Dionne shook his head. "No, all he was thinking about was how he might kill you without getting any closer to the church."

"Why did he leave?"

"The time wasn't right, and he probably knew I was behind him. It was enough to chase him away."

"We should go after him?"

"We could try, but it would be like finding a shadow in the darkness. The demon will have people hiding him, lying for him..." He nodded toward the police cruiser, which was still parked a few yards away. "Besides, I don't think the officer there will let us do anything but go back to bed."

Karl and Father Dionne started walking back to the rectory.

"We can't just wait for him," said Karl.

"Oh, but we can. After all, he isn't going to kill anyone else besides you."

"Right." Karl swallowed, and found that his throat was dry, despite the rain.

"Come," said Father Dionne, picking up the pace. "When we get back to the rectory, I'll make you a nice espresso coffee."

"Sounds good."

"It will be."

The two men broke into a slight run.

The police cruiser inched along Dominicus Circle, shadowing them all the way.

CHAPTER TWENTY-SEVEN

1

Karl and Father Dionne were having breakfast in the rectory dining room – a meal of bacon, eggs, and toast prepared by one of the Jesuit brothers on campus – when Constable Tremblay came calling.

"Constable," said Father Dionne, getting up from his chair and shaking hands with the policeman. "Won't you join us?"

"I've already eaten this morning, thanks."

"Then a coffee, perhaps."

"Yeah, sure."

Father Dionne looked over at the brother, but he was already preparing a cup for the constable.

"What brings you here? Not more bad news I hope."

The brother slipped the steaming cup of coffee in front of the constable. "No, not really...No one was killed or went missing overnight so I guess considering what's happened the last few days, that's good news."

Karl nodded. Yes, he thought. At least the killing has stopped. For now.

"But you didn't come here to tell us there was no news."

The constable spooned two sugars into his coffee, and then a single container of cream. "No, I came to check on Karl, here."

"Me?" said Karl. "Am I a suspect again?"

"No, you're likely the next victim and I just wanted to come by and make sure you were alive and well."

Karl patted his chest with both hands. "Very much so."

"But you were out walking late last night." He turned to Father Dionne. "And you were with him."

"Surely that's not a crime," said Father Dionne.

"No, but it is curious. I'd like to know what you two were doing out so late."

"I couldn't sleep," said Karl, before Father Dionne could say a word. "I went for a walk – I know it was stupid of me – and I ended up at the church, praying. When Father Dionne noticed I was missing, he came to get me."

The constable nodded. "And of all the places on campus to look, how did you know he'd be in the church?"

It was a good question, and for the first time Karl imagined that without the interference of the demon, the constable – perhaps even the entire Abbotville Police Department – was capable of doing a competent job of policing and investigating. This morning, it was obvious that the demon wasn't clouding his thought processes.

Luckily, Father Dionne was the constable's equal on this morning. "I awoke in time to see Karl enter the church. Considering the deaths and everything else that's been going on, I knew he'd be praying inside for some time." The elderly priest's face changed its visage for a moment with just a hint of a smile. "We are men of God, you know. Prayer to us is like coffee and donuts to policemen. It's part of our lives and you see, God doesn't punch a clock, so he's there any time we need him to listen to our prayers. More coffee?"

"No thank you," the constable said quickly, and then seemed to be at a loss for something to say. Judging by his face and his body language, he was out of his element talking about prayer and spiritual matters. At last he let out a sigh and said, "Well if you're going to be praying, I ask that you do two things for now."

"What's that?" asked Father Dionne.

"One, if you have to pray in the middle of the night, do it in your room. I don't know all that much about God and religion, but I can't imagine it makes much difference to God if you pray to Him in church or alone in your room…"

Karl was impressed. The constable was absolutely right.

"…but it does matter to me. I don't need anybody daring the killer to kill them."

"Point taken."

"And if you are going to be praying anyway, put in a good word for me, you know, for catching the killer before anyone else dies."

"Consider it done," said Father Dionne.

"Speaking of catching the killer," said Karl. "Any word on Brick?"

"No." The constable looked disappointed. "Coach Chambers said he hasn't seen him, so if he is back on the campus, he's laying pretty low."

Father Dionne nodded.

"But we'll be looking for him today, searching the campus. The Cardinals have a practice this afternoon, so we'll be there waiting for him." The constable drained his coffee.

"Good luck," said Karl.

"Yeah, thanks."

2

By the time Father Dionne got to his office, there was an army of people outside waiting for him. Martine came running out to meet him looking absolutely exhausted, as if she'd spent the best part of her morning beating back the angry mob before giving up the fight and hoisting a white flag in surrender.

"I couldn't redirect them or put them off anymore," she said, apologetically. "There were just too many of them."

Father Dionne took her hand in his and gave it a comforting pat. "That's all right, Martine. Quite frankly, I'm impressed that you held out as long as you did."

Martine smiled in thanks. "I think you're going to have to do a scrum here on the steps of the rectory, Father," she said.

"A scrum?" said Father Dionne, unsure of the term.

"Like they do in the House of Commons and Queen's Park."

Father Dionne looked over at the closely packed group of reporters and added, "Oh, all right. If I must."

"I think you'll have to do another one in the main lecture hall this afternoon as well."

"But what if there's nothing new to report."

Martine shook her head. "It won't matter. Judging by the calls I've been getting this morning there will probably be a dozen or more news organizations arriving this afternoon who will be starting from scratch."

"New ones? Like who?"

"There are crews on the way from A&E's *Investigative Reports*, CNN, *Rivera Live*, even two freelance writers from

Toronto who say they've got book deals."

"Oh God," said Father Dionne, looking rather weak.

Martine took his arm and led him toward the rectory steps. As they neared, the crowd opened up to let them pass. Father Dionne took four steps and then turned around.

The scrum suddenly came alive. Cameras began to click and whir, microphones and cassette recorders appeared out of nowhere and the roar of voices asking questions was almost deafening.

Father Dionne put up his hand to silence the crowd and he was as surprised as Martine obviously was when the ploy worked and the crowd fell silent.

"I think it's only appropriate that before I answer any of your questions, we begin with a short prayer for those who have died, their family and friends, and ask that no more lives be taken before the evil monster who is to blame for all this grief and sorrow is caught and punished by either man or God."

The crowd was silent for a moment, probably wondering what he had meant by his last few words, and then erupted in a shouting match as each reporter tried to be the first to ask a question.

"What's the significance of the upside down crosses?"

"How many more students were on the mission study?"

"Will there be funeral services on campus for the other students?"

But it was the strong voice of a black woman at the back of the crowd which outlasted and overpowered the rest of the throng, "...how is it possible that such evil can occur in such a sacred place as a Jesuit college?"

The rest of the reporters said nothing, waiting for Father Dionne's answer.

"Evil is all around us, young lady, and Ste-Claire College is no more immune to it than any other place in this world. To the layman it might seem that God has abandoned us, but I assure you that God is very, very interested in what's happening here at Ste-Claire College, and I don't think I'd be wrong in saying that it's very likely that we currently have His absolute and undivided attention."

There were a few moments of silence before the rest of the reporters erupted in a roar of questions.

3

The day dragged on.

There were dozens of police moving about the campus with great urgency, all seemingly intent on getting things done, but for all their effort they were no closer to catching the killer than they'd been the week before.

And they'd never get any closer, either.

The murders might end, but the killer – the real killer, Astaroth – would never be caught. Realizing this had come as a sort of blessing to Karl because he'd wondered for days about how one might go about destroying a demon. After all, Karl was merely a mortal man while the demon Astaroth – depending on which account you believed – was either the former prince of the order of thrones, an ancient god of Syria, a beautiful angel riding a dragon and carrying a viper in his right hand, or one of the seven princes of hell.

Karl Desbiens, Regent in the Society of Jesus versus Astaroth, Prince of Hell.

Not much of a contest there. In fact, it sounded downright one-sided, and yet, the Jesuits before him had been able to best the demon and send him away, so there was no real reason he couldn't achieve the same results.

He had to believe in himself.

He needed to have faith.

And he had to put his trust in God.

They would fight the demon together and good would surely triumph over evil. How could it not?

But before anything could happen in terms of the demon, Karl first had to find Brick and get the dagger from him. At the moment it seemed as if that was never going to happen. Brick had apparently disappeared from the face of the planet and he was only going to return when it suited him, or more correctly, suited the demon…and who could tell when that might be?

So in the meantime, they would all try and live their lives as best they could. For Karl that meant teaching class again – something he was actually looking forward to – and trying to make a difference in young people's lives.

Karl had no classes on Monday, but he did have a tutorial on Tuesday morning. Although few students had ventured out to attend classes the last few days, Father Dionne had refrained from officially canceling classes. Karl didn't really expect any of his students to show up tomorrow, but he still needed to be prepared, just in case some of them did. With that in mind, he decided to head over to the college's Centre for Theological Studies to make sure the room he'd be using in the morning had an overhead projector and a screen. It was a silly notion, especially so late in the day, but it gave Karl somewhere to go and something to do, a welcome diversion from constant thoughts of saving the world from encroaching evil.

He crossed Dominicus Circle and headed north between the science building and a small building housing six classrooms that was used for tutorials and exams, then turned left and passed the main lecture hall on his right. He crossed Dominicus Circle once more and entered the Centre for Theological Studies by the door at the south end of the building.

His class was held in Room 113. He taught a freshman theology class there and the room was adorned with a half-dozen posters, both religious and literary in nature. Karl's favorite poster was one that looked down onto a cityscape which provided the backdrop for a dying Jesus on the cross. The view of Jesus was from above, his haggard face looking up, eyes half-closed and indicative of terrible pain. Above this image were seven simple words: "Dare to be a priest like me." Karl had always felt the poster was a powerful message and he'd heard that when it was part of a campaign to recruit new priests – complete with billboards and subway posters – it convinced eight young men to enter the priesthood. Elsewhere around the room were stacks of books, including the Bible, the Koran, the Veda and Upanishads, the Torah and Talmud, and a few books by Billy Graham.

There was always a projection screen hanging just above the blackboard at the head of the class and there was usually an overhead projector in the corner of the room. But it had been a while since Karl had been in the room and the projector could have been moved, taken, or just plain broken in the interim. If he needed to, he could easily pick up a new one from the school's AV department today, or at least request one for tomorrow morning. But if he left it for tomorrow morning, none of it would be done in time.

Before he entered he could see that the screen was hanging

down at the front of the room.

No problem there.

But what about the projector?

He stuck his head into the room and took a quick look in the corner. Although it was dark, he could see the projector in its place...but there was something else.

The first thing Karl felt was the collar of his jacket being torn by something big, heavy and sharp. Next he felt a fluid warmth beginning to flow down onto his shoulder and chest.

He looked to his left.

There was a man, standing in the shadows, holding a knife.

"Brick?" Karl said.

The young man took a step into the light and lunged at Karl with the dagger thrust out before him.

Karl dodged right and the blade just caught the edge of his midsection, slicing through his jacket and cutting flesh on his left side, just above the waist.

Karl felt a fire burning on his skin where it had been touched by the dagger. The pain was intense, and for a moment he thought he was going to black out, but the ache eventually faded and he was able to get out a few words through his tightly clenched teeth. "Brick," he said. "Don't do this."

"Fuck you, asshole!" Brick answered.

But it wasn't really Brick doing the talking. Karl knew that. Sure, it was Brick's body, but his voice was a lot deeper, more resonant than usual. And the words...well, Brick was known to talk trash, especially out on the ice, but never with such crude language.

Obviously Astaroth was pulling the strings.

"Show yourself," said Karl. "Let the boy go and we'll talk."

But instead of answering, Brick rushed forward, his huge body looking like a truck barreling down on him. He was holding the dagger close to his chest and was obviously intent on knocking Karl over with his bulk. After that, Karl would be easy to kill, and Astaroth could do it at his leisure.

As he tried to move out of the way, Karl reached into his jacket pocket and took out the crucifix he'd been carrying and raised it in the air. The big brass crucifix didn't stop Brick dead in his tracks, but it did cause him to hesitate a moment, allowing Karl just enough time to take a step to one side. Brick still crashed into him, but the impact didn't knock him backwards. Instead, Karl went flying sideways, bouncing off a desk before hitting a chair and tumbling heels over head.

When Karl opened his eyes, he was lying flat on his back with one foot tangled up in the chair he'd fallen over. There was a pain in his back like a spike had been hammered into his spine.

Brick was standing over him, smiling demonically.

Karl wondered if the demon was enjoying this. The other murders had been necessary to achieve an end, and while Karl's own death was as necessary as the others had been, he was also a man of God and that had to provide the demon with a bit of a thrill. At the same time, Karl's link to God was probably the thing that had prevented him from being killed by the first blow of the dagger. Either way, God was on his side and His presence was giving Karl at least a chance to fight back.

But how?

He could strike Brick in the leg with the crucifix, but that would probably just anger him. He needed something else, and soon.

Karl's right hand flailed around for something to grab hold of. There was nothing to hang onto, but his wild movements knocked over a stack of Bibles, sending several of them skidding across the floor.

"I think you will die slowly," said Brick, his voice deep and rich, as if his throat and vocal chords were covered in a thick, dark oil.

Karl took one of the Bibles in his hand, and for a split second he thought about keeping it there, fighting the demon with a crucifix in one hand and a Bible in the other. A nice image for a portrait, but it wasn't going to scare off Astaroth, or his designate, Brick, who was presently hunched over Karl with the dagger raised to strike a blow at Karl's shoulder, just left of the socket. It wouldn't be a fatal blow, but it would hurt like hell. And there were going to be a lot of wounds like that, making him suffer in agony until he bled to death or mercifully fell unconscious from the pain.

Karl couldn't let that happen.

If he was going to die, he was going to die fighting.

So instead of using the Bible as a source of inner-strength, Karl threw it at Brick's head.

A corner of the book struck Brick in the left eye, forcing him to pull back and grasp at his face with his hands.

Karl threw another Bible at Brick's head. It bounced harmlessly off his skull, but managed to push him off balance.

Karl rose up off the floor to a sitting position and swung the crucifix at Brick's crotch. There was a soft thudding sound as the heavy brass cross smashed into what appeared to be an erection. Karl took another swing and this time caught one of Brick's testicles.

"Owf," Brick cried, the wind rushing out of him in a gush.

The big man doubled over in pain, grabbing at his crotch with one hand while managing to keep the dagger in front of him with the other.

Karl took the opportunity to get to his feet.

He'd hurt Brick, but with Astaroth behind him, it wouldn't be long before Brick was recovered and intent on killing Karl as quickly as he could.

Karl reached out with his left hand and grabbed the sharp end of the dagger.

An energy suddenly began to course through his body, numbing his arm and giving the rest of him a tingling sensation unlike anything he'd ever experienced in his life.

It was power.

It was evil.

And if felt good.

Karl raised his right hand and brought the crucifix down hard onto Brick's head.

There was a hard crunch of bone, immediately followed by the wet slurp of soft tissue as the end of the crucifix's cross piece broke through Brick's skull and put a hole in his brain.

Brick was staggered by the blow.

He released the dagger...

And Karl held it in his hand.

Dark power flowed through the weapon, charging him with thoughts of pain and suffering, murder and death.

He wanted to kill Brick.

Bash his head in.

Karl knew it was wrong, but the power of the dagger was too strong. He tried to cast it aside, but it wouldn't let him.

It wanted him to finish the job.

Kill Brick.

Karl looked up at the young man. He was holding his head with both hands, the left hand over the spot where Karl had hit him. Blood flowed freely through his fingers and it looked as if his brain was beginning to swell, pushing its way through the newly created hole in his skull.

But he was not dead.

He would not die.

Karl had to kill him.

Kill him with the dagger.

It was wrong.

But it was what the demon wished.

He tried to resist the urge to stave in Brick's skull with the dagger, but the urge was just too strong to fight. He raised his right hand, the one with the crucifix clenched tightly in his fist, and brought it down onto the back of Brick's head.

Again there was the satisfying crunch of shattering bone.

But Brick would still not die.

He was in utter agony.

The blood was now spurting from his head in bright red streams that his beefy fingers could not contain.

Now even the small part of Karl, the part not affected by the wishes of the demon, wanted Brick dead. He was suffering far too much, was in too much pain.

How could he possibly still be alive? Karl wondered.

He hit brick again with the crucifix. This time the cross-pieces became buried inside his skull all the way to their junction. Karl had to yank and pull on the crucifix to work it free, braking bone and spreading brain matter with each twist and turn of the cross.

Brick screamed in pain.

"Why don't you die, dammit!" Karl screamed.

The dagger tingled in his hand.

He looked at the dagger a moment, all aglow and glinting with highlights, and without another thought he brought the dagger's handle down onto the base of Brick's caved-in skull.

And suddenly Brick fell, hitting the blood-drenched floor tiles with a splash.

He grunted once, his left leg twitched, and then he was still.

Dead.

Karl stood there, trying to catch his breath, waiting for the haze that was swirling through his head to fade.

The crucifix in his right hand was covered in blood, but the dagger in the left was clean, unstained...immaculate. Looking at the dagger, he wondered how it had got there.

But then he saw Brick's dead body lying on the floor in a pool of blood.

And knew.

He had won.

4

"Hello?" said Father Dionne.

"Brick is dead...I killed him."

"Is that you, Karl?"

"I had to...had to kill him."

"It was inevitable. Either you killed him, or he would have killed you."

"He tried, but..." said Karl, his breath ragged. "I have the dagger."

"Good, bring it with you and meet me in the church."

"What about the body? I can lock the door, but someone will be–"

"Never mind that now, we've got more important things to worry about than a dead body."

"But–"

Father Dionne cut him off. "There are things we must do, and quickly."

There was no response, only the sound of short, choppy breaths.

"Meet me in the church."

"Yes, Father," said Karl.

Father Dionne hung up and headed out.

CHAPTER TWENTY-EIGHT

1

There was still a hint of light left to the day when Karl exited the Centre for Theological Studies and headed over to the church to meet Father Dionne. Although he left the building by the south doors, he decided not to walk along Dominicus Circle, but to head north and take the long way around past The Head pub and Fine Arts Building, around the main Administration Building and then down past the rectory to the church.

If he was lucky, he'd be able to make the trip unobserved.

That was important. Karl had so much blood on his hands and clothing that anyone seeing him on the Circle would immediately call the police, putting an end to whatever plan Father Dionne had planned for ending this whole ordeal.

As Karl walked along the path between The Head and the Fine Arts Building, he had a feeling that someone was with him. It was a presence, like a shadow viewed out of the corner of the eye, or the faint image on a storefront windowpane.

He stopped on the path and turned around abruptly.

Nothing.

No one there.

Yet the feeling was still there, prickling the flesh of his arms and making his hair stand on end.

"Who's there?" he said.

Nothing.

No answer.

"I know someone's there," he said, wondering if it might be the demon's presence he felt, and then realizing it could be no other. "Why are you hiding?"

Silence.

Karl knew he should run, but he refused to show the demon any weakness. He could feel God's strength running through him and was emboldened by it. "What are you afraid of? I'm just a man...A man of God."

He turned around in place, examining the darkness between the buildings. Drops of rain began to fall.

"I have what you want," he said, holding up the dagger. "Take it and kill me if you dare."

More silence.

If the demon was out there, he obviously wasn't willing to show himself. Why not? Karl wondered. Why doesn't he just confront me and take the knife?

But the feeling of being watched was gone. The shadows no longer held any secrets.

Karl was alone in the rain.

He turned back around and continued on his way to the church.

2

Egidio DeAngelis pushed the broom along the hallway, glad to be working indoors for a change. Just a couple of days ago he'd been sweeping up in the courtyard between the church and the arena and discovered the body of a dead student hanging upside down from one of the flagpoles. The sight of it had left him shaken, and he'd almost taken a few days off because of it, but he'd never taken a day off that wasn't part of his vacation in the twenty years he'd worked at the college and he wasn't about to start now.

Egidio believed that work was the thing that defined a man and taking a day off without pay was unthinkable. He had a family to think about, two daughters who had school to be paid for. The fear he felt working at the college the last couple of weeks would pass. Things would eventually get back to the way they had been before, and soon he'd feel good about coming to work each day.

He had faith in God that this would happen.

And God had yet to let him down.

Just then Egidio's broom seemed to get snagged on the right side in front of one of the classroom doors. After gliding along with ease, the broom suddenly got sluggish, as if it had come upon something sticky on the floor.

Spilled coffee most likely, thought Egidio. Or pop, or some sort of candy. He looked up to make note of the room number, 113, just in case this problem started happening here on a regular basis.

Then he reached behind his back and took the small spray bottle filled with water that he used on such trouble spots, a few spritz from the bottle and a wipe from a paper towel and Egidio would be on his way, finishing his circuit of the first floor and heading to the second.

But when he pulled back the broom to spray some water on the floor, the broom left a bright red smear on the floor tiles.

"No," Egidio said, as his heart fell into the pit of his stomach. "Oh, Dio!"

Another dead body. Another young student, brutally murdered, here among the Jesuits.

Egidio shook his head in disbelief.

Ste-Claire College was no longer a House of God.

It had become the devil's domain.

Egidio turned and ran, wanting to get as far away from the school as he could.

3

Father Dionne was waiting for Karl at the main entrance to the church, a tiny white-topped figured dwarfed by the giant wooden doors that led inside.

He stood just inside the doorway, allowing a sliver of light to glow out from behind him and cast a long, faint shadow on the rain-soaked front steps.

Karl ran the last few yards, as much eager to speak to Father Dionne as to get out of the now pouring rain.

"Did anyone see you?" asked Father Dionne as he let Karl inside and locked the door behind him. The lock sounded loud and solid as it fell into place.

Karl shook his head, and for a moment he wondered if Father Dionne was locking the door to keep people out, or keep him inside.

"You have the dagger?"

Karl raised his bloody left hand. The dagger gleamed.

"Good," said Father Dionne, turning and heading for the altar.

"It's over, right?" Karl asked. "We have the dagger now. It's in our possession, just like the walking stick...so it's over. We've won...I bested the demon..."

Father Dionne said nothing.

Karl could feel himself starting to ramble with his words. He'd been so physically and emotionally charged during his confrontation with Brick that now he seemed drained and weak, just glad it was over and not really caring all that much about what happened next. "Of course, I'll have to turn myself into the police now for killing Brick, but at least there will be no more murders."

"No!" Father Dionne said with a sharp turn to face Karl.

Karl stopped in his tracks.

"It's not over...The killings are not over."

"What do you mean?"

"There must be one more."

"But I'm the only one left that was on that trip."

Father Dionne nodded.

"You're not asking me to kill myself, are you?"

Father Dionne shook his head. "No. But I am going to ask you to kill me."

4

Constable Tremblay was one of the first to arrive at Room 113 of the Centre for Theological Studies.

The room was a shambles, with blood on the floor and spatters against one of the walls, and books strewn across the entire room as if several piles had been knocked over.

Even though half the victim's head had been caved in by a blunt object, Constable Tremblay was still able to recognize Brick from what remained.

He'd been a great hockey player with a really bright future ahead of him. And all that was gone now...thanks to the killer.

But as the constable looked closely at the corpse, he noticed that there were no trademark upside down crosses on the body as there had been with all of the previous victims. It was possible that this murder wasn't connected to the rest, but there were too many good reasons not to treat it as a totally separate homicide.

First and foremost was the fact that Brick had been on the field trip to the mission, just as the others had. When he'd been the last remaining student from the trip, he'd been a good candidate for the killer. He was strong enough to do the killings, he knew all of the other students and knew his way around campus. Besides hard evidence, the only thing lacking for Brick was a motive. Why would he want to kill his fellow classmates?

Why would anybody?

That part of it just didn't make sense, and was one of the reasons they were having so much trouble solving the case.

The murders were being committed for no apparent reason.

That meant anyone on campus could be the killer – another student, faculty, staff, even the priests and brothers who ran the school.

Constable Tremblay stepped back from the corpse and gestured to one of the other constables to toss something over the body.

As he stepped away from the body, all he could think was why?

From what he'd read about the Society of Jesus, Constable Tremblay knew they were also known as the Pope's army, as soldiers for the Catholic Church who followed orders without question and without hesitation, even if it meant killing someone for the good of the faith.

But why kill these students?

Maybe the students saw something they weren't supposed to up there at the mission site and, not trusting the students to keep their mouths shut, the Jesuits had ordered them eradicated, just to be sure.

The thought of it turned the constable's stomach.

Surely the Jesuits couldn't be that cruel. They were men of God, for Christ's sake!

But as much as Constable Tremblay didn't want to believe such a wild notion, there was no way he could ignore it as a possibility. After all, how was it that Karl Desbiens, a regent in the order, was the only one left who'd been up to the mission site? Even the God damn archeologist from the Royal Ontario Museum had been killed recently, officially by a thief in a robbery gone bad, but Constable Tremblay had trouble believing that.

Karl Desbiens was close to becoming a fully ordained priest within the order. What if he'd been told by his superior, hell maybe even the Pope himself, that he had to kill these students in order to show his loyalty to the order, to show that he was worthy of being a Jesuit?

It was all crazy stuff, but it fit better than any rational reason he could think of.

Just then an O.P.P. officer came by and gave a little tug on Constable Tremblay's sleeve. "We got the class schedule for this room and guess who teaches here most often."

Constable Tremblay let out a sigh. "Karl Desbiens."

"That's right, and he's supposed to be teaching a class in here tomorrow."

"Well, let's not wait to see if he shows up," said Constable Tremblay. "Let's find him...Now!"

5

"What?" said Karl.

Father Dionne sighed. "You must kill *me*...with the dagger."

"No, I, I can't do that."

Father Dionne grabbed both Karl's arms at the wrist. "You must."

"But why?" Karl looked about the church, as if searching for reason. "What if...what if we destroy the dagger? We could have it melted down, or broken into pieces and then have the pieces sent to the ends of the earth, the ocean depths, maybe even into space...there are Jesuits who work in the space program, aren't there?"

Father Dionne simply shook his head. "No we can not. There is only one thing to do with the dagger. Only one thing we *can* do."

Karl was silent a long, long time. Finally, he said, as if defeated, "What is it?"

"In order to offset the evil inherent in the dagger, it must be surrounded by a shroud of good."

"Shroud of good? How?"

"According to Trudel's diary, the Ste-Claire martyrs ended the killings when he plunged the dagger into the chest of Daniel Sernine, and then buried Sernine's body with the dagger still inside it."

"Evil shrouded by good."

"Yes. They were men of God, their bodies and souls were devoted to the service of the Pope."

"But we didn't find any remains at the mission site."

"You didn't, but Brick did. You told me that you sent Brick back to do one last check of the site. With the help of the rain, Astaroth must have unearthed Sernine's remains, pushed them up from below...a place where his kind have some measure of control."

Karl was silent, considering the idea. It sounded all too plausible.

"After the body became visible in one of the pits, all Brick had to do was reach down and take the dagger."

Karl felt sick to his stomach. "So if I hadn't gone digging around, none of this would have happened."

Father Dionne put a sympathetic hand on Karl's shoulder. "It's possible, but if it wasn't you, then it would have been someone else...next year, a hundred years from now...what's time to a demon? It would have happened eventually, Karl." Father Dionne said the last half-dozen words slowly and clearly so that there could be no misunderstanding.

Karl was silent.

"At least we know what to do to make sure that it will never happen again."

"I have to...kill you?"

"Yes, and then bury me at the mission site in such a way that no one will ever go digging around there again."

"But I don't, I can't..." Karl was having trouble finding the words. "I love you Father, you've been like, well, like a father to me. I couldn't possibly kill you...you of all people."

"No, that's exactly why you must. The Ste-Claire martyrs died willingly at the hands of their fellow men of God. It was the *only* way to truly defeat the demon. I believe that to be true with all my heart. It had worked to best the demon for hundreds of years, and it would have worked for an eternity if not for us."

"But Father..."

"Karl, listen...I'm an old man, and to be honest, I never felt that I was a very good Jesuit. Ste-Claire College pretty well ran itself, and for the past few years I felt as if my life had passed without much meaning. But this...how could I not do *this*? It's what the Society of Jesus is all about, what being a Jesuit is all about. Do you realize I'll be following in the path of, not only the Ste-Claire Martyrs, but of Jesus himself? I will be giving my life for the good of all mankind." He shook his head. "It's something I don't have to think twice about."

Karl let out a sigh, knowing what he had to do, but still wishing there was some other way.

Father Dionne reached out and grabbed the dagger in Karl's hand, then raised it so that Karl was holding the tip directly over his heart.

"Don't deny me this, Karl," he said, removing his jacket and unbuttoning his shirt.

"Do I have to do it–" He glanced around the church. "–here?"

"There is no holier place for miles around."

Karl's hand was trembling.

Father Dionne reached out to steady it, then pulled it closer so that the dagger's point was pushing against his skin. "The car is parked outside the door. There are shovels and picks in the trunk."

Karl's entire body was beginning to shake.

"Do it!" Father Dionne ordered.

Karl hesitated.

"Do it now!"

With tears beginning to stream from his eyes, Karl pushed the dagger forward. The tip of the blade pierced Father Dionne's flesh, then sunk a couple of inches into his chest.

Father Dionne's mouth opened wide.

At first Karl took the gesture to be one of pain, but as the knife continued to slide deeper into his chest, into the muscles and then into his heart, it was obvious that Father Dionne was experiencing not pain, but rapture.

Karl felt his body go numb. He had no more strength left to push the dagger further. It was hung up on the bones of Father Dionne's ribcage. Karl wanted to pull back the dagger, felt a faint hope that what had happened could somehow be undone, but he resisted the temptation.

But he couldn't bring himself to push the dagger any further into the old man's chest.

For a moment the dagger's hilt just hung there, jutting out

from Father Dionne's chest like a handle, or someplace to hang a coat.

Then Father Dionne's eyes popped open. He looked at Karl with a hint of terror. "Finish it!" he said.

Karl nodded and pushed the dagger with all his strength.

At first the blade scraped harshly against Father Dionne's ribs, but then something strange happened....

Father Dionne's body seemed to open up around the dagger. The blade slid easily the rest of the way in, past the ribs and through the heart.

Karl kept pushing, letting go of the hilt and then pushing it from the end until it was swallowed up by Father Dionne's chest.

Gone.

Father Dionne stood for a moment, a smile on his face, and then fell over onto his side.

Dead.

PART THREE: SHRINE

The enemy snatched from a Mother her infants, that they might be thrown into the fire; other children beheld their Mothers beaten to death at their feet, or groaning in the flames…

– *The Jesuit Relations and Allied Documents*

CHAPTER TWENTY-NINE

1

When Constable Tremblay arrived at the rectory looking for Karl, Father Dionne's secretary had told him that he had gone for a walk several hours ago, and hadn't returned.

"Where's Father Dionne?"

She shrugged. "He left a while ago, and he was in an awful hurry."

"Do you know where he went?"

"He mentioned something about the church–"

Constable Tremblay turned to leave before the woman had time to finish speaking.

"Stay here," he told an O.P.P. officer standing idly on the steps. "In case one or the other of them come back."

The officer nodded.

Constable Tremblay hurried down the steps and ran across the rain-slicked lawn toward the church.

2

It had taken Karl a few extra minutes to get Father Dionne sitting up in the passenger seat of the car, but it had been the right thing to do. It would have been quicker just to throw Father Dionne into the trunk, or across the back seat, but it was more dignified this way – fitting for someone who had just given their life for the good of all mankind.

The sky had grown dark in the past half-hour and the rain was now streaming across the windshield.

Karl hoped it wasn't a bad omen.

3

The church was empty.

If there was somebody inside, they were hiding.

Constable Tremblay sent officers to cover all the exits, and then he and several others began a systematic search of the building, starting with the confessionals at the back of the church.

The constable drew his weapon as he moved past the shadows and dark corners surrounding the confessionals. As he did, he wondered if the killer had been by this way, confessing his sins knowing the priest hearing them could never reveal his identity.

Perhaps that was what had caused Karl and Father Dionne to remain so distant the past few days. While they hadn't been uncooperative, they hadn't exactly helped push the investigation forward. Karl had suddenly given up trying to convince him that Brick was the murderer, and Father Dionne had virtually disappeared from the campus. If the killer had confessed to Father Dionne, then perhaps they might have been trying to draw him out, confront him themselves, or administer their own brand of Jesuit justice, whatever that might be.

Constable Tremblay shook his head. Such a wistful notion. Of course the killer had *not* confessed, and Karl and the priest were *not* out somewhere trying to punish the murderer. If anything Karl was the killer, or he knew exactly what was going on, or both.

The constable moved into a small round room with a large and heavy bowl set up on a pedestal where baptisms were performed. He was wondering when the last baptism had been performed here when someone called to him from inside the church.

"Vince!"

He stepped out of the small round room. "Yeah?"

"You better come here."

"What is it?"

"Just come."

Constable Tremblay followed the other officer to the altar at the west end of the church. Off to the right, there was a large pool of blood on the floor, black around the edges and beginning to harden across its surface. There were footsteps leading away from the pool of blood, as well as a long, S-shaped smear that wended its way between the footprints and an exit door at the north side of the building.

"Another murder," said the other cop.

"Looks like it," said Constable Tremblay.

"Like the others?"

The constable shook his head. No, not like the others, he thought. The other bodies had all been found where'd they'd fallen, but this one had been dragged away. Why?

And why, after seven students had been killed in similar fashion, the eighth had differed significantly, and then the ninth had been altogether *unlike* any of the previous murders.

What was so special about this victim that the killer wanted to take the body with him when he left?

And, perhaps more importantly, just who had been killed here?

At that moment, a call came in over the radio for Constable Tremblay. He reached to his waistband, picked up the portable radio that linked him with his cruiser and said, "Constable Tremblay. What's up Gina?"

"I'm on the phone with someone who wants to talk to you about the murders."

"Who is he? What does he want?"

"He won't tell me anything," Gina said, her voice broken only slightly by static. "He says he wants to talk to you directly."

"I can be back at the station in ten minutes."

"He wants to talk to you now."

Constable Tremblay looked up. "Does anyone here have a cell phone?"

One of the O.P.P. officers put up his hand.

"What's the number?"

The constable relayed the number to Gina.

Minutes later, the provincial policeman's cell phone chirped. He handed the phone over to the constable.

"Constable Tremblay."

"Just the man I want to speak to." The voice was deep and low, and definitely foreign.

"You want to tell me something about the murders."

"Yes-s-s." The word slithered into the constable's ear.

"What?"

"Just this-s-s. If you're looking for Karl Desbiens, you might try the mission site."

"What's he doing up there?"

"Let's just say it's a good place to bury a body."

"How do you know this?"

The person on the other end hung up.

The line went dead.

"You two stay here and look after the crime scene," the constable said to the officers standing on either side of the pool of blood. "The rest of you come with me."

4

It was dark by the time Karl reached the mission site.

And the rain was steady.

The ground would be soft, and heavy, but it had to be done tonight.

Karl pulled off the highway and parked the car under the overhanging branches of a maple tree. Leaving the body of Father Dionne in the front seat for the time being, he popped open the trunk and gathered up all the tools he'd need and carried them down the path to the mission site.

When he got there, the ground looked strange. Most of the pits had been washed out and were slowly being filled up by the surrounding earth. In another year, they'd be little more than pockmarks in the soil, and in ten there'd be no trace that anyone had ever been here.

Just as it had been when he'd arrived the first time.

But at the far end of the clearing, there was a huge hole in the ground, or more precisely a gaping wound where it appeared much of the topsoil had been washed away by rain.

Karl walked over to the edge of the clearing and peered down into the muddy water of the pool that had formed in the bottom of the large pit. The water swirled and roiled, as if it were part of some ocean, and not a dirty puddle made by the rain.

Karl wondered if this had been the spot where Brick had found the dagger. It was possible since Karl didn't remember any of the crew's pits being so large, or deep.

Karl stepped cautiously away from the edge of the pit and made his way back to the near end of the clearing that was closest to the woods. He would dig Father Dionne's burial plot here, as far away from the sluicing water and as deep as his tools would allow.

It might take him all night to dig just six feet, but Karl was up to the task. After all, he'd killed Brick and took the dagger from him, he killed Father Dionne according to the old man's wishes and had saved humanity from the plague the demon Astaroth would have undoubtedly wrought onto the world. What was a few hours of back-breaking labor compared to that?

Karl dropped the tools at the edge of the clearing and headed back to the car for Father Dionne's body.

5

Constable Tremblay led a train of five cruisers through the pouring rain. He'd radioed ahead, informing the local O.P.P. attachment that they were on their way.

It was possible, maybe even probable, that the local officers wouldn't wait for him to get there to catch Karl himself, but at this point, he didn't care who stopped the killings, he just wanted them to be over.

The mission site was another ten or twelve kilometres up the road. If he kept the cruiser's speed constant at one-forty, he'd be there in five minutes.

Maybe less.

6

The smile was still on Father Dionne's face, as if he were truly resting in peace.

Who knew? Maybe he'd already been met by Saint Peter and escorted directly to the right hand of God, who was at this very moment congratulating Father Dionne on a job very well done.

It would explain the smile.

Karl reached into the car and undid the seat belt.

Father Dionne's body did not move.

Karl had to push, pull, tug and heave, to get the old man's body out of the car, and even when it was free of the car's interior, it was still almost impossible to move.

Before setting off down the path, Karl made one last check of the inside of the car. There was a blood stain down the back of the passenger seat, and a larger stain on the seat itself, but he'd be able to clean those, and perhaps even get the seats recovered before anyone suspected anything.

After closing and locking the car door, Karl moved behind the body, hooked his arms under the armpits of the corpse and began dragging it down to the mission site.

It would have been easier to drag Father Dionne by his legs, but having his body and head bump along the muddy, rocky path, was too undignified for such a hero.

Karl took several breaks to rest along the way, but he eventually reached the site where he would bury Father Dionne. After setting the body up against a tree and out of the rain, Karl began to dig.

The ground was softer than he remembered, and he was able to dig a foot-deep pit in just a few minutes. If he could continue on at this pace, he'd have the body safely in the ground well before morning.

And then he'd seal the site forever with layers and layers of concrete that would serve as a base for a splendid new monument in honor of the Ste. Claire Martyrs, and the students who died as a result of their search for the truth, and of course, for Father Dionne.

Brave, strong, Father Dionne.

The monument would be huge, massive, and no one would ever be able to break ground here again.

Not in a year.

Not in ten years.

Not in a hundred.

The demon's dagger, the key that would unlock the gates of the underworld and bring forth hell on Earth would be lost forever.

For the first time in weeks, a smile broke across Karl's face.

He had won. He was a worthy Jesuit, the equal of all those who served the Order before him.

Victory was his.

And it tasted sweet.

Karl began to laugh with joy.

It was over.

Finally over.

7

The other officers were waiting for Constable Tremblay when he reached the mission site.

"We were told to secure the roadside and wait," said one of the provincial officers. "What are we looking for?"

"The serial killer from Ste-Claire College."

"No shit!"

The constable shook his head. "No shit."

The officers gathered around.

"If he's armed," said Constable Tremblay, "he'll probably only have a knife. But everyone keep their distance just the same. He's killed eight people so far, and I doubt he's going to care much if the next one is a cop."

They started to move.

Constable Tremblay could hear Karl long before he could see him. At first he thought the man was crying, but as they neared it became apparent that he was laughing.

"Jesus Christ!" the constable whispered under his breath.

He *was* laughing, and smiling, as if he didn't have a care in the world.

A jury was going to be all over that.

As they came to the end of the path, Constable Tremblay saw that Karl was filling in what looked to have been a fairly deep hole. He was throwing dirt into it, sending mud and water splashing up onto the ground surrounding it.

Just then one of the other officers nudged the constable's arm. "Over there," he said. "Under the tree."

Constable Tremblay squinted, not wanting to shine his light just yet. But even in the dark it was obvious that there was a large swatch of bright red blood staining the trunk of a big birch tree less than ten feet from where Karl was working.

"Let's do it," said Constable Tremblay.

Suddenly the woods erupted with movement and lights as each one of the police officers stepped out from the bushes, guns drawn and pointed, lights switched on, and barking orders.

"Drop the shovel!"

"Get away from the hole!"

"Hands on your head!"

Karl turned around, the smile still on his face.

"You're under arrest," Constable Tremblay said.

Karl nodded, as if resigned to his fate and ready to accept punishment for his crimes.

"Take him away," said the constable. "And dig up that hole

and find out what's in there."

"No!" Karl suddenly cried out. "You can't dig here."

He turned around to reach for a shovel, perhaps to protect the grave, but before he could lay a hand on the tool, he was tackled by three officers.

"No," he said, twisting and turning in an attempt to get away. "It's over...The ground must be left undisturbed."

"Get him out of here!" said the constable.

Karl was carried up the path, his hands and legs bound, screaming like a madman the entire way.

8

Minutes later, one of the officers in the pit said, "Feels like there's a body down here." He reached down into the mud and water with his right hand, and nodded. "Yeah, one at least."

"All right," said the constable. "Let's get it out of there."

9

In the distance, a dark figure stood partially hidden behind a rise of jagged rocks.

He nodded in approval.

EPILOGUE

Two Months Later

1

Constable Tremblay put the last of the Abbotville Police Department files on Karl Desbiens into a large cardboard box in preparation for shipment to the Crown Attorney's Office.

The trial was slated to begin in Toronto in two weeks and although it was a fairly open and shut case, the Ontario Government wasn't taking anything for granted. Word was that the Society of Jesus had sent a team of lawyers from Rome to defend Desbiens, and they would be working with the best criminal defense attorneys the Catholic Church's money could buy.

Everyone was expecting some wild defense theory and there had already been hints that the Church would argue that this was an otherworldly battle between good and evil and couldn't possibly by judged by mortal men.

Sounded good, but they'd found Karl Desbiens burying his last victim. He'd all but confessed to that murder, and the dagger recovered from inside Father Dionne's body had traces of Desbiens' own blood on it.

Thoughts of the dagger reminded the constable that it hadn't yet been shipped to the Crown Attorney's Office. It was *the* crucial piece of evidence and it had been put in the department's lock-up the moment Dr. Hussein at the Centre for Forensic Science in Toronto was finished with it.

Constable Tremblay took his keyring from his pocket and singled out the key to the lock-up. He opened the door to the room, then found the key for the locker containing the dagger.

He had to admit it was a beautiful piece, shiny and golden,

with a sort of goat-shaped head on the hilt and a sharp cross-shaped blade that made holes in flesh that looked like upside down crosses. He was curious where it might end up since both the Society of Jesus and the Royal Ontario Museum had put in requests for it following the trial.

He opened the locker and looked inside.

The dagger wasn't there.

Maybe the chief had already removed it, or it had been sent to the Crown Attorney's Office earlier in the week.

The constable stepped out of the lock-up. "Gina!" he called down the hall.

"Yeah?"

"Has the dagger already been transferred?"

"No," she said. "Why?"

2

Karl had been sitting alone in his cell in Toronto's Don Jail for almost two months waiting for his trial to begin. He didn't expect to be acquitted, although the Jesuit lawyers from Rome were very impressive and if anyone could make a case for his actions on religious grounds, they were the ones who could do it.

Over the past few days political protests at Queen's Park had filled the jail to the point where many of the prisoners had to be doubled up in their cells before being released on bail. As a suspected murderer Karl wasn't eligible for bail, and he wasn't a good candidate for sharing his cell, since few of the others prisoners had committed such a serious crime.

Still, he hoped he might get a cell mate. It would be nice to have someone to talk to, even if it was a criminal, and even if it was just for a little while.

Just then one of the guards, Officer Shapcott, stopped in front of Karl's cell.

"Straighten up that cell, Desbiens," he said. "You've got a cellmate coming in within the hour."

"Really? Who?"

The guard looked annoyed with the question, but answered it anyway. "Guy by the name of Roth."

Karl felt his heart jump up into his throat. "Does he have a first name?"

"Course he does," said the guard. "Question is, do I

remember it?"

"Do you?"

"Uh, it was a strange sort of name, like an old New York money type of name."

"Astor?"

"Yeah, that's it. Astor. Astor Roth."

Karl said nothing.

"I'm sure you two will get along just fine."

Karl doubted that, doubted that very much.

When the guard was gone he studied his cell. There was no light fixture he could hang himself from, no bedsheet he could wind around his neck. There was nothing sharp he could cut himself with, nothing pointed he could plunge into his heart.

He wanted to kill himself, *needed* to take his life before the demon did, but there was nothing in the cell that could help him do the job.

Not in the cell, but perhaps outside of it.

Karl clasped his hands together, fell to his knees and began to pray, asking God for His help.

The door at the end of the cell block rolled open.

Karl looked to the ceiling, pleading that God give him the strength of will to overcome his body's natural reflexes.

And then…Karl felt his body begin to tremble as it was pervaded by the power of God.

A smile broke over Karl's face as he knew that God was there with him in the cell.

By his side.

Helping him defeat the demon.

Karl took one last breath.

And held it…

Forever.

ABOUT THE AUTHOR

Bram Stoker and Aurora Award winner Edo van Belkom is the author of over 175 stories of horror, science fiction, fantasy, and mystery to such magazines as *Parsec, Storyteller, On Spec* and *RPM*, and the anthologies *Northern Frights 1, 2, 3, 4, Star Colonies, Shock Rock 2, Fear Itself, Hot Blood 4, 6, 11, Dark Destiny, Crossing the Line, Bad News, Alternate Tyrants, The Conspiracy Files, Queer Fear, Robert Bloch's Psychos, Year's Best Horror Stories 20*, and *Best American Erotica 1999*.

In addition to winning the 1997 Stoker Award from the Horror Writers Association for "Rat Food" (co-authored with David Nickle), he won the Aurora Award (Canada's top prize for speculative writing) in 1999 for the short story, "Hockey's Night in Canada. His novels include *Wyrm Wolf, Lord Soth, Mister Magick*, and *Teeth*.

His short story collections include *Death Drives a Semi*, and *Six-Inch Spikes*. Non-fiction books include the interview book *Northern Dreamers* and the how-to titles *Writing Horror* and *Writing Erotica*. He is also an editor with four anthologies to his credit, T*he Aurora Awards, Northern Horror, Be Afraid!* and *Be Very Afraid!*. And, Edo is the author of *"Mark Dalton: Owner/Operator"* an on-going adventure serial published monthly in *Truck News* since 1999.

Born in Toronto in 1962, Edo graduated from York University with an honors degree in Creative Writing. He then worked as a daily newspaper sports and police reporter for five years before becoming a full-time freelance writer in 1992. Since then he has done a wide variety of writing-related work ranging from trivia questions to book reviews, opinion pieces on professional wrestling to speeches and special letters for Toronto Mayor Mel Lastman. As a broadcaster, Edo is a horror movie host on SCREAM, Canada's all-horror digital television channel. A frequent guest speaker and panelists at writing conferences and conventions in Canada and the United States, Edo was Toastmaster of the 1997 World Horror Convention in Niagara Falls, New York.

He lives in Brampton, Ontario, with his wife Roberta and son Luke. His web page is located at *www.vanbelkom.com*

The best in all-new neo-noir, hard-boiled and retro-pulp mystery and crime fiction.

FLESH AND BLOOD SO CHEAP

A Joe Hannibal Mystery
1-891946-16-1
Wayne D. Dundee

The popular St. Martins hardcover and Dell paperback series is revived! Hard-boiled Rockford, Illinois P.I. Joe Hannibal is at it again, this time swept up in a murderous mystery in a Wisconsin summer resort town. Deception and death lurk behind the town's idyllic façade, when a grisly murder is discovered and Hannibal knows for a fact that the confessed killer couldn't have done the deed!

It'll take two fists and a lot of guts to navigate through the tacky tourist traps, gambling dens and gin mills to get to the truth, while dangerous dames seem determined to steer Hannibal clear of the town's darkest secrets. In the end, Hannibal himself, and everyone he cares for, may be in jeopardy as he learns that murder may be the smallest crime of all in this lakeside getaway!

WAITING FOR THE 400

A Northwoods Noir
1-891946-14-5
Kyle Marffin

They found the first girl in the Chicago train station, a dime-a-dance and a quarter-for-more chippy. Suicide. A train ticket still clutched in her hand: Watersmeet, Michigan, the end of line…

400 miles north, Watersmeet station master Jess Burton wastes away in his tiny northwoods depot with big dreams of big city life, watching the high-rollers and their glamour gals hop off the train for their lakeside mansions and highbrow resorts. Till the night Nina appeared on the depot platform.

Nina…Big city beautiful and clearly marked 'property of'. The kind of dame that can turn a man's head, turn him inside out and upside down till danger doesn't matter anymore, till desire can only lead to death. Because folks are dying now, and Jess is in over his head, waiting for the 400 and the red-headed beauty to step off the train with his ticket out of town.

THE BIG SWITCH

A Brian Kane Mystery
1-891946-10-2
Jack Bludis

Hollywood, 1951. Millionaires, moguls and movie stars dazzle in the land of dreams. Money talks, when desperate glamour girls are a dime a dozen. There's a seamy underbelly beneath the glossy veneer. Scandals lurk in every closet, sins too dark for the silver screen. It's all a sham, everything's a scam, everyone's on the make, no one's who they seem.

This is Kane's turf. Brian Kane, Hollywood P.I.

It's a standard case, as un-glamorous as they come: Hired by a mega-star's wife to catch her cheating husband with another casting-couch hopeful. Till one starlet winds up dead. Then another. When Kane's client turns out to be an imposter, and thugs are trying to scare him off, he's suddenly suspect #1 in his own case. And the body count keeps growing…

But it's personal now, and not even a vicious murderer can keep Kane from getting to the bottom of the big switch.

Now try the finest in traditional supernatural horror!

NIGHT PLAYERS
1-891946-11-0
P.D. Cacek

Welcome to Las Vegas, home to glittering casinos, to high stakes, high-rollers, high priced call girls. 'Round the clock vice, where the nightlife never ends. It's the perfect place for a new-born vampire to make her home.

Meet Allison Garrett, the unluckiest gal who ever became a vampire, with an irreverently sharp tongue to go along with her sharp teeth. Meet her sidekick, Mica, a Bible-thumping street corner preacher. Both of them are on the run from the catty coven of L.A. strip-club vampire vixens they narrowly escaped from in P.D. Cacek's Stoker Award nominated debut novel Night Prayers. Hiding out in Las Vegas, Allison's now a night-shift showgirl, while Mica tries in vain to bring the good book to gamblers, crooks and hookers. And everything's as idyllic as it can be for a preacher and a vampire setting up house in sin city. Till the evil vampire that cruelly turned Allison shows up along with his bloodthirsty minions, and it'll take more than a gambler's luck to save Allison and Mica this time!

...DOOMED TO REPEAT IT
1-891946-12-9
D.G.K. Goldberg

It's a miracle that sassy, self-proclaimed punk-cowgirl Layla MacDonald hasn't gone off the deep end: Her mother gruesomely murdered in one of Charlotte, North Carolina's most scandalous love triangles, 'Daddy-Useless' drinking himself into despair, another temp job leading nowhere fast, and the painful memories of her boyfriend's abuse still as fresh as open wounds. Till she meets Ian. And suddenly, dormant desires are awakened. Madness is unleashed. Surreal violence explodes.

Because Ian is a ghost...

...The wandering ghost of an 18th century Scottish rebel, compelled by dark forces neither he nor Layla understand, seeking vengeance for 300 year-old horrors from the bloody highland battlefields. Their fates are bound together, and Ian is driven to protect Layla, with violent consequences, as madness and lust simmer amidst the ethereal world of lost spirits. Now under suspicion for Ian's rampages, the law's on Layla's tail, and her only escape may be to join her spirit lover, both of them doomed to repeat an endless cycle of ghostly horrors.

The Horror Writers Association
BELL, BOOK & BEYOND

An Anthology Of Witchy Tales
1-891946-09-9
Edited by P.D. Cacek

Stoker Award winner P.D. Cacek brings you 21 bewitching stories about wiccans, warlocks and witches, all written by the newest voices in terror: the Affiliate Members of the Horror Writers Association. From fearsome and frightening to starkly sensual and darkly humorous, each tale will cast its own sorcerous spell, leaving you anxiously looking for more from these new talents!

"If these authors are indeed the future of horror, the genre is in good hands...If you care about where horror is headed and who's going to take us there, this fine, spooky volume is a must read"
Garret Peck, Sinister Element

"Genre fans will obtain a taste of the destined in this witchcraft anthology"
Harriet Klausner

A FACE WITHOUT A HEART

A Modern-Day Version Of Oscar Wilde's The Picture Of Dorian Gray
1-891946-08-0
Rick R. Reed

Nominated for the 2001 Spectrum Award for "Best Novel": A stunning retake on the timeless themes of guilt, forgiveness and despair in Oscar Wilde's fin de siecle classic, The Picture Of Dorian Gray. Amidst a gritty background of nihilistic urban decadence, a young man's soul is bargained away to embrace the nightmarish depths of depravity – and cold blooded murder – as his painfully beautiful holographic portrait reflects the ugly horror of each and every sin.

"A rarity: a really well-done update that's as good as its source material."
Thomas Deja, Fangoria Magazine

"Depicting modern angst with unerring accuracy"
Reviewer's Bookwatch

GOTHIQUE

A Vampire Novel
1-891946-06-4
Kyle Marffin

International Horror Guild Award nominee Kyle Marffin takes you on a tour of the dark side of the darkwave, when a city embraces the grand opening of a new 'nightclub extraordinaire', Gothique, mecca for the disaffected Goth kids and decadent scene-makers. But a darker secret lurks behind its blacked-out doors and the true horror of the undead reaches out to ensnare the soul of a city in a nightmare of bloodshed, and something much worse than death.

"An awfully good writer...this is a novel with wit and edge, engaging characters and sleazy ones for balance, a keen sense of melodramatic movement and a few nasty chills."
Ed Bryant, Locus Magazine

"Bloody brilliant! A white-knuckle adventure filled with plenty of chills and thrills...this book just never lets up."
M. McCarty, The IF Bookworm

WHISPERED FROM THE GRAVE

An Anthology Of Ghostly Tales
1-891946-07-2

Quietly echoing in a cold graveyard's breeze, the moaning wails of the dead, whispered from the grave to mortal ears with tales of desires unfulfilled, of dark vengeance, of sorrow and forgiveness and love beyond the grave. Includes tales by Edo van Belkom, Tippi Blevins, Sue Burke, P.D. Cacek, Dominick Cancilla, Margaret L. Carter, Don D'Ammassa, D.G.K. Goldberg, Barry Hoffman, Tina Jens, Nancy Kilpatrick, Kyle Marffin, Julie Anne Parks, Rick R. Reed and David Silva.

"A chilling collection of ghost stories...each with a unique approach to ghosts, spirits, spectres and other worldly apparitions...Pleasant nightmares."
Michael McCarty, Indigenous Fiction

"A landmark collection...I loved this anthology"
A. Andrews, True Review

"This timely work refutes the current charge that ghost stories have lost their appeal... buy this book. Read it. Rediscover what is means to be a child cowering in the dark, listening for shuffling feet...and whispers"
William P. Simmons, Folk-Tales Review

STORYTELLERS

1-891946-04-8
Julie Anne Parks

A writer who once ruled the bestseller list with novels of calculating horror flees to the backwoods of North Carolina. A woman desperately fights to salvage a loveless marriage. A storyteller emerges — the keeper of the legends — to ignite passions in a dormant heart. But an ancient evil lurks in the dark woods, a malevolent spirit from a storyteller's darkest tale, possessing one weaver of tales and threatening another in a sinister and bloody battle for a desperate woman's life and for everyone's soul.

"A macabre novel of supernatural terror, a book to be read with the lights on and the radio playing!"
Bookwatch

"A page-turner, for sure, and a remarkable debut."
Triad Style

"Genuine horror and the beauty of the Carolina wilds. It's an intoxicating blend."
Lisa DuMond, SF Site

CARMILLA: THE RETURN

1-891946-02-1
Kyle Marffin

Marffin's provocative debut — nominated for a 1998 International Horror Guild Award for First Novel — is a modern day retelling of J. S. LeFanu's classic novella, Carmilla. Gothic literature's most notorious female vampire, the seductive Countess Carmilla Karnstein, stalks an unsuspecting victim through the glittery streets of Chicago to the desolate northwoods and ultimately back to her haunted Styrian homeland, glimpsing her unwritten history while replaying the events of the original with a contemporary, frightening and erotic flair.

"A superbly written novel that honors a timeless classic and will engage the reader's imagination long after it has been finished."
The Midwest Book Review

"If you think you've read enough vampire books to last a lifetime, think again. This one's got restrained and skillful writing, a complex and believable story, gorgeous scenery, sudden jolts of violence and a thought provoking final sequence that will keep you reading until the sun comes up."
Fiona Webster, Amazon

"Marffin's clearly a talented new writer with a solid grip on the romance of blood and doomed love."
Ed Bryant, Locus Magazine

THE DARKEST THIRST

A Vampire Anthology
1-891946-00-5

Sixteen disturbing tales of the undead's darkest thirsts for power, redemption, lust...and blood. Includes stories by Michael Arruda, Sue Burke, Edo van Belkom, Margaret L. Carter, Stirling Davenport, Robert Devereaux, D.G.K. Goldberg, Scott Goudsward, Barb Hendee, Kyle Marffin, Deborah Markus, Paul McMahon, Julie Anne Parks, Rick R. Reed, Thomas J. Strauch, and William Trotter.

"Fans of vampire stories will relish this collection."
Bookwatch

"If solid, straight ahead vampire fiction is what you like to read, then The Darkest Thirst is your prescription."
Ed Bryant, Locus Magazine

"Definitely seek out this book."
Mehitobel Wilson, Carpe Noctem Magazine

THE KISS OF DEATH

An Anthology Of Vampire Stories
1-891946-05-6

Sixteen writers invite you to welcome their own dark embrace with these tales of the undead, both frightening and funny, provocative and disturbing, each it's own delightfully dangerous kiss of death. Includes stories by Sandra Black, Tippi Blevins, Dominick Cancilla, Margaret L. Carter, Sukie de la Croix, Don D'Ammassa, Mia Fields, D.G.K. Goldberg, Barb Hendee, C.W. Johnson, Lynda Licina, Kyle Marffin, Deborah Markus, Christine DeLong Miller, Rick R. Reed and Kiel Stuart.

"Whether you're looking for horror, romance or just something that will stretch your notion of 'vampire' a little bit, you can probably find it here."
Cathy Krusberg, The Vampire's Crypt

"Readable and entertaining."
Hank Wagner, Hellnotes

"The best stories add something to the literature, whether actually pushing the envelope or at least doing what all good fiction does, touching the reader's soul."
Ed Bryant, Locus

SHADOW OF THE BEAST

1-891946-03-X
Margaret L. Carter

Carter has thrilled fans of classic horror for nearly thirty years with anthologies, scholarly non-fiction and her own long running small press magazine. Here's her exciting novel debut, in which a nightmare legacy arises from a young woman's past. A vicious werewolf rampages through the dark streets of Annapolis, and the only way she can combat the monster is to surrender to the dark, violent power surging within herself. Everyone she loves is in mortal danger, her own humanity is at stake, and much more than death may await her under the shadow of the beast.

"Suspenseful, well crafted adventures in the supernatural."
Don D'Ammassa, Science Fiction Chronicle

"Tightly written...a lot of fun to read. Recommended."
Merrimack Books

"A short, tightly-woven novel... a lot of fun to read...recommended."
Wayne Edwards, Cemetery Dance Magazine

NIGHT PRAYERS

1-891946-01-3
P.D. Cacek

Nominated for the prestigious Horror Writers Association Stoker Award for First Novel. A wryly witty romp introduces perpetually unlucky thirtysomething Allison, who wakes up in a seedy motel room — as a vampire without a clue about how to survive! Now reluctantly teamed up with a Bible-thumping streetcorner preacher, Allison must combat a catty coven of strip club vampire vixens, in a rollicking tour of the seamy underbelly of Los Angeles.

"Further proof that Cacek is certainly one of horror's most important up-and-comers."
Matt Schwartz

"A gorgeous confection, a blood pudding whipped to a tasty froth."
Ed Bryant, Locus Magazine

"A wild ride into the seamy world of the undead...a perfect mix of helter-skelter horror and humor."
Michael McCarty, Dark Regions/Horror Magazine

Look for these other titles from
The Design Image Group at your favorite bookstore.
Or visit us at **www.designimagegroup.com** to order direct
online, and for links to your favorite on-line
and specialty booksellers.

To order direct by mail, send check or money order
for $15.95 per book, payable in U.S. funds to:

The Design Image Group, Inc.
P.O. Box 2325
Darien, Illinois 60561 USA

Please add $2.00 postage & handling for the first book,
$1.00 for each additional book ordered.

Please allow 2-3 weeks for delivery.

Manufactured by Amazon.ca
Bolton, ON

32205091R00176